THE HORN AND THE FOREST

THE HORN

AND THE FOREST

JAMIE LEE COOPER

THE **BOBBS-MERRILL** COMPANY, INC.
A SUBSIDIARY OF HOWARD W. SAMS & CO., INC.
Publishers · INDIANAPOLIS · NEW YORK

for my parents
ESTHER and LEE

NOTES FROM THE AUTHOR

Location of Story

Most of *The Horn and the Forest* takes place along the Wabash, Salamonie, and Mississinewa rivers in northern Indiana. During his captivity, Nathan was taken into Michigan.

Nathan's Totem

His totem group (that is, the group into which he was born) was Bird's Cry of the Delaware. His totem was inherited through his grandmother, Night Dog's wife, who was a Delaware. But Night Dog, Potawatome on his mother's side, brought up his children as Potawatome after his wife died.

The Delawares inherited through the matriarchal line, and this made Strange Rain and her children related to the Delaware clan group instead of the Potawatome.

Voyageur

Voyageurs were French-Canadian traders who usually traveled by boat. Often they transported goods for the large fur companies in Canada. One definition calls them "half Indian, half French, and half prairie wolf." They were bright in their dress, and wore earrings, colored sashes, caps with coins sewn on. Often they married into Indian tribes and remained with them.

Candlewood

This term was used for any resinous wood which could be used as a torch, such as pine knots.

Names of Months

The names of the months used in this book are Winnebago, a tribe that lived along the western shore of Lake Michigan, traded with Indiana tribes, and allied with the Shawnee chief Tecumseh in the War of 1812.

Winnebago names were chosen because they were simple and expressive, often used by long-hunters, and in some cases were shortened forms of the much longer Potawatome names. Many tribes counted thirteen months (moons) but the Winnebago counted twelve. This is more in keeping with our own system and makes it possible to translate a month as June and not May-and-a-half.

Animals

Wild bull was the name given to the black bison that once lived in the forests of Indiana, migrating to Kentucky in the fall and going north to the Illinois prairies in the spring. The black bisons were not the same as the brown bisons of the plains, which were smaller and more numerous.

Devil dogs were the coyotes which ranged freely through the Indiana forests in the early days.

Night dogs were wolves. The name was in general use among the white men.

Hunger wolves was the name commonly applied to wolves during the seasons when hunting was bad for them and they became desperate for food. The term was in general use among the Indians, and often used by the white men.

Asanzang (Wildcat Creek): The word means *sunshine,* and was the name of a Miami village and its creek.

Onzalamonie (Salamonie): Miami word for *bloodroot.*

Pwakanna (Pipe Creek): Miami word for *pipe.*

Micisagiengan (Lake Michigan): Ojibwa word for *great lake.*

Manjinikia (Big Frame): The name of a Miami chief, his village, and its creek.

Namatcisinwi (Mississinewa): Miami word meaning *it slants.*

Kitapikonnong (Tippecanoe): Potawatome name for *buffalo fish.*

Wapehani (White): Delaware word for *white, clear water.*

Wabaciki (Wabash): Miami word for *white.*

Kolcisasipi (St. Joseph): Miami word for *bean blossom.*

Kinapikwomakwa (Eel River): Miami word meaning *snake fish.*

Meskwawasipi (Cedar Creek): Potawatome word for *cedar.*

Tcanktunungi (Fall Creek): Miami word meaning *makes-a-noise-place.*

Waythowkahmik (Yellow River): Potawatome name.

THE HORN AND THE FOREST

1

You could smell the dark blowing through the vast woods. Already the blackness stood branch-deep, but outside, the sky still hung blue and there was day a-plenty. Down in here you knew the sun had crossed the top of the world when the green woods-light flickered out, and when you saw the bright will-'o-the-wisp running ahead of you. As for the dark, the monster trees lost themselves in it and let you slam into them for pure spite.

The ground hid in the mist, and went up and down under your moccasins teasing you with humps and bumps you didn't remember. The trail to your own cabin seemed a stranger-trail. Night birds and beasts woke up. Day ones crawled off to sleep. The owls known as hill-hooters boomed back and forth. Feet padded up and down the paths. Even the wind turned lurky, and sneaked around acting mysterious. And when it rained, as it was raining now, the woods was stranger still with trees dripping all about, and every drop like the footfall of some beast or mortal man.

Lannard slouched down the twisty river trail. He had a fresh-killed deer wrapped in its bloody hide slung from his back. He scowled into the dark, daring something to jump him.

"Here I am," he muttered into the fearsome shadows, "and thunderin, savage mad! If you got sunthin else to fling at me, fetch it!"

The words flew up around him like pigeons from a fallen roosting tree. Some hung in the leaves and some drifted on up the trail. It seemed as if he kept hearing them over and over, again and again. But it was only the wind, mocking him with its echoes.

"I been in these old woods too long, without a decent breath of good sky air. . . ."

He shook his head and hoped he'd hit a blaze-mark soon, before he mistook a will-o'-the-wisp for a hunter's fire and got deeper lost. There were beasts about, hungering after any prey. And there were Indians, too.

"Too dang many," he fetched out, eying the Indian tree ahead. But only the fog hunkered on its bent-out limb, and he slipped on past.

He bobbed on faster now, for here the trail was made by Indian feet and was worn a handspan deep into the ground. He wondered if it went to Asanzang Town, or to some stranger-village like the one he'd skirted before the light was gone. He stopped then, stiff and alert, thinking he'd seen the yellow shape of a panther stretched above him in an elm. But the dark and the fog were fooling him, and it was only the hollow burying log of an Indian babe lashed there. He wondered why its folks had been so hurried that they hadn't dug a proper grave.

A rifle shot away, something stood out ghostly white on a limestone ledge. He stood as still as the trees themselves, till he made it out to be the picked-clean hipbones of a deer. They were tied with strips of trade-cloth, a gift for the Indian hunter's god.

He started on, but the mournful cry of a peewee snapped off and when it didn't come again he was wary. Crouched in damp giant fern he watched a dozen horses with grass-stuffed bells swinging from their necks, and Indians on their backs, come silently out of the fog and go into it again. Potawatomes, he frowned, on their way to raid. Bands of them were everywhere these days, and all hankering after trouble. Some rode as far west as the Spanish settlements on the Missouri for a handful of scalps and a few starved horses. He thought of the unlucky cabins they would burn this night, but not for long. Out here a man, to keep his right mind, daren't waste much thought on other folks. He had his own self to look out for.

When he heard a screech owl calling down the way, he knew he was safe and went back to the trail.

"But tarnal," he whispered aloud, "if I jest knew I was headed right. . . ."

As white as moths, the blaze-marks showed themselves suddenly. He'd most missed them in the smoky fog. He stopped a while and studied them. There were three up-and-down blazes with a long slash to one side, telling him there was a trap off to the right.

What white man loved his life so little that he trapped up here? Then he made out a fancy curved mark above the blaze. Micajah's own mark. Now Lannard knew where he was, and he cut his glance away from the rolling bank where he'd stumbled on Micajah's body the day before. His grey eyes took on their distance look as he tried to rake something over the memory to hide it.

"*Micajah*," he said gruffly, with his head turned away from the bank, "I done the best I knowed."

A sudden wind beat past him down the trail, a wild wind out of the north and west, the wind of the Illini, The Men. It had run all the way from the Mississippi, across the man-high bluegrass where not one tree stood to hold it back. It had the smell of prairie fire on its breath. Far behind him, the Great Prairie was burning, as it burned every fall.

Lannard sniffed it like a hound, and grinned to himself. He reckoned things weren't as bad as they had seemed that morn. Then, when the man he'd been following had slipped away from him in a great swamp, he had turned broody. Now it came to him that beyond that swamp there wasn't a blessed thing but the prairie, and the prairie was burning.

"The wind's done a better job than me," he said to himself. "It's birthed a fire with feet enough to run him down." He looked toward the bank now. "Don't you worry none, Micajah . . . that man's days on this green earth are done."

Now he jogged along the trail and the tiredness fell behind him in his tracks. Soon the trees gave out, and he was on the Asanzang barrens. Here nothing grew but a few stunted oaks and haws.

Ahead he saw a misty blob of light with four humpy shapes against it. They looked like four shaggy bears squatted on their haunches by a honey log, and they might have been. Now that the days were shorter, the great beasts were always on the prowl. But the shapes weren't beasts . . . they were men, the four Lannard had been long-hunting with. And that was no log between them. It was a thing you saw in the back-East settlements. A burying box.

Lannard padded up to them so quiet that Tinch jumped when he saw him, then stammered shamefaced, "I heerd you stompin this way . . . a far piece off."

"Got it done?" Lannard jerked his beard at the dark box.

"Yep," Kerman answered. "Just puttin in the last pegs." The sound of his tomahawk closing down the lid was the only mortal sound for miles around.

Lannard eased the bloody hide of venison off his back and crouched down beside it. Across from him, he could hear Rocreuse muttering a French prayer, whether against the night or for the soul of Micajah he couldn't be sure. At first Rocreuse had balked against riving out a box for the lad.

"We're woodsies!" he flared, reminding them. "A woodsy buries in a hollow log, same as an Injun."

"Or in nothin at all," answered Lannard. He'd found woodsies in the forest before now, with precious little dirt scraped over them. "Looked more like a male painter's sign-

16

heaps than a proper grave! If I'd grub up one when I was diggin for ginseng, I wouldn't know whether 'twas a woodsy or an Injun. A white man ought to be laid away in a decent box."

The others thought so, too. Specially since it was Micajah.

"You find anybody?" Kerman fetched out slowly.

"Yep," Lannard came back. "I tracked the man clear to the newfound lakes. At noon hush, I was so close on his heels that I left off blazin my trail, for fear the sound of my tommyhawk would give him warnin. But his sign turned as twisty as a shrew's trail. He knowed I was behind him. Once I found where he'd stood watchin me while I picked over stones and sticks to see which way he was headed. He lost me, though . . . in a stranger swamp." He rubbed his beard. "May be an Injun, judgin from the way he toes in. But . . . may be a woodsy, too. Most of us takes to walkin like Injuns. I never seen him at all . . . and there wasn't nothin in his sign to tell me any more about him."

Tinch sighed.

"Sure is a shame," he put in softly. "Goin to be mighty hard on Jonathan, losin a son like Micajah. . . ."

Lannard nodded. Many's the man had jawed at his own boy on account of Micajah. Micajah, they would snap, didn't sulk when the meal bag shook out empty. Micajah turned his hand to whatever was needful. Micajah could split a leaf at forty paces. Micajah. . . .

The other youths set their mouths as hard as pignut trees, and their bones turned mean against Micajah. Micajah, they said shortly, wasn't like the rest of them. And unless he was bewitched by Auntie Gentry, he'd come up missing some fine day. No man or boy ranged alone into stranger-Indian country. Or hunted by his lonesome. Or wandered the forest of nights. They ran onto him often, tall and lean in his seventeen years, with a look of yearning that fetched many a gal from her cabin door. When some bit of foolishment sent his laugh ringing down the trace, the other youths clapped him on the back and grinned with him. But their honeyed words turned sour as swill in their mouths, and their eyes went cold from envy.

"Micajah had enemies a-plenty," Lannard muttered. "Could have been some white man had a grudge on him. Or some crazy, drunk Injun got to hankerin after that red hair. . . ."

"If some Injun kilt him, he's kilt his luck for sure," Scuddy put in, and all craned round to look at him.

It had long been whispered that Scuddy was too down-right friendly with the Indians. Some folks swore he'd even gone through the heathen rite that drew out his white blood and made Indian in its place. Kerman himself had circled Tedapaschit's Town* and seen Scuddy seated among the totems of the chiefs. Suspicion had gone up and down the trails that Scuddy was fixing to set himself up as another Simon Girty. But one half-crazy renegade like Simon Girty running in and out of Indiana territory was God's plenty.

Settlers and woodsies had fretted about Scuddy. In the end, four men were picked to feel him out. They had brought him to this extra-lonesome part of the great forest to go long-hunting . . . they said.

"Wal, it's true," Scuddy flared, then. "It's mighty bad luck to kill a red-haired body. Why, everyone knows that Blacksnake, Little Turtle's own white boy, wouldn't have been spared down in that Kentucky raid where he was took, 'cept that he had red hair." He looked at them with his flat eyes. "Wal . . . leastways, that's how the Injuns think."

"If I knowed as much about Injuns as you," Lannard said slowly, "it'd be a real worry to me."

It came still.

"You know," Lannard went on, casting a glance at the others, "we ought to send word on ahead. But if it was an Injun kilt Micajah, maybe they got their backs up . . . and one man . . . alone. . . ."

* Muncie, Indiana.

18

"I ain't got no fambly nor kin," Scuddy said, right off. "I'll go on ahead."

"Sorta figured you would."

Scuddy checked the priming of his gun and hefted up his pack of pelts. "I'll light a torch and start right out," he said. He stuffed his shirt with loose hunks of shellbark to light when his candlewood went out. "Don't you fret none bout me," his voice was bold. "I'll be all right."

It was plain to all that Scuddy would rather take his chances alone in the dark of the woods than hole up any more with them. Of late, he had talked too much. He'd seen how they'd taken to looking at him. He knew they were onto him. But now Lannard had given him a choice . . . he could either clear out of the Territory and leave them be, or he could be found dead on the trail.

"Reckon *you'll* be safe enough," Lannard slanted his eyes at Scuddy.

At the woods' edge, Scuddy held up and hollered back a "much obliged." Then he was gone that quick.

"I think we should have kilt him," Rocreuse growled. "He may be runnin from us like a rabbit now, but he'll bring us trouble yet."

"He knows we know," Kerman glanced up from the box. "I don't allow he'll come back. I think he'll go on ahead, like he said . . . clean to the southern ocean, likely."

"No sense in killin a feller lessen you have to," Lannard spat, "even when he's deservin of it." Then he shrugged and added, "Could be, though, some Injun'll take keer of that little matter. I reckon he's as shifty with them as he is with us."

Lannard whacked off some chunks of venison and set them to roast over the fire. Kerman finished pegging down the lid of the box. Rocreuse went to packing his pelts. They talked some little more about Scuddy, then about the south-running trail they'd take tomorrow, the heavy Indian sign Lannard had seen to the north, the far-off prairie fire, and the stranger they hoped was trapped there. But after a while, they fell quiet. Underneath everything else was the thought: *Micajah is dead. He was most like my own boy.*

"Miserable wet, ain't it?" Tinch mumbled.

"Yep." Lannard stared at the dark caught in the trees.

South on the barrens, a pack of wolves tried to tree the moon with their howling.

"Reckon they smell the death?" Rocreuse put in, of a sudden.

Beyond him the venison was roasting on some sticks. None of the men were very hungry.

The drizzle turned to a light coon-track rain, so they slept inside a half-face camp, with the fire spluttering at their feet. All night they kept the fire going, for Lannard remembered that Micajah never liked the dark. They reckoned it was mighty dark in that burying box, but they all had the feeling Micajah wasn't there. No, he was sitting by the fire, keeping watch while they slept.

The howling of the wolves grew louder.

"Night dogs is bad tonight," Lannard muttered. "Sounds like they're movin this way."

Toward daybreak, he was awakened by a scratchy sound near the box. He took a lighted pine knot and shuffled over to it. A panther sprang out of its shadow and went cat-fast into the woods. Lannard cussed the beast through his beard, went back to the fire, and lit his clay pipe. He was sitting on his heels and blinking at the box when he heard the wild geese call. And of a sudden, he knew Micajah was really gone. Gone with the south-flying geese. *Gone. . . .*

The woods turned grey and Lannard roused the others. They stomped out the fire on its stone hearth and got their packs together. But when they started to heft the box up on their shoulders, Rocreuse held back. He was against lugging Micajah home. Why, not even a settler would lug a body home! No, he'd hack out a buryhole right where he found it, and slash a cross-mark on the nearest tree. When word got down the trace, kinfolks could hunt out the grave and plant flowers if they wanted. . . .

They stood around while Rocreuse had his say, but when he was done, they lifted the box just the same, and started off. Their pulled-down faces said as good as words that he'd shamed them all with such talk.

"Were it one of our own kin," Lannard said, hard-voiced, "Jonathan would fetch him back to us if he had to come clear from the Mississippi with the box on his back."

Rocreuse scrambled after them, his sooty eyes full of worry. Beyond the barrens, they'd have to fight that box every step of the way, for it would never squeeze itself down the man-wide trails. Times a-plenty, they'd have to stop and cut a path for it, and the whole woods would know they were coming, and be waiting. And they'd get so weary, they'd be easy prey. Three days on the trail with that box was too much to ask of any mortal man, he stormed.

Lannard and the others slanted their eyes away from him. They knew what he said was true.

"Still . . . there's things has got to be done," Lannard said quietly.

They went on. It was close in the forest already. A hot sun was rising outside, but you'd have to be a red-tailed hawk above the roof of leaves to see it. Here was only the still green light. A mockingbird flew up near them, and the men listened to hear what had scared it. A copper cloud of monarch butterflies quivered past, migrating south, and for a while the flight stretched as far as a man could see both ways.

"Sun must be higher'n we thought," Lannard picked up his gun, "cause I seen them flitters yesterday, way to the north, restin in a locust grove. Likely they've been flyin since daybreak."

"The woods is pretty quiet yet," Rocreuse said softly. And later, when he had shouldered one corner of the box, he added, "We might make it home alright, at that."

They left the river trail and cut their own, following the blaze-marks they had axed a month back. The woods turned thicker, and they turned even more cautious. To stay alive in here, a man had to mind what he was about. He might find a tomahawk in his gullet, or a rattler waiting for him in the bushes. Or, like the Carson man who'd drunk a mess of rum and fallen on the trail, he might wake up and find a panther scraping leaves on him, taking him for dead.

They had lived among these monster trees so long that they carried the mark of the woods as trees carried their blazes. Their dressed buckskins were stained and out of shape from animal blood and river water. The long queues of their hair flapped out behind and tangled in the heaps of skins slung from their backs. Their tomahawks and knives swung from loops at their belts. Their beards ran on where their furry hats left off. And their loose, lapped-over shirts were stuffed with jerky meat and bags of Indian meal and pouches for tobacco and clay pipe. For all the world, they looked like the tamed bears down at Fort Washington * . . . bears that reared up like men and carried packs on their backs. But they were long-hunters and they brought their living right out of the woods. No cursing a wooden plow through rooted ground for them, nor sitting over crops at night to guard them from hungry beasts! Woodsies, the settlers called them, and growled the word out. No good, the settlers would tell you, no good could come from folks that wouldn't stay put, but always had to be drifting after game like a pack of starving night dogs.

"Looky thar!" Tinch chuckled. "We've skeert us a bear!" He spat at the manlike tracks.

"No wonder he's skeert, gittin *your* scent," Lannard answered. "You sure don't smell like no bed of mint."

They had to pick their way around the wild bull wallows, and the hunter in them stopped and sniffed at the hair torn from the old bull's backs and blowing on the spikes of the haw trees. They reckoned these wild bulls were on their way

* Cincinnati.

to Blue Licks across the Oheyo that some folks called "the Ohio." (The same folks that called a wild bull a "buffalo.")

The mist lifted and showed them ground as black and soft as otter fur. They pushed through spider webs hitched across their trail, and kicked at roots which caught at their moccasined toes. They ducked vines as thick as a bobcat's body, pointed out patches of sky that showed through where the leaves were beginning to fall.

The forest was tight about them now. If a man got lost in here, he was lost for fair. Boughs were as big on the north as on the south, and no longer could you tell directions from them. Moss spread every which way, saying, "This is north . . . no, *this!*" There was no grey goldenrod before them now, with its wolverine head looking to the North Star. Game trails petered out in places where human feet couldn't follow. Your only hope was to run by old blazes or Indian sign, and even then it was a puzzle where they would take you. Many a stranger lost in here just lay down to die, or went daft from stumbling into trees so high he couldn't see where they left off.

The third day they hit the Onzalamonie * (Blood Root) trail just before dark. They tried to make their feet go faster, as if they could beat the day to its end. Since they'd left the barrens they had not seen another mortal, but there was sign a-plenty, both beast and Indian.

Most of the day something had prowled along with them, just across the ravine that ran with the trail, and they'd marked its movements by the little things scared out of its path. But when they waded the Passeanong † it stayed behind and yelped and yurred after them. A fox, and a sick one, they reckoned, for it to be ambling around in broad day.

Once, silent as panthers, they slipped through the tall fern and stood in the chest-high waters of the Mississinewa, where canebrake hid them. Their shoulders turned heavy as walnut

* Salamonie.
† Deer Creek.

from the weight of the box, their faces were swollen from the biting of thumb-long mosquitoes, their joints seemed jelled in the raw water. But even Tinch stood steady when a leech slipped in through a rip in his hunting shirt.

They waited, mute and grave, till the first night dog gave his deep-throat growl, and the turkey calls of the Indian hunters left off. (Likely the Twanh-twanhs, the Crane People, called by the Potawatomes the *Miamis,* they told one another.) And when they went down into Hole-in-the-Sky gorge, they knew they were watched. Word of lugging a burying box would be told in every village.

"It'll set them Injuns to wonderin," said Lannard, as they hurried on.

Now, with night setting down, they were so tired that they staggered, but Lannard could see as good as any hill-hooter in the dark, and wanted to go on. They sighed. Lannard was smaller than the rest, but he was hard built and could best the lot of them any day, so they followed after him without a word.

Their feet knew the trail now, and they bobbed along easily, talking to keep the tiredness from their minds.

Kerman told how it was the wheels (making them had been his trade) that had brought him out here. The wheels had made him restless, and finally he'd turned out a set for himself. Tinch told how he'd just wandered in here because he heard the game was plentiful. Rocreuse said he was born here. Lannard said that, back in the settlements, he'd been warned not to come so far west.

"Thar's a boundary line that marks the Indiana Territory, and white men dassn't cross it!" he was warned.

"But tarnal!" he flared now. "When a man's movin after game, it don't stop fer no boundary . . . lessen it's real learned game that can read and write!"

So he had crossed the line, with his woman and his young ones straggling after. And he found that a few others had crossed it, too. Back East, game was so scarce a man could barely get enough hides to trade for powder, he claimed.

This was the reason for moving west that he gave his woman when she pulled her mouth down. But, he said to the others now, it was more than that. He just couldn't stand folks living in his pouch. It had got so you couldn't tramp the woods half a day without stumbling onto a cabin. True, there were times when he missed the green fields worked by human hands, seeing settlement roofs from a hilltop, and knowing Indians were as scarce as hen's teeth.

Here, all was different. Bigger trees than he'd ever heard tell of did the crowding. The Indians were wild and fearsome. No wonder the first thing a man did was to hack himself a jit of a clearing where he could get a glimpse of the sky, and draw a breath of air that came to him across open ground.

"You'd think," said Tinch, thoughtful-faced, "that a back-East doctor couldn't stand this wilderness."

"I don't notice we're bein overrun by them," Lannard put in. "The only one we got is Jonathan. . . ."

He broke off, and they listened to their moccasins slipping along the trail. The wind rolled over on its back in the leaves, and kicked a few onto the burying box. The men were glad Lannard had hushed when he did. There were words they too wanted to say about Jonathan, but they hid them back in the dark of their mouths, and gritted their teeth around them.

They would talk of him when they were inside man-made things, like cabins that had doors to shut the outside out, and the inside in. But here, in the open woods, it might bring bad luck. Like when a young one gets his hands on something he never had before. It might be a bit of cloth with a needle stuck in, a needle more precious to his ma than salt itself. The young one would stick it into his shirt. It was his to wear for a little space, to look at and wonder at. His, till he started crowing about it. Then his ma would catch up with him. "I didn't know you had that!" she would scold, and the wonder-thing would be gone. Like that young one's ma, Something might snatch Jonathan away

25

from them and slap their hands. And their hands were just learning tenderness from him.

Dark set down so quick and hard it seemed to each man that he was alone, save for the weight on his shoulder. The grunty breaths and rustles he could hear from the others seemed more like spook-noises than sounds made by the living. Cut off from the others, each set to thinking of Jonathan. For the hundredth time they said what a good thing it was that he had come out here, and the furry heads bobbed and the beards jerked.

Before Jonathan came, they hadn't given much thought to the right and wrong of things. Whatever a man's temper might be, he fed it. There were plenty of broken heads, plenty of single gals with babes in those days. But now, since Jonathan had come among them, they began to wonder if they weren't beasts of the woods also, and Jonathan the only real mortal.

True, he had never said a word to them about their wild doings. But more and more they mistrusted their own way of settling things and came to him to decide the right and wrong of matters. Like the time they'd found a not-bright Indian boy wandering by his lonesome. They'd fought among themselves over what to do with him. Most of them were for turning him loose bloody-headed and clean-scalped. Some were for selling him to a Wyandot trader who bought slaves. But one or two of the women (whose men had eaten bear meat until they gagged, and still hadn't fetched a babe from behind the chopping block) took pity on the miserable little fellow. They wanted to keep him for a pet, like folks sometimes keep wild wolf cubs.

When they fetched the scared and kicking young one to Jonathan, a wonder-thing happened. The boy stopped making anxious owl calls that begged help from the village he'd lost. And he quit trying to turn his nose from the white man's smell, which was worse to him than rotted flesh. No, instead he buried his face against Jonathan's tight leather shirt. For it smelled of the herbs that Jonathan used in his doctoring, and had been made by grateful Indian hands. And when he looked up at Jonathan, they could see that he knew in whose cabin he stood. Who of The People hadn't heard of this redheaded Light Person who made medicine for men of both skins, and asked for nothing in return, not even for a squaw with a soft mouth?

More than one young squaw, however, had slipped love medicine into the stew she made for him, and some had even played the love flute when he passed by. Many a one was still hopeful, as were certain of her white sisters, of having his handsome face and hard body to light her wigiwam and warm her bedmat the way her cooking-fire never could.

Jonathan listened gravely while the woodsies told what they had thought of doing with the boy. But in the end, when he cut the thong they'd tied around the young one's neck to lead him by, there was a shamed look about him. And all the time, he was talking soft to the boy in the tongue of the Southerners, the Shawnee, who called themselves *Sawano*. But he never said much to the woodsies in any tongue. No, he just took the boy back to his own village.

Puzzled that he had tossed away their notions, Lannard and the others trailed after him. They were surprised to see the boy's mother so glad to get him back she near bruised him with her loving. And his pa! His pa couldn't thank them hearty enough! He even loaded them down with bags woven of wild-bull hair and filled with dried Indian meal. He gave them buckskin just slashed from the bark lacings of its stretching frame, and kinnikinnick, the Indian tobacco, from his own pouch.

Somehow, they told each other, Jonathan had known that Indians loved their babes, same as white men. When they thought on it later, they reckoned it had been a wrong thing to talk of scalping or selling the young one. And the more time went by, the more wrong it seemed. It just showed, they said, how far a civilized person's thinking could stray. And they were glad that Jonathan had set them right.

At first they'd sworn up and down that a man like Jonathan couldn't last a year and stay good. The woods would change him, too. But now it was three years since his coming here. And he was still whistling along the trail of nights, stooping through their cabin doors, laughing at their nonsense tales with those quick eyes of his, making pets of little wild things, and passing the time of day with any stranger-Indian he met along the way.

The woodsies and settlers just couldn't understand him, but they did admire him. Even though he wore a linen shirt with ruffles, under his leather one, and heavy boots instead of moccasins, they did admire him. Had another man dressed like that, and kept his face shaved as smooth as an Indian's, and combed his hair every day, and tied it back with a piece of ribbon instead of a piece of whang, they'd have hated him out of the Territory. But since it was Jonathan . . . well, some men had strange habits. They pointed out that even Rocreuse wore a sash over his belt and rings in his ears, and wrapped his head in a bright cloth under his furry hat.

Once they had been awkward with Jonathan, and their tongues had been numb, for what could they say that a learned man like him would want to hear? But all that passed away when they saw that he smoked a clay and drank rum like the rest. And now they told him of traps and game and trading and Indian lore they'd picked up. He'd sit there, quiet, and his face would flicker like the fire in the cat-and-clay chimney. They could see he liked them and liked to be among them, even if they didn't know any doctor-talk, and had never lived in a two-story brick with blackamoors to scurry at the wave of the hand.

In return, they tried to please him and to be like him. They tried to hold back tempers, and wash their faces more than once a month, and keep the lice down in their beards, and go less often to the Indian girls' bedmats, and be a mite kinder toward each other. They watched his every move and tested his every word, and followed as best they could in the furrow he made for them. They hung onto him as tight as a young one to his ma's paps. And they tried to fight down the badness that was in every one of them. But it was hard.

"Law!" Lannard stopped of a sudden, slamming into a windfall of branches. "I wonder why the Lord ever made these woods so all-fired thick? Sure proves He thought on makin trees before He thought on makin men!"

They stopped to rest a minute, and Kerman stretched out on the mossy ground. He was weak and shaky from the slow sickness in his chest.

"You'll be all right," Lannard told him, squinting into the back of the woods. "Soon as we get out of here, and you get a breath of clearin-air, you'll be better. Law, this old woods chokes me, too. A man could drown in here, same as in the Wabash."

The rain started in again, and they could hear the wind booming in The Bucks, their name for the twin elms that marked the turnoff to Jonathan's cabin.

"Sounds for all the world like Injun water drums," Lannard muttered.

Then he saw light from a cattail torch rammed into the earth.

"Jonathan," he whispered, and his mouth went dry.

2

THEIR looks circled Jonathan like hawks as they stood in the cave of light the torch hewed out of the dark. Then they dropped their heads and watched a ragged moth going in and out by the flame. There was no place else to look, save at Jonathan's face, and that was too stricken a thing for eyes to rest on.

Lannard opened his mouth and studied on something to say, but acorns rattling down, foxes barking, the restless trees tossing their leaves drowned out the words in his head. The woods was doing all the talking this night. Nothing came out of Lannard's mouth, but the wind blew into it.

Why hadn't Jonathan met them like any mortal man, clench-fisted and maybe drunk, crying out, "Oh, my God . . . *Micajah!*" They had hoped it would be this way . . . that he'd scream the grief out of him, and that would be an end to it. But the mark that Micajah's dying had put on Jonathan's face, turning his gentle eyes to stranger-eyes, told them more than all the words he could have howled aloud. They knew they were right in fearing that this sad hurt might drag him down, and they were uneasy. It came to them now that when anything happened, they all ran to Jonathan. But who was there for him to run to?

They bent to ease the box down on the soggy ground. Tinch kicked twigs out of its way, and Kerman stomped down a knobby root. They acted as if Micajah could feel the rough things of the earth through the heavy puncheons. They knew he couldn't, but they knew, too, that a pa would feel those things for his dead boy, so they were uncommonly tender with the box.

Jonathan knelt down beside the box and picked off the wet leaves that flapped against it. They crouched down across from him.

"Mighty fine pegs," he said slowly. He touched the wet box lovingly. His long fingers pried at the lid. The men about him stirred.

"I wouldn't, if I was you," Lannard said.

Jonathan's eyes flared up.

"We sort of cleaned him up and laid him out. If you look at him now. . . ," Lannard fumbled. "Wal, there's better ways to remember him."

Jonathan looked down at the box.

"I tracked the man that kilt him," Lannard offered. "Read his sign clear to a swamp where Injuns are as thick as the hairs on a hound. But the man . . . I never even got a look at him. If I had," his voice turned hard, "I'd have fetched him back to you alive, but in such miserable shape that even you couldn't cure him up!"

Jonathan bit his lip.

"One thing, though," Lannard added hopefully, "he's headed into the prairie, and it's afire. . . ."

They craned closer now, to hear what Jonathan would say. It seemed that even the woods left off its jabbering to listen.

"Likely now," Jonathan said, after a while, "that man's own pa is looking for him and saying: Why doesn't he come? No, if the fire got him, that's no mortal's fault. But you, Lannard . . . you lost a boy once. You shouldn't be the cause of another mourning and another empty cabin waiting for one who'll never come again . . . not if you can help it."

They all sat back on their haunches. Yes, it was the answer

they knew he would give. Him, with his doctoring of folks . . . you couldn't expect him to be vengeful, not even for his own flesh.

"It's a downright shame!" Rocreuse flared up. "To lose a son like Micajah! If he'd been some cussed boy . . . worthless, brawlin, drunken. . . ."

"You talk like the trees, Rocreuse," Jonathan said softly.

He picked up the torch and they hefted up the box again, but Rocreuse was slow to get it on his shoulder.

"I'm too weary," he said. "I can't go another step."

"We could make camp here for the night," Tinch put in hopefully. "Come morn, it'd be a lot easier to track through that old swamp."

"*I* favor stayin the night here, too," Kerman said slowly. "After all, it's a mighty tricky place. . . ."

"Oh, hesh up!" snapped Lannard. "If you're afeerd, admit it!"

Without another word, they moved ahead. The swamp spread out before them, and they bunched together nervously, all save Jonathan. It was a queer place, the queerest in the whole of the Territory. Birds heard nowhere else called over these marshes. The trees grew as tight as the woods trees, but they didn't stand on solid ground. And any moss you saw was likely not stretched over rocks, but over soggy earth that had a lot of sand mixed in.

Folks said the ghosts of Indians who'd trapped along these streams still set their traps, hoping for a human foot. There was the murdered hunter whose cut-off head still floated about, looking for its body's resting place. And there was that soldier of Wayne's who'd hanged himself above the hedge last year. You could see, if you cared to look, the two grooves in the honeysuckle made by the restless swaying of his ghost-feet.

Tinch yelped as a vine dropped round his neck.

"Looks like you're next," Kerman snickered, "if you believe in signs."

32

"You'll have me jumpin all over the place if you don't hesh," said Lannard testily. "Let's stop a minute and rest. It'll do us all good."

They stood together and stared out from the trail. They wiped at the mist of rain that clung to their matted beards and made the leather of their faces and the leather of their buckskins look the same. They had come all the way through the woods with Micajah, and now they were as jumpy as hunted foxes with having to cross the swamp at night.

"You're all bone-tired," Jonathan said.

They turned to look at him, and the tightness that had built up in them melted away. The world turned itself right-side up again. The trees backed down and quit threatening them, and the screechy cats and night dogs could howl and yowl all they liked, for they could see these beasts weren't bold enough to jump four men lugging a boy. No, likely they hadn't even needed to be quite so wary of those stranger-Indians. The woods was only made of trees. And the beasts were only animals going about their business. And the Indians were just men, like them. It was funny how things always dropped into their proper places when Jonathan was around. You couldn't put a finger on why, but there it was.

Lannard stamped the cramp out of his short legs. Rocreuse lit his clay. Kerman and Tinch fell to talking. Jonathan went on ahead, and the others followed slowly with the box.

The rain had quit when they began to climb out of the swamp. As they stepped into the half-moon clearing, they could even make out the belt and knife of the Warrior Stars, just showing above the trees. The clearing was hills that went up and away from the swamp stalking it on three sides. On the fourth, the woods rose again.

"Looky thar!" Kerman ducked his head toward a light that was bobbing across the clearing toward them.

But it was no ghost-light, such as the women talked about. It was Docia, Kerman's little girl, scooting along with her shawl flapping behind her, and a burning shellbark in her hand. The way Jonathan looked when he saw her, so confused and surprised, they knew he'd forgotten all about her, till now.

"Your wife stopped in for a tonic," he said to Kerman. "She was there when Scuddy brought the word, she and Docia. She stayed to help."

Kerman brightened, seeing his young one coming close, thinking of Retta in the cabin just ahead, but he uttered only a soft, "Keerful, honey!" when Docia ran up and hugged his leg.

Then her eyes fell on the dark box, and they all looked for her to set up a keening at this sight, her being such a little tyke, and so set on Micajah. But she just stood there with her head on one side, squinty-eyed from the glare of the torch her father had taken from her.

"It's a heap better than an old log," she spoke right out and surprised them all. "But where's Micajah's ghost-body?"

It gave them a kind of a shock, her saying such a thing. But, they nodded, that was just like Docia. She was full of the strangest notions, for a young one.

There was light in the double cabin on the clearing's highest hill. Its oiled-paper windows faced west, over the swamp. Its back was hard up against the trees. It was two cabins, side by side. One was the living cabin. The other, the medicine cabin. There was a wide dog-trot between them that had a roof of clapboards, and a floor of beaten clay. The puncheon door to the living cabin stood wide.

A young woman came into the light. She was tall and as slim as a willow whip, and she stood with her toes curled over the doorlog, and her head held high. It was Retta, Kerman's wife, that all the settlement turned to in time of trouble. She watched the group coming toward her, but her face gave no sign of what she saw. Her brown eyes were calm, just as if the clearing were empty, with only the night standing over it.

When they set the box down in the entry, she didn't even look at it. Her eyes were for her husband, and the glance

34

between them was a thing to see, even though she said nothing but, "I see you're safe back."

Docia, however, sank down by the box.

"Micajah," she said gently, "I'm sorry you're dead."

Her pa picked her up in his arms, and they stood awkwardly, all with throats too tight for a sound to come out of them. Then Lannard turned to Jonathan and said how they'd thought an awful lot of the lad, and would be proud to stay and help with the burying. They would sleep in the entry tonight and watch the box, they said. There would be plenty of nights for them to sleep in their own cabins with their wives, but never another night to spend beside Micajah. They'd go and greet their families and come back.

"Better eat first," said Retta kindly. Of a truth, she had laid the table for the lot of them, and behind her, you could see a roast on its spit over the fire. They shuffled past her, suddenly starved and empty, and waited to be bidden to pull up a stool. Jaded as they were, they wouldn't offer to make themselves at home without being asked.

"Help yourselves," Jonathan told them, but he didn't look at them. He stared at Docia instead, and his eyes were far off, like he was seeing his boy years back. Even Lannard had to turn his head away from the heartbreak look on Jonathan's face.

It was Retta who spoke up and said the men could drop their packs in the corner, Retta who fetched out a jug of rum and said would they have a dollop while she finished dishing up the supper? In just a shake, she was flipping hot johnnycakes onto a wooden trencher, slicing down the roast and scooping pumpkin out of its shell and setting dittany to steep.

The long-hunters ate with quick jerks and little talk. They paused often to crane their heads round to the wind that blew in over the doorlog, and to wipe their sleeves across their faces where the sweat came thick. All the time, their moccasined feet kept up a restless shuffling under the table.

They were always like this when they first came back. It

35

was hard to know what to do with the legs that suddenly hung down from stools, and they ached to sit cross-legged, as they did in the woods. Their hands kept forgetting the use of two-tined forks, and they wound up by just holding them politely and eating with their knives. Their noses twitched, trying to get used to the cabin smell of dried-out chinking and strings of herbs and softsoap and polished logs. The smell of their wet buckskins, too close to the fire, somehow didn't fit in. Their eyes, when they raised them, were dazed from seeing things beyond this door, and their lips quivered to tell about them.

Now they had to get used to looking only at a cabin again. They stared and stared around it. A cabin was a smaller thing than they'd thought for, and the loft lower over their heads, all so bright when outdoors it was dark, so hot when outdoors it was cool. Even their faces and voices seemed strange. Now they longed to feel the movement of their legs on the trails, and the always-talk of the trees above their heads, and the closer cries of the beasts. They looked out across the doorlog toward the awesome swamp and the woods beyond, and wondered that they had ever cursed these things.

Retta knew. Her own husband always came back like this. Many's the time she had seen him cast his eyes around the clothespegs where hung his sleeping shirt and other things, and his face had that stranger-look.

"They go, and every time they go, some part of them don't come back," she told herself. "From the time they begin to walk and wander, they're stranger-men. Their lives belong to the woods, and ours to the cabin."

Later Lannard fetched out of his pack the things he'd taken from Micajah's body. His skinning knife, his tomahawk, the crooked Indian knife with its beaver-tooth blade, his bag of powder and shot, pieces of flint and steel and punk. Rocreuse handed over a thin gold ring that Jonathan put on his own little finger, and a page torn from one of Jonathan's books. All wondered why the boy had carried it and what it said, but were shamed to ask. Kerman had a bird skeleton, splinters

36

of bone, a ball of thong, feathers from a flicker, a rough map scrawled on bark. Tinch took out of his polecat pouch a few Spanish bits and some dried, leftover cherry cakes.

They spread the things out on the puncheon table and poked at them and peered at them. There was a lonely look to these poor left-behind possessions, now that the boy who had carried them against the warmth of his chest was dead. It was powerful little to show for seventeen years of living, just these few things gathered up by his slim hands, kept and carried for why?

In the end, Jonathan scooped them up off the table and put them away in the wooden chest Micajah had made, alongside his clothes. Now all that was left of Micajah's living was his own body, and when it was let down into the earth, what would there be to show that he had lived?

"My restless son," said Jonathan softly. "Maybe I'll happen on his moccasin print along one of the streams. And when I do . . . I wonder . . . will I know it for his?"

But Docia, babe that she was, couldn't quite get it through her head that Micajah wasn't ever coming back to them again. She was worried by their sad-eyed looks, and shinnied up the legs of the men to shove her bright face into their gloomy ones. And when that did no good, she pressed her cheek against Rocreuse's knees and whimpered. Gal-like, she knew which of the rough woodsies was the softest toward young ones.

Before long, Rocreuse had taken off his Frenchy earhoops and slipped them on her fingers for her to marvel at, and was tossing her in his arms to the husky song a voyageur sings when he hears the river rapids close. His black eyes looked on a far-off land, and his back stiffened as if he were balanced against the roll of the river. The others, watching him, could near see that dark woods-country of pineys and raw waters and skies blue with cold, where the stars of the Northern Cross hung above, and there was a curious beast called the *carcajou*, the wolverine, that had a human way of rearing upright and shading its eyes with one paw. They could hear

37

the swish of the paddles, and feel the far-north wind that came down from the forever-ice. And they could imagine the babe Rocreuse held safe in the canoe's bottom by his pa's hard thighs.

Of a sudden, Rocreuse broke off and muttered a curse. They looked at him quiet-faced, as if they didn't know he'd been thinking of that distant time and country, of the pa he hated who had taught him that song and, afterward, abandoned him.

The woodsies finished eating, anxious to be gone, for none had his cabin or half-face camp nearby, and all but Kerman had to come back yet this night. Then Lannard stiffened, and craned his head toward the dark of the doorway. Of a sudden, all heard it, a jogging, rattling sound underneath the thin rain, the sound of Indian runners.

The men came up from the table, stumbling over the stools in their rush. They cursed the door for standing open to the whole sneaky world, the light of the fireplace for showing them up as men with noggins in their hands instead of guns. They hated the walls of the cabin for hiding the forest from their eyes, the rum for lulling them into the peace of their long-ago homes, where they had had watchmen with lanterns, close-by neighbors, and Indians who slunk down the streets of nights, like tamed devil dogs. Their knotty hands groped hastily in polecat pouches for shot, their feet hit the floor so hard that the herbs on strings rattled against the chimney, and dust shook out of the loft boards. But once they began to move, a hunters' calm came over them, and silenced the crazy words that were tumbling down their tongues like otters down a slide.

"No need to stampede like a wild bull herd!" Lannard flared. "Since when do Injun runners come up the trail rattlin shells and bones to make an attack?"

"Especially here," added Jonathan quietly.

They sucked in their breaths and nodded. They had forgotten in their panic that in Jonathan's swamp, both Indians and white men could go and come as they pleased, and no one would lift a hand against either, no matter how deep the hate. The Miamis had promised, and Jonathan had promised, too, because the swamp was sacred Miami ground. Still, the woodsies would have felt better if they could have hauled the heavy door shut, dropped its bar in place, and stood by with their rifles in their hands.

Jonathan stepped out into the misty rain. The men crowded out after him, and pushed the door to behind them. It wasn't long until they made out the bobbing lights of tall mullein torches coming up the trail. Then Indian runners, holding them, broke through the chest-high mist, carrying a burden on their wet shoulders. They loped along at a pace that looked almost restful, but even the best horse in the Territory would be hard put to keep it up for a night and a day as they could, and cover a hundred miles from sunset to sunset. Yet no weariness showed in their coppery faces. Their long, corded legs never wobbled, their shoulders never bent.

The men by the doorlog frowned, trying to make out what it was these runners had fetched. It put you in mind of a skinned animal, was all they could say.

The Indians came on steady, their bare upper parts gleaming in the flare of their torches under the dripping trees. Their moccasined feet carried them forward as if nothing stood before them, no cabin, no trees, no men. They put you in mind of Indian tales which told of hunters who'd run right up into the hills and into the sky and turned into stars.

An Indian who looked too old for running trotted at their head. There was a hard and set look to his face, as though he were driving himself to something he'd never dreamed of. He alone had on a buckskin robe, and a headband with feathers trailing down its edge like a tail. But his face was smeared with soot, and he wore no ornaments. All could see he was an Indian in mourning.

"Shawnee," Kerman muttered.

Now they could see that the burden the runners carried was a boy about Micajah's age. He lay on their shoulders with his belly turned up to the sky and his arms thrown out

39

stiff, across their backs. His head had fallen back, so that it bobbed between the chests of the two front runners, and he saw all upside down. His eyes, the only alive-looking things about him, stared out fierce and black, and when they fell on the white men, they went slitty. His long hair was singed and hung in rags. He was naked.

With him came the heavy, rotten smell of burned skin. They saw that his hide was peeling and in some places the flesh was torn away in chunks. He was covered over with dried blood, black and caked. Those who tried to help him had bled their chests and arms over him, hoping to heal his burns.

They came into the light of the oiled-paper windows of the cabin. The old Indian looked into the entry, where a fire burned low to keep prowling beasts away from the bury-ing box. He nodded toward the box and the runners moved slowly toward it, and laid the boy down upon it. Lannard and the others chewed at their beards, and their faces dark-ened. Those Indians had no right to fling down one of their own on Micajah's burying box, which the woodsies had made so carefully with their own hands. Their mouths twisted to say so, but Jonathan held them back.

"Likely they don't know what it is," he said gently, "and take it for a platform like the Shawnee wigiwam has."

The old Indian stopped close to Jonathan. He reached out and touched Jonathan's chest, then his own. It was a sign of friendship. He spoke the formal greeting.

"I have come."

The runners squatted on their heels behind him, and rammed their torches into the ground. They crouched with their heads down, panting hard. A small boy none had noticed before came out of the mist and went to stand be-side the tall boy lying on the box.

"Those are my sons," the Indian nodded toward the two boys. "The little one, still my son. The big one, no longer my son. In the Miami village where we have been welcomed as brothers, he has disgraced my name and theirs." He looked at Jonathan. "Again and again, I have told my son, no longer my son, to abide by the Miami ways, for we live by their bounty. Yet he will not. Always he hates the whites, the Morning Light People." He broke off and turned to the boy who stared bitterly up at the roof of the entry built by white men's hands. "Now, with no shame, he comes and tells me that he has killed your son. With no shame he comes, falling down from his wounds. Not the honorable wounds of battle, but the wounds of the great God's punishment for breaking faith. With shame for this son, no longer my son, I bring him to you." He bowed his head.

Lannard choked.

"So that's who I was follerin," he whispered, twisting round toward the tall boy. "That's who I run into the prairie."

"Tomorrow the Indian law will be obeyed when you throw my living son, no longer my son, onto your son's dark box and fling the dirt in his open mouth. Killed and killer will be forever in one grave."

The tall boy's eyes looked out from his black lashes hurt and wet, but he didn't make a sound, or even flinch at his father's words. Yet the hurt in his eyes was not for the pain of his body. To giving and taking pain, he had been hardened from a babe. No, the hurt was for his father's weakness, turning his back on the warrior ways of the Shawnee, and becoming as an old woman at the will of the Miamis. His shame was as great as his father's. But it was for his father, not for himself. He cast his eyes at his little brother beside him, and murmured something too soft for the others to hear.

Jonathan walked over to the tall boy and looked down at him, but none could tell from his face what he was thinking. One thing all noticed, though. His doctor's hands, so quick to reach out to a stricken mortal, stayed shoved down in his sash. After a while, he went back and stood by the Shawnee man.

"I leave this one to you," the old Indian fetched out, softly. "All his Shawnee blood I have taken away. His name also. He is nothing. Of no race, of no people. Now I must go to where his mother waits for me on the trail. Already, being a woman, she forgives him, for she cannot forget the love and pain that gave him life. But I am a man. I forget."

He turned away, and the runners fell back and picked up their torches. But the smaller boy would not come away from the tall lad on the box.

"*No!*" he cried out. "I have not cast him away. I still speak his name. He is Shining Sun, my brother. I will not leave him!"

"Obey me," said the Shawnee.

"*No!*" screamed the child. He rushed at his father and twisted loose the knife which hung from his belt. He turned the blade against himself. "If you leave him here, I will kill myself! I will die with him!"

But he was such a little babe that the knife was easily wrenched from his hands, and he writhed and fought in his father's strong brown arms.

"This is not the way of a Shawnee," said his father coldly.

But Jonathan stopped it all.

"I cannot accept your son," he said. "Take him back. Take him." He paused. "I give him back to his people as a gift. I give him back his Shawnee blood. I give him back his right to be born again."

The old Indian and Jonathan looked at each other, but the others looked only at the tall boy. They could see now that he was dying. Already his eyes were glazing over with the slow film that crept from under the lower lids. Already his soul was going, while they talked there in the rain.

At a nod from the Shawnee, the runners eased the boy gently upon their shoulders again. They started down the trail.

"Brother," the Indian murmured, "I am a defeated warrior, driven from my south home, and made to beg from the Miamis a place to spread my blanket. Were it not for this, I would pledge you great things. But I . . . I have nothing left to pledge." He lifted his head to the shifting wind. "When the Shawnee moon shines on you in the nights, may our Grandmother, the Moon Woman, protect you."

But the little boy spoke boldly.

"*I* will give you a pledge!" he declared. "Someday I will do you a great service." He untied from his neck a piece of whang with a bear claw tied on. He held it out to Jonathan. "This is my friend-totem. Keep it, with my pledge. Someday I will come to you with the strength, the cunning, and the speed of our cousin the bear. My feet, no matter where they go, will find you again!"

He and his father went off together, following the lights of the runners. Jonathan and the woodsies stood in silence, watching the torches quivering beneath the wet trees, and the misty rain falling.

Finally Lannard said, "It was a fine thing you done, Jonathan, givin his boy back. Did you do it because. . . ?"

"Let's not study on why we do things," Jonathan shook his head. "It makes things turn cheap."

They turned to the entry, then, and looked over the box, wanting to make sure it hadn't been hurt by the Indian lying on it. Kerman scraped some rags of burnt flesh from the top of it. The others turned homeward.

Later on, they came back and watched with Jonathan, all stretched out beside the box with their feet toward the fire. Jonathan sat with his back to the rough logs. For hours he watched the rain misting, the smoke blowing, the tired woodsy men with their faces pulled down into their blankets of beards.

From the south, across the Salamonie river, came the sad singing from the Miami village called Manjinikia after their chief Big Frame. He heard the slow drum start to beat. He heard the high-pitched tones of the singer. It was a windsong, so called because it was lonely like the wind in the trees, or across the great prairie, or down the river. The song fell slowly.

43

"On the Pathway of Souls, I stand and wave,
See, alone my shadow-soul waves.
Give me life again,
For none are here that I call Father."

He knew the Shawnee boy was dead. He looked at the box beside him, then toward the wind-song, and the rain ran down his face like tears.

The rain was pouring now. You could hear it beating on the bark-hide roof and running down the ridge poles and splatting in the narrow trench it had dug around the cabin. Till daybreak, the wind shook the old chieftains of the forest, until their bones were picked clean of leaves. Young whips of trees were lashed until you thought they'd snap apart, and the rotten widow-makers were pushed over. Many a woman harkened to hear them thudding down, and came up from her pallet. Many a man was on the trail this night, and maybe trapped beneath that very tree. Grateful the woman whose man was safe beside her. Wakeful the woman whose man was off somewhere, and she lit pine knots and stood on her doorlog, peering out into the rain listening for a call on the wind.

Jonathan stirred, remembering. No longer would they need to fret after Micajah on nights like this. Never again would he wonder if the lad had slept on the bank of a rising river, was caught beneath a fallen tree, or was prey to hunting beasts giving their blood-drawn howl. No, Micajah was safe forever, where he was.

But Jonathan turned the bear claw over and over in his fingers.

"Little Shawnee," he murmured, "do me the great service now. Bring back my son, so I can worry about him once more."

3

OLD Death was not a choosy fellow, and was talked of familiarly by all. But Micajah's death was different because Jonathan was his pa, Jonathan who kept watch over their sick, soothed their dying, listened to their worries, brought needed things to their cabins without shaming them. Many's the grateful man who had lugged him fresh-killed meat, the first of the garden patch, extra fine skins . . . and he would always say there was no need to feel beholden. But they never felt they could do enough. Now, here was their chance to do something big for him. They'd give his boy a burying that folks would talk about for years to come.

Anyway, in secret each thought Jonathan liked *him* best. "He'd be mortal offended if *I* didn't come," they bragged back and forth.

The Carsons and the McCutcheons came, but slowly, for Sally Carson was making a babe, and was poorly. To look at her bleak face you'd never think she had hiked in here, lightsome and strong, but a year ago.

Mrs. McCutcheon put you in mind of a heron, the stiff-legged way she walked. She'd worked hard enough to be a hundred, but she'd just eased over the forty line.

"I been dragged from Caroliny to Pennsylvany to *here*," she complained, with her mouth going puckery. "I said to my boy Abe we *got* to stop here, or one day we'll wake up in Chiney!"

The Simontons came, dragging their crippled boy on a poplar sled. Ellen Simonton spoke to them real pleasant.

"Seems like we never could get down here before, what with gettin settled in our camp and all. . . ," her words trailed off, for she felt a shyness at coming face to face with the settlers, and she'd seen how hatefully the Callis and Stiles women eyed her youthful prettiness. "I . . . I brung the purtiest persimmons and pawpaws from down my way. And I put in a big chunk of bread, fresh kilt this morn, and wropped in the hide."

Pansy Stiles sniffed.

"Us farm folks don't call venison and turkey-breast bread. It's all meat, same as bear." She pushed in beside Retta. "*I* brung some coffee."

The others poked into the calabash.

"Tain't the boughten kind, but it's as good as common. You know, *we* got a Kentucky Coffee Tree."

"I recollect you harpin on it," Sally said sourly, "more'n once."

But Pansy ignored her and turned to Dove Callis.

"Maybe this-here coffee'll do you some good," she said. "You got an awful queer look about you."

Dove stepped back nervously.

"I been fightin the ager," she said.

But they all knew she'd been stayin with Lannard's babes and woman while he was long-hunting. Somebody had to be with them all the time, for ever since her last babe was born, Lannard's woman had been down with the crazies.

"Sure is nice to see plain folks again," Dove added, as if she knew what they were thinking.

They were gathered underneath the trees, all but Retta, who had gone in to see to the cooking. Now Ellen trailed after her.

46

"Ain't they someways I can help?" she asked, pausing a moment on the doorlog, the way a real lady did when she was visiting for the first time.

"My, what a grand place!" she burst out, going in. "It's like the cabin my man has swore to build for me, now that he's done with his wanderin."

"They ain't never done with their wanderin," answered Retta quietly.

"Yes, but *he* is! He swore when we left the Youghiogheny that we'd settle on the banks of the Salamonie."

She stared wistfully at the things around her. The cabin had chinked walls, four of them, instead of three, like down at her half-face camp. And this floor! Well, she would settle for a beaten-down earth floor, but this one of rough puncheon with its creaky oval pegs seemed mighty homey underfoot. She marveled at the two doors of split-out logs that hung on wooden hinges. One opened at the front of the living cabin, and looked out over the clearing. The other opened on the entry and faced the medicine-cabin door. A body wouldn't have to have two doors, she told herself, but to have just *one,* and to pull a latchstring in at night and know that you were safe and sound, with something more between you and dark than a bearskin flapping over the open end of the half-face camp, beyond the fire.

"He's even got greased-paper winders," she said, in awe. Then added, "But I reckon scraped animal hide'll do for us."

Sally Carson waddled tiredly through the door and eased herself down on a three-legged stool. The bed in the corner caught her eye. Its one leg was a forked stick set out from the corner and pounded down through an auger hole in the floor. Two strong poles ran out from the walls to form the foot and one side of the bed. They crossed at the fork and were tied firmly to it.

"Has it got a wove deer-thong frame?" she asked Retta, in hushed tones.

"Yes, and a corn-husk mattress."

"That's a sight better than a mess of skins and hides," she

47

said wistfully. "I wish I'd be took sick now. It sure would be a cozy place to have my babe."

Mrs. McCutcheon hobbled in and eyed them sharply. She stood watching Retta shape the johnnycakes and lay them on their curved boards by the fire. Right off, she had to nosy in. She snatched a ladle from its hook and used it to jab every calabash and kettle. Some she tasted . . . "this'd make a dog sick." Some she moved . . ."a body can see it's ready to burn." The meat on the spit she basted with venison drippings . . ."make it a lot more tasty."

"You jest set and rest, Mrs. McCutcheon." Retta bit her tongue to keep from flaring at her, because meat basted with the tallowy venison fat wasn't fit to eat. "We can take keer of all there is."

"Jonathan lives high," Mrs. McCutcheon remarked sourly. "Ain't no one needs a fireplace that big. Why, it's as deep as my Abe is tall, and wide as this cabin! And such a lot of extry trash!" She nodded toward the front of the fireplace, the pegs for calabashes and rush brooms and ladles. From the mantel hung strings of sassafras and dittany and mint for teas, basil and sage and ginger for seasoning. On top of the mantel was the pewter box with flint and steel inside, and there were even clay saucer-lamps with cotton wicks floated in bear grease. Behind them was a long row of worn books.

"Read 'em once, and what have you got?" she asked. "My man was a reader, but he's jest as dead as if he hadn't known one curlycue from another."

On pegs along the west wall hung Jonathan's clothes. At the back of the cabin, on the east wall, was a long shelf. It held a mug-shaped potato bowl made of maple, a squashlike masher, wooden mixing bowls, a tin corn-grater, a box for pewter spoons and two-tined forks, the cabin knife, maple mugs and bowls and trenchers that had been burned and scraped until they shone like glass.

"Oh," sighed Mrs. McCutcheon, "things is lots easier for women today than when I was a gal. Now, you take *that*. . . ," she jerked her head toward the hollow stone trough on its upended log. "I never had nothing so nice to warsh my dishes in. And the spoons we had was made of shells stuck in twigs. Many's the time I had to do my cookin in a clay pot, and the grease come right through." She thinned her lips. "Many's the time I ground roast acorns into flour cause thar wasn't nothing else to eat. And I've seen folks back in the Caroliny hills stand up to get wed with their young ones rompin round 'em. The preacher, he come so seldom. And I didn't live within ten days' walk of a doctor. . . ."

"You just set," murmured Ellen, pulling herself to her feet. She moved out the door and the other women followed her, anxious to escape Mrs. McCutcheon's garrulous tongue.

Outside, they sorted their mugs and bowls and trenchers. Down the middle of the log table that had been laid before the cabin, they heaped piles of nuts and apples and rose hips, tart wild grapes, pawpaws and persimmons. They fussed around the table, setting the spoons just so, acting as if they were back on the Susquehanna or the Yadkin or the Rappahannock. But it was only to hide what each was thinking. One would pause and stare out toward the open grave, then they'd look to their own young ones rolling and screaming in the fallen leaves.

Lannard trudged up the hill to where Jonathan stood by the buryhole. It was damp from the rain. Other men stood around in bunches. Some leaned against the warm cabin walls, some squatted in the entry, admiring the box. Some lounged on logs dragged near the table. They smoked their clays, whittled, or talked softly, but all fell quiet when Jonathan and Lannard stepped into the entry. At the same time, little Docia came flying up the swamp trail, clutching in one fist a bunch of wilting asters and goldenrod.

"For the box," she said.

The same four men who had carried Micajah home hefted up the box on the hickory withes they had run beneath it. Others stepped up, anxious to help, but the four shook their heads at them.

49

"We've brung him this far," Lannard drawled. "It wouldn't be right if we didn't bring him the rest of the way. Anyway . . . as tall as he stood, he's only the weight of a boy."

The men shuffled their feet. The women left off their work, pulled their shawls tighter about them, and walked after the box.

"Death ain't no stranger to me," said Retta bitterly. "I seen my own ma laid to her lonesome rest on the trail, and my two no-name babes right in this buryin ground. I heerd the rattlin in their throats and shut their eyes with my own fingers. But, Lord Almighty . . . Micajah."

The young ones stopped their playing coon-and-dogs with the Stiles boy, and he came down out of his tree.

"I'm still coon when the buryin's done!" he yelled, and was smacked by the nearest grownup.

"Some day you'll be gettin laid away," they told him, "and if you don't act proper now, folks won't act proper then."

Jonathan's burying ground was the only one for many a mile, and some said it was just so much flapdoodle, but settlement ways were catching on, even though the nearest settlement on good dry trails was five days' hard ride. But that wasn't counting the new fort, Fort Wayne, or any of the others to the east, on the Wabash trail.

"Anyways, it ain't so lonesome for our dead," Kerman's woman said, "if they're buried together, instead of scattered over the land like seeds from a cottonwood."

Ellen said wasn't it a pity they couldn't open the box and touch him, so they'd be able to let him know they wished him well? And Pansy said she hoped the menfolks who found him had remembered to untie his ankle thongs, so he wouldn't be twisting forever. Dove stayed far enough away from the box to make sure none of her tears fell on it to weigh him down.

"*Her* tears would weigh anybody down, she's so free with 'em," Kerman muttered.

But most of them thought it was a real honor to have the

best Weeper in the Indiana Territory living among them like a common person.

"It's a perfect day for a buryin, if you got to have one," Ellen said gently.

They stood in a knot around the buryhole, Jonathan right at its edge. The box went down slowly on its withes into the empty dark, and the mud settled around it with a squishy sound.

In the swamp, all sound had quit. Then, suddenly, a mocker called when it should have been asleep. The men cast their eyes toward the guns they had left leaning against the cabin walls.

"Likely that's the Sin-Eater comin," said Dove reassuringly. "My man went to get him, and they should have been back afore now."

On the trail, however, were three men. Two were Indians, but the third. . . .

"Who in tarnal?" Lannard puzzled.

"It's the breed, the Frenchy Injun, Night Dog they call him," Kerman muttered.

"Is it?" All eyes turned to Rocreuse, whose face had darkened at the name.

So this was the breed all had whispered about. They slanted their looks at him, for everyone had heard how this breed and Rocreuse had the same pa. Their pa had been a voyageur from the Frenchy settlements way up north, by the great English Lakes. His woman had tramped after him on the stranger-trails with her babe, Rocreuse, in her arms. But one day, down at Vincennes, her man had left them with the padre at the mission, and they never laid eyes on him again. Later, word came back to them that he'd run off with an Indian girl who had gleaming eyes and a husky voice. Night Dog was his other son.

The Indians halted at the edge of the clearing and talked. The breed listened to what they said, his face grave, then shook his head. He laid his gun, knife, and tomahawk by the trail, and rammed a stick in the ground beside them as a

51

marker. From one of the Indians he took a hide *parfleche* and heaved it onto his shoulder. They turned back, but he came on toward the people on the hill, walking on the silent, rolling feet of a brave.

Rocreuse hooked his thumb over his skinning knife.

"Look at that!" muttered Kerman. "Big as life!"

The breed walked straight to Jonathan.

"Brother. I am Night Dog."

The others drew close and looked at the woodsies. Most folks knew but little of any Indian tongue. Settlers flatly refused to learn it, but the woodsy men all spoke Indian, for many of them stayed in the villages when they were long-hunting alone. The Indians had no hate against them, inasmuch as they were only wandering hunters. It was the settlers, with their fencing and land clearing, that made the Indians rise up.

"Brother. We have never met," Night Dog went on, "but I know of you. I am here because I was a friend to your son. Because, were it my son, you would do this for me."

With everyone straining to catch his words, the young ones were forgotten. Now they squirmed from the arms that had held them back, and pointed and jabbered in whispers about the Frenchy Indian. They saw that his hair was worn loose, not in queues like their pa's, nor chopped short with a skinning knife, as some men did. They gaped at his golden earrings and bracelets, and the more daring among them reached out to touch the bright beading on his buckskin shirt and the seams of his leggings.

Jonathan looked back at Night Dog, who stood nearly as tall as himself. You could see he was putting things together in his mind . . . the long times that passed when no one had seen Micajah on the trails, and then he'd come swinging in, but not scrubby like a long-hunter who'd been sleeping in the open. It came to Jonathan how little he had known of Micajah, after all.

"Perhaps Micajah never told you of my cabin. Perhaps he thought it not important," said Night Dog quietly.

"No," Jonathan lied. "He loved to talk of you."

Night Dog's voice warmed.

"He was much like my own son, long dead, murdered also."

They shifted their eyes to look down at the box in its hole. It was one thing to stop in a village, or to see an Indian girl on the sly. But to think on an Indian the same as you'd think on a white man, to visit him as you would a neighbor! There were a lot of things we didn't know about Micajah, their eyes said.

"Brother. It is good that you have come," Jonathan said.

Night Dog swung the *parfleche* down from his shoulder and laid it at Jonathan's feet. The men crowded closer. None of them had ever seen one of these carry-alls, but they had heard tell of them.

"Likely stole it from some west Injun he murdered in his sleep," Stiles muttered.

"This is my gift of food," Night Dog said simply. "Today I observe your ways."

"My thanks to you."

Jonathan turned back to the grave. When the Stiles saw that he was going to say the burying words with the breed right there, they sniffed and started off down the hill. But when he didn't come after them, they shambled back and stood a little way off from the others.

"We got to stay till Micajah's laid away," whispered Pansy sharply.

The fur hats came off and the bonnets dipped.

As was their way, all who had anything to say to Micajah stepped to the grave and spoke his name as if he were living.

"Don't go wanderin off too far," Kerman said. "We'll go huntin together again afore too long."

They swallowed at that, for it was true that sick-faced Kerman probably wouldn't live to see another spring.

"I'll keep an eye on your traps for you," Tinch said, with his face all puckery.

"Don't you worry none about not bein baptized keepin

you out of heaven," Rocreuse mumbled. "When we found you, I went ahead on my own, and baptized you myself." He started away, then came back. "Micajah, you know I didn't mind carryin you home." He ducked his head.

Lannard was the last. You could see by the way he kept jerking his beard that he was feeling Micajah's death deeper than most.

"Micajah. . . ," he began, but broke off. "I . . . I can't say arything!" He choked and stepped back.

Now came the hard moment for Jonathan to speak, and somehow they knew that, though the anguish in his voice was his own, the words in his mouth were not.

"Would that he had died in my arms, then we would have wept and wailed our fill. Wherefore should I live, in my pain, now that you are dead, who day and night were my boast throughout the city, and a blessing to all? Both men and women hailed you as a god, for an exceeding glory were you in your life . . . now death and fate have overtaken you."

Afterward, they asked him if these stranger-words were from The Book and he said no, they were written by a man named Homer. Likely, they said to each other, some preacher he had known back East.

Suddenly Dove Callis sniffed and burst into loud cries.

"Good gramine!" Sally glared at her.

"I heerd tell of a place where they hire weepers for bury-ins," Lannard muttered, coldly. "She ought to make tracks for thar. She sure could make her a fortune."

Jonathan took up the wooden shovel and put the first earth on the grave. The men stayed behind with him, each taking his turn at the shovel. The women hurried back to the cabin, now that the sad part was done.

The venison roast was dripping on the hearth. The johnny-cakes were golden brown. The turkeys were stripped of their casings. Pone was taken from the spider. Squash was carried to the table, along with the boiled corn, the potatoes, and cucumbers. Sassafras steeped in its kettle, and jugs of rum came out of the bushes. Trenchers were heaped, and woman-talk rose above the sound of skirts dusting over path and floor.

But when they called the men to come to the table, they found they needn't have rushed. Callis was back, and he had the Sin-Eater with him.

"Wal, it's about time!" Dove snorted. "You should of been here before the body was covered over!"

The Sin-Eater looked at her coldly.

"I ain't used to walkin," he informed her. "It's usual fer me to be sent a horse to ride."

Hastily, they shushed him and the airs he was putting on. It wouldn't do for Jonathan to hear such talk, as he hadn't wanted the Sin-Eater in the first place.

A johnnycake was brought from the table, and the Sin-Eater stood by the grave and ate it slowly, thoughtfully.

"Tarnal, man!" Lannard growled. "Hurry up! I'm as hungry as a she-bear!"

"Well?" Dove kept jabbing at him. "Do you feel arything?"

Finally he nodded.

"As I was chewin, I felt the poor lad's sins settle on my shoulders. Now all's well with him. Lucky fer him, and you too, to have a Sin-Eater close by. Sin-Eaters is scarce as hen's teeth. . . ."

"For heaven's sake, let's eat!" Sally flared.

Talk went fast, up and down the table, and food went from hand to mouth, so quick you'd think they'd bite their fingers. Day was a precious thing and a person got used to eating on the run, so he could hurry back to his choring.

But they didn't eat as peacefully as they'd expected to, for when the breed was brought to the table, Rocreuse turned sullen. In his mind this Indian, his hated half-brother, was somehow to blame for the loss of his pa and the heartbreak of his ma.

"Simmer down," Lannard poked at him.

Finally he settled down to chewing on a pigeon leg and everyone hoped his dark mood was past.

"Mrs. McCutcheon," he called, after a while. "How'd you cook these here pigeons? They're jest like my ma used to fix em."

"That's good," Lannard scowled. "Eat 'em, and shut up."

The rest went on with their chewing, but their eyes were uneasy.

"How?" he called again.

"Wal, I don't think *I* brought that mess of pigeons," she faltered, finally. "Down *thar's* my trencher."

"Wal, who then?"

"I brought them," Night Dog's voice was soft. "My daughter cooked them."

Rocreuse stood up so sudden that he jarred the heavy table, and mugs slopped over, and piles of fruit collapsed.

"*You!*" he spat. Then, snatching up a mug of rum, he filled his mouth and spewed the rum into the Indian's face. He lunged and was halfway across the table. One knee scattered a heap of nuts.

"Come down from thar!" Lannard snapped. "Afore you fall and break your tom-fool neck!"

But Rocreuse had no aim to come down. Instead, he yanked his knife loose from the thong at his belt. Night Dog stood up slowly, his arms spread wide, showing he had no knife or tomahawk. He looked at Rocreuse coolly.

"Brother," he said, "I have never known fear of men. I would not turn on my heel to save my life."

"Is that a fact?" sneered the Stiles man. He came around the table.

Some of the other men stirred, seeing trouble. Then Pansy yelled for Rocreuse to kill the breed. That decided it, and Rocreuse jumped. Lannard grabbed for him and missed. Jonathan was on his feet and in front of the breed before they could catch their breaths, and Rocreuse saw him there too late. His knife blade sliced the tight leather shirt that Jonathan wore.

The sounds quit like crickets do when they feel somebody

56

walking on the grass. You could even hear a wild goldfinch calling down in the swamp.

Rocreuse sank down on the ground and Lannard stood over him, red with fury. No one wanted to be the first to move or say a word, for they were shamed to the heart by what had nearly happened.

There was a scramble among the young ones for the knife Rocreuse had dropped.

"I'm Rocreuse and you're the Frenchy Injun!" one screeched.

"I ain't goin to be no Injun!" another stormed.

"Shame on you young ones!" The women stamped in among them, yanking them apart and flinging slaps on either side. "Shame! You act like varmint cubs or worse!"

The men turned flushed faces to Jonathan.

"I reckon it went a mite too far," they mumbled.

But he stared back at them with a look so fierce that it took their breath away, though he said not one word about the shameful way they'd acted. It wasn't like Jonathan to let them carry on with such antics and not give them at least a gentle setting down. They were frightened, for none had ever seen him like this.

"I . . . I guess we're jest so used to livin in these old woods that we're gettin like the creatures," one of them fetched out, after a while.

"Wal, it sure ain't no way to act at a time like this!" Tinch said, tight-faced.

"I reckon we didn't think," added Kerman.

They had forgotten the promises he had made, Jonathan told them sternly. He'd sworn the swamp would be a place of safety for all men, and that if anyone were slain in the swamp, the Miamis could not only take it back, but kill those who violated the promise. What place would be safe for them then? Where would they turn for help?

"But you'd be here! You wouldn't up and leave us . . . no matter what!" one burst out.

"No," said Jonathan slowly, and the stranger-look went from him, leaving his face more natural.

He leaned down and picked up Rocreuse's knife and held it out to him, but Rocreuse had rolled over on his back with his arm across his face, and wouldn't look at Jonathan or take the knife. Then Jonathan straightened up and threw it at an oak. It hit so hard that acorns shook down on them, and the long hilt quivered in the bark while all eyes looked at it.

"Wal," Callis cleared his throat. "I reckon we're jest a mite edgy."

"Don't make no neverminds how edgy we are!" Lannard jerked his beard. "It ain't a proper way to act, or to show respect for the dead. Jest like a pack of varmints howlin at the sight of the moon, hamstringin their prey!"

"That's right!" the Sin-Eater said around a mouthful of food, and they all glared at him.

"Ain't it time you was goin?" one asked angrily. "This here's a private matter that we cain't talk of in front of strangers."

He got to his feet all frothy.

"Danged if you ain't the orneriest bunch of people I ever seen!" he flared. "I'm goin . . . and don't you ever call me again to do your Sin-Eatin, cause I won't come!" He snatched the half bit Jonathan had laid down for him, and stamped off into the hills. "It's a Christian work, you know," he yelled back at them, "but you can all go to hell afore I eat for you again!"

Someone laughed and the rest of them took it up. Soon rum and trenchers were going around the table again and Abe, whose head was full of riddles, fell to telling them. Even the young ones stopped their play and squatted by him, to try their hand at guessing the answers.

The sun was going from the clearing when they began to pack up their fixings and divide the food. When they called their young ones and they didn't come, they went to see what devilment they were into now, and found they'd dragged ashes over the ground and were standing around, staring at them.

"Thar, you see!" chirped one. "It does look like Ellen's foot!"

"Tain't no such thing," another said back. "That mark don't fit *nobody's* foot!"

"Land, ain't there been enough unhappiness without you wild ones tryin to figure out who'll die next?" snapped Mrs. McCutcheon.

They snatched up their young ones and, one by one, went off down the trail. Dark was right on their heels, and the cabin snuggled against the wind that started up behind them.

4

CAME December, and still no sign of winter. The grass grew green on the graves and all knew it for a bad sign. The ground was soft as a new-plowed field when it should have been shank-deep in snow and frozen hard as a limestone ledge. Scattered blossoms whitened the wild hawthorn, and bloodroot pushed its fresh leaves through dead ones.

Roots and herbs were plentiful, but the womenfolk turned their mouths down at them. Plants that came up out of their time were likely to be poison. So they ate bitter meal ground from roasted acorns, for game was scarce, and only the wind walked the trails and salt-licks now.

Tinch went hunting all the way south to Makes-A-Noise-Place, and with his own eyes he saw a *wendigo*, a beast-man, an Indian brave turned animal, hankering after human flesh.

"It's jest fool's luck you ever came back," Lannard flared. All felt beholden to Tinch for bringing word that the *wendigo* was on the trails, and they warned their young ones to listen for his bowstring in the forest.

A stranger, a trader asking to trade his goods for a silver spoon, stopped at Jonathan's cabin. He needed it to run a silver bullet, he said. He'd been hauling on the Black Swamp

Trail when his oxen had died on him, his bound-boy had run off, and some of his best trade goods had been snatched by some Shawnees.

"I heerd they is a witch-woman, name of Gentry, hereabout," he said, "and I aim to get her with that bullet! Ef she hadn't put a spell on the weather and made it mild, I wouldn't of come up here this time of year!"

But Jonathan sent him packing and warned him not to show himself around there again.

The wind shifted and came from the west when it should have been blowing from the north. Rain set in. It fell morn and night. Bark swelled on the monster trees. Cabin doors got out of kelter and wouldn't shut nor open without a struggle. Trails were just muck. Kerman happened on a bogged-down deer and clubbed it to death with his rifle butt. Birds got washed out of their nests and popped into stewpots. Women took to hiking their skirts up around their middles when they stepped outside, and all left off wearing moccasins, for the mud sucked them right off your feet.

The night came when the rain quit. Folks stood on their doorlogs and their ears rang. They listened to the little creatures of the woods squishing in the mud, and the trees dripping, and the runs gushing, and behind those sounds they heard another.

"Drums," Rocreuse said.

They lit pine knots and peered out into the black, and sloshed to the edge of their dooryards, listening. But they couldn't say for sure where the drums were beating.

"Likely they'll stop, come morn," Lannard said reassuringly.

But they didn't stop. All day the men heard the sound as they slogged along the streams and checked their traps, as they patched their roofs, deadened trees, fell down to sleep. The drums pounded on their ears worse than the long rain had pounded. They got jumpy, barred their doors, ran more bullets, crowded together and listened to the distant thrumming. Finally Lannard and Rocreuse went down the trail to find out what it was all about. In a little while, they fetched back word.

"They're sacrificin in the villages," Lannard said. "They got the ager."

The drum-talk, then, meant only sickness. Folks drew quiet, relieved breaths. Then they too came down with ague.

Lannard was the first, and he shook as if his teeth would rattle right out of his head. Rocreuse was next, took sick right on the trail. The ague stopped in at every cabin and not a soul was spared, not even a babe.

Jonathan did all he could. He was on the trail before sunup, for the sickness was worse than he had ever seen it. Young ones, plump and full of go, were sickened in the afternoon and dead before the moon came up. Women were taken at their chores and hardly able to drag themselves to a pallet. Men crept in from hunting camps, trailed every step of the way by hungry beasts. Night dogs, sensing death, turned the darkness frightful with their howling.

Jonathan dosed his patients with a purge of snakeroot, white-walnut bark, sassafras and calomel. Of nights, he mixed and boiled this medicine. Of days, he packed it out to the sick himself, and spooned it into their mouths. He wouldn't hear to leaving some in a noggin, for they were too likely to bury it under the floor with some charm of Auntie Gentry's, or drink it all at once.

It struck him that the sickness was always worse in places where water had backed up along the streams. He told the others so, and asked them to meet, on their good days, and drain off the water standing near their cabins. But they turned down their mouths.

"Ager comes out'en the mud," Rocreuse flared. "If we drain the water, there'll jest be more mud!"

Jonathan gave up trying to get any help from them, and took to carrying his ax with him. When he happened on a dam, he tore it loose. When he found a dip with water scummed over, he filled it up. All day the others heard his shouts to the mare, the sound of his ax in the woods.

"Why in tarnal is he wastin his time on such foolishments?" Mrs. McCutcheon stuck out her lip. "He's got all of us to look after, and he's wearin himself out. By hokey, if *he* gets down, we're done for sure!"

The sickness hung on, and Jonathan ran out of calomel. Night after night, he sat up with the worst of his patients. Their cheeks were caved in, their faces turned yellow, their eyes burned with fever. Their skins couldn't have been stretched any tighter if they were pegged to a cabin, like drying hides. When at intervals the shakes seized them, it seemed to him that he could hear their very bones rattle.

Those who died were laid to rest in the little graveyard. Those who survived rose up, gaunt and raddled, to go about the matters of living once more, some bitter and not-caring because of empty cradles and vanished faces. Jonathan again ate his meals at the table instead of on the trail, and slept in his bed at night, instead of propped up near some fever-racked patient.

Then one evening, a little past moonrise, he sensed someone near his doorlog and heard a voice call his name. Rising from his place by the fire, he put down the book he'd been reading and opened the door.

The Frenchy Indian stood on the path before the cabin, and the rings in his ears shone bright in the moonlight.

"Brother. It is to ask your wisdom in curing the sick that I come. My daughter lies stricken, and the medicine of our healers has brought her no help. Brother, if you would but come to my cabin, for I fear to bring her out into the dampness of night. . . ."

His head was lifted proudly, his words were fetched out strong and calm, but his eyes were tortured with the fear and the pleading. *Say that you will not turn from me because I am a breed. . . .*

"I will come," Jonathan said, and went back inside for his medicine case.

When he entered Night Dog's cabin and saw the half-conscious girl lying on a pole bed in the dim light, his heart was stirred by wonder at her beauty. And he knew, as he took her small hand in his own, that he would never let it go.

Sitting through the night beside her, he looked at the hand many times. There was a delicate look about it, yet the palm was roughened by cabin work, and there were callouses inside the thumbs. He told himself that even if he had not seen the callouses, he would have known of them, by looking at the scrubbed and tidy cabin.

As he watched firelight flicker across her closed eyes, he thought how easily she could be mistaken for a highbred daughter of the Spanish settlements. It was the French blood that came to life in her bewitching features, the Indian blood that brought a dusky warmth to her skin, gave her lashes as thick and black as cobwebs, lips the color of rose berries in the fall. *Strange Rain,* her pa called her, a name like the murmur of the forest.

The cabin in which they lived looked oddly like a white man's cabin, for Night Dog had taken his girl to an up-north mission a few years back, and she had stayed a whole winter. They had taught her a little about the white man's tongue, and some about the white man's God, and much about white woman ways of scrubbing and sewing and cooking. She had learned to coil her hair into a close knot, to wear cowhide shoes that tapped when she walked, and a calico dress that came all the way to the floor. But these she cast aside, once she was back under her own pa's roof, to return to her easy Indian clothes, her bright silver earrings, and the soft little moccasins that made no sound on the puncheon floor.

All night Jonathan dosed and sponged her. Toward morning, her fever broke and she opened soot-black eyes and looked up at him as if she had known, all along, that he would be there.

After that, Jonathan's step took on a new swing. He looked young and high-spirited, and there was a jaunty air about him. Folks got to wondering what in tarnal had come over him, and, they sniffed as he went by, wasn't he using Ellen Simonton's sassafras soap?

64

Most of the menfolks reckoned that Jonathan was courting some woman, but the women said no, he was above such lustful things. He didn't look on a woman as a woman, but only as a bunch of bones and innards that were always getting out of fix. A man with nothing on his mind but game and crops and skins had little else to do, when day was over, but crawl onto his pallet with his woman. But Jonathan, him with his books and study and far-off thoughts and such-like. . . .

"Pshaw!" Mrs. McCutcheon said, and followed her opinion with a bawdy, sniggering laugh.

But this time, the men were right, for Jonathan was courting Strange Rain. There was a gentleness about her that drew him to her as strongly as her beauty. Sometimes when he looked at her, he thought her eyes said the things his own eyes tried to hide. For it had been a long time since Jonathan had thought of taking a woman, and now he was fumbling and shy.

When he tried to talk with her, the words he wanted to say kept sticking in his throat, and he could only ask questions about her early life on the trails when Night Dog was still trading, or speak about the falling weather, or the game. Sometimes, when he spent the night in Night Dog's cabin, he lay before the fire and listened to her breathing and thought that she didn't sleep either, and once when she washed a cut place on his hand, he felt her fingers tremble, and saw how she kept her eyes cast down.

But she is so much younger than I, he would remind himself, and then days would go by before he was in the cabin again. He would think of his first wife and his back-East home, the two-storied brick where he was born. It was a pretty house, a shiny house, with candles in candlesticks that threw back light, and walls that were smooth and painted. They'd had real furniture, not these cabin fixings he had made himself, but soft beds, deep chairs, couches covered with satiny cloth. They had had draperies at the windows, and the people who came and went had worn starchy clothes and always smelled clean.

He thought of the Yadkin river that he had been able to see from his bedroom, and how he'd stared out at it, dreaming a lad's dreams. He used to walk up its banks thinking that maybe, just over the next rise, he'd find its source. He remembered the time he had gone around the third bend, and had never been so far from home before. It was then that he knew there was a world beyond that house, then that he began wanting to go away from that house.

He thought of the time he'd run off with some food tied in a silken scarf, and had followed the river to places where the trees thickened and the stumpy fields gave out. He must have been about seven then, and he had climbed the tall hills and seen the world, all of it, for one whole day, he chuckled.

"Then Father sent the blackamoors after me, and whipped me in front of them."

He had never hated the domineering man who sired him, but there were years when he had feared him. Now, though, thinking back, he could say to himself, "He was a good man, an upright man. It was just that he loved his world, and wanted me to love it. But no. . . ."

No, Jonathan had loved the world beyond the hills, those hills that stood between the settlement and the rest of the continent, never letting the forest winds come in, and never letting the sea winds get past.

"I was not lost when I went into the hills. I was lost on the settlement streets, but not on the trails that led away from them. I never belonged in the settlement . . . yet it was a mighty pretty place."

There was the day his father had said to him, "You're to marry Martha Heath, my son. It's fitting that the children of partners should wed."

He always thought of it as a marriage of polite indifference. Though he could remember Martha with pity now, when he remembered her at all, the pallid, spiritless girl who had received him into her bed with a dutiful sigh. Life together had been joyless for both of them. And when Micajah was born . . . it always seemed to Jonathan that Martha

66

had died as wearily as she had lived, folding her hands and closing her eyes as if settling down to a nap from which *none,* she thanked God, could awaken her!

For nearly five years, he had stayed on studying and practicing, but after his father's death, there were no ties to keep him, no kinfolks to argue that the wilderness was no place for a child. And Micajah had loved being on the trails . . .

He tried to see himself as he might have been, walking down the settlement streets, bowing to the prim settlement folks. He thought of the Saturday night suppers with quiet, proper music, the meeting house on Sunday, Martha directing the servants to wash on Monday, iron on Tuesday, mend on Wednesday . . .

"Not for anything!" he said aloud. "I wouldn't trade this cabin, this woods, or a single one of these rough people for such a life!"

He opened his door and leaned against the frame. The night air was cool, with snow on its breath. The weather was breaking, and down at Manjinikia's village they were having a stomp to guide the god of winter to them and kill the evil that had made things bloom out of their time. The sound of the shouting and drums was sweeter to his ears than all the cultured voices on Yadkin streets.

"I've always known my place was here. And if the woodsies and settlers don't take to my marriage, then I'll move to a deeper woods where a doctor is so badly needed nobody will care that his wife is Indian."

The first snow came on New Year's Eve. The sickness died. And Jonathan rode for Cincinnati, with hides and pelts for trading. But this time he spent nothing on medicine and books. No, he bought a fresh-water pearl on a gold chain and a Spanish shawl brought in by a trader.

"Now," he said, "all I have to do . . . ," but the old shyness overcame him.

He took to riding between Asanzang Town and Night Dog's cabin, hoping to see Strange Rain alone, for he knew she often walked that trail, going to the village to trade or visit. One evening he caught up with her, and asked if he could take her on to Asanzang Town.

"*Ae*," she told him, without lifting her eyes.

But when she was in front of him on the mare, the words he'd planned to say went from his mind, and they rode for a while in silence.

"It is the time of tale telling," she said presently, in her mixed English and Indian speech. "It is the Snow Moon, when the gods will be too cold to wander in the forest and listen to what we say. I go to hear the old tales, and to stay a few days in the wigiwam of the mother of Yellow Rock."

"Yellow Rock?" a swift jealousy seized Jonathan, for he knew this youth, a handsome Miami, with girls sighing after him. "He is your kinsman then?"

"No," she answered slowly. "He has spoken for me. He has come to my father's cabin and asked my bride price and looked at my dowry. He will bring a fresh-killed deer to seal our marriage whenever I say."

"I . . . I had not known . . . ," he began.

"My father says I must marry. I am very old," she added, looking up at him. "I was born when the Three Fires still burned, not long after the last great war when all The People fought the Miamis. I have twenty-five winters, more perhaps, or less. My father did not keep my count. He knew I would grow up anyway."

Jonathan slowed the mare to a walk. Already they could hear the dogs barking at Asanzang Town.

"My father dreamed . . . that I must marry a medicine man," she sighed and cast her eyes down. "Yet there is a certain man . . . I have a great feeling for this man. . . ."

Jonathan tightened his hands on the reins and glanced at her sharply. If she loved another why had she looked at him as she had? The way she spoke, and her touch. . . . He flushed.

"Could you ask my father to let me wed this certain one?" she demanded suddenly.

He tensed.

"*I* cannot say such a thing to my father," she went on. "You know he would not listen to such words. But you . . . you walk with him often. He respects what you tell him. . . ."

"No!" Jonathan said harshly.

"You could say to him," she persisted, "that if he made the sacred fire once more and said the prayers and read the smoke, and dreamed again. . . ."

Jonathan set his jaw.

"My words would not help," he said shortly.

"*Atawa*, alas!" her voice was sorrowful.

Now the forest was dark and the lights of the Indian village were shining through the trees.

"Listen!" she said. "It is the love flute. Yellow Rock is playing it, waiting for me. . . ."

But Jonathan wouldn't let her go.

"Wait!" he said, for suddenly he was bold, knowing that if he did not tell her this night, she might consent to marry another. "I . . . I would bring the deer to your door," his words came out in a rush. "I would meet your bride price."

She looked at him out of the corners of her eyes, and he began to speak the words of an old Potawatome love song, "*The love flute is playing, and thy hair smells like honeysuckle. Dark and deep are thine eyes, thy touch warms me. And above all, I love thee. . . .*"

He held her slight body close to him and kissed her as a man would kiss his bride, with deep tenderness and searing hunger, until she pulled away, startled and confused.

"You . . . you must talk with my father," she said, blushing at the strange thing that was a kiss.

"I think I know what he will say," he told her. "I am waiting to hear what *you* will say."

She looked down.

"I love you," he murmured, against her hair. "Are you happy that I love you?"

"*Ae*," she whispered. "I am very happy."

"You will have your father send runners to say that we are

69

wed, so that the young braves will come no more to your cabin, and will step aside without speaking when they meet you on the trail?"

"*Ae. . . .*"

"You will wed me also in the white man's way, with a paper to witness it, and the prayers of my own God?"

"*Ae. . . .*"

"You will not be afraid because our skins are different colors? You will never wish to go from me and return to your old ways?"

"Never!" She pressed her face against his shoulder, then slipped lightly from the mare to the path.

He spoke thoughtfully.

"Your father . . . what of the medicine man in his dream? Perhaps. . . ."

She began to laugh, a soft sound of mirth that was almost a girl's giggle. He remembered then that he was called white medicine man in the villages, and grinned at her sly trickery.

"We'll both go to your father tomorrow," he promised, and turned the mare.

When word was passed up and down the trails that Jonathan had taken him a woman, and that she was a breed, lots of folks found good reason to drop in and set a spell.

All had to admit that she was a pretty thing. Her long hair in its beaded roll was thick as a man's arm. Sally Carson said her eyes were as dark as pawpaw seeds, and her mouth purely beautiful. She was smaller than they had expected, for she didn't even stand as tall as her man's shoulder, and lighter skinned than they had thought, too.

"She looks more Spanish to me," Ellen Simonton said.

Strange Rain spoke to them shyly, remembering the white man's tongue she had learned at the far-north mission. A few of the womenfolks held that Jonathan could have gone to Cincinnati, or to the new state of Kentucky, and got himself a fine white woman. But the menfolks said what fine white woman would be willing to live in this godforsaken wilderness? It was an unfortunate remark, and their wives didn't take kindly to it. A few menfolks were made to sleep outside for several nights before things were patched up again.

Nobody really resented Strange Rain, though, except the Stiles. They stopped by and told Jonathan that if he was only living with this Indian girl, they'd stay on and let him be their doctor. But if he was really *wed* to her, then they'd move on to someplace where they could have a white woman for a neighbor.

"It's a pity I never took up the Fool Language," Jonathan told Stiles coldly. "Then I could understand you and your woman."

Looking haughty, the Stiles packed up their plunder and left. Nobody knew just where they had gone, since they went without speaking to a mortal soul, but Tinch heard they'd moved in with kinfolks near Fort Wayne.

"Never seen a better riddance of bad rubbish," he said, pleased.

As the winter passed, talk of Jonathan's wife died away, and by spring, nobody gave the matter two thoughts. Anyway, by spring they had decided that no matter *where* he looked, he couldn't have done better. The womenfolks were pleased, when they dropped in, to be treated so welcome and polite, as though they were fine back-East ladies who had come in a carriage through cobbled streets, instead of on foot, through a beast-filled wilderness. It flattered them that Strange Rain asked their advice about cabin work and such. They were touched by her shyness, surprised by her tidiness, and gratified by her modesty. In no time at all, they were paying her compliments among themselves by saying things like, "She's so ladylike, a person would think she was white."

As for the menfolks . . . as Lannard said, they were all so beholden to Jonathan that if he brought home a she-bear, they'd try to act nice to her. But all of them liked Strange Rain, and most of them secretly envied Jonathan.

Her efforts to please him and take up his ways stirred Jonathan's heart. She told him firmly, and he thought a little sadly, that she had put aside her Indian clothes and would wear the long calico skirts of white women, for it was a proud thing to be a doctor's wife, and she didn't want to shame him. But when she went to the woods for herbs and berries, or to visit Night Dog, she wore her Indian clothes again, and Jonathan saw that she put them away as tenderly as she folded her bright, costly shawl from the Spanish settlements, which he had bought for her in Cincinnati. She still wore her hair in a beaded roll and put on silver earrings, and often he heard her husky voice singing some song of the villages as she knelt before the fireplace, intent upon basting the roast.

Spring came. The forest turned green, the geese came north, the wild-plum thickets and hawthorns bloomed. Mrs. McCutcheon came up the trail with a mess of fresh greens for Strange Rain, having decided that the Indian girl was "about as good as any, and better'n most." Ellen Simonton had a spell of the ague and shook for three days. The Circuit Rider stopped by and talked about hell. Kerman died and was laid to rest in the graveyard, and Retta took little Docia and went back to her folks in Pennsylvania.

When summer came, with its wind-song days and soft nights smelling of wild roses, Strange Rain was making a babe.

5

THE dust was whirling in the wind, making the dancers veiled and ghostly. The drums beat like a runner's heart. The bells and shells whirred on the dancers' stomping legs. The babes in their cradle-boards watched all, and choked in the dust. The fires leaped up. The camp had the pungent smell of sacrificial tobacco, sweat, grease, and dogs roasting on their spits. The dust rattled against the leather and bark of the wigiwams, rattled and rattled till it woke her.

"Wild Wind Running," she murmured, and raised up, seeking the long form of her brother somewhere in the dark. "It is the time of the Dog Feast. . . ."

But her brother was not there; he had been slain long ago. The dancers had vanished with the dream. And the sound was not dust against a wigiwam, but snow against an oiled-paper window.

Ae, now she remembered. Strange Rain fell back clumsily, the mound of her belly bearing down on her and making little gurgling noises in the still cabin. *Ae,* she wept. I am here. I am alone. And when his step comes again on the path, I will be gone.

Jonathan had left before daylight and would be gone until

late afternoon. By then, she said to herself, I will be back in the cabin of my *noss,* my father, where I can dream the dreams of my people with no shame, where I can talk of the trails I walked in my childhood, where the Morning Light People need never look on me again.

More and more she'd been waking, of nights, to listen for the wind in the cottonwoods along the river. But the same wind didn't blow here, and the cottonwoods grew by the cabin of Night Dog. She missed the cabin, which she had helped her *noss* to raise, and the ever-changing sky that ran above the ever-changing river. How could she have fetched herself to this stranger-swamp with a stranger-man, now to bear his stranger-child?

She thought of the things she had brought here, the clothes, the copper kettle, bits of jewelry, beaded pillows. She had thought they would make the cabin of Jonathan her home. But they hadn't. They looked like things taken away, during an Indian visiting dance, to other wigiwams, things that cried out when their owners stepped into the wigiwams. They called up memories of places they had been with you, hands that had touched them, tears shed upon them, joy in possessing them, words spoken about them, so that you rushed to your own wigiwam again, unable to bear seeing them.

Even when she looked in the shiny glass Jonathan had fetched her from some far-south place called Cincinnati, it showed her a face different from the one the river showed her.

"I am lost," the girl said mournfully. "Stolen from my *noss's* cabin, from the cottonwoods and the river."

Slowly, she pulled herself up, for the light was bluing. She drew her feet from under the blanket and felt new pains stab at her, dull pains that made her teeth come hard together. After a while they passed, and she got out of the one-legged bed. She stood for a while, looking at it. A bad taste came into her mouth.

"I was under a love spell."

She dressed carefully. She tied her hair into its long roll with the beaded streamers that dragged after her as she walked. The silver brooches sewn to her buckskin top jingled as she put it on. Her leggings caught at her moccasins, leggings so thick with beading that they seemed heavy and awkward. But this was the proper dress of Night Dog's tribe, and she thought it best to wear it now, for otherwise the gods might take her for some Morning Light Person. A few settlers had. They asked if she'd been snatched from the Spanish settlements and brought up as an Indian babe. Since she was what they called a "half-burnt wood girl," the gods might not be sure which blood she favored, but one look at her would tell them now. And they must know, for she was returning to her gods.

It was a grave sin she had committed, this marrying a Morning Light Person who had no household god in his medicine bag, no charms, only herbs and roots, and whose *ototeman* was a book he called The Bible. She had seen him fetch in boughs of cedar and willow, sacred wood, for her cooking fire. She did not explain to him about the wood, for she thought he knew and meant to change her. But she refused to use it, and saw his eyes grow angry. When the fire snapped, he did not say, "Hear! The little lightning hearts are breaking." So she feared the wrath of *Animike*, the lightning god, and prayed hard during the summer storms. No, her man did not even offer food on the hearth for his dead, not even for the beloved Micajah. Nor did he keep hair snipped from their heads to throw on a field of battle, and thus avenge and ease their souls.

Many were her sins, for she had eaten of the first fruits without a chief to offer them on a birch-bark tray and cry out to the four winds, "I tell you, we are going to eat of the first fruits!" And when her man brought home bear meat, and she asked if he'd apologized to the bear, their cousin, for killing it, and had hung the head in a high tree, he said no. None of the game she had eaten had been properly handled, or soothed in its dying. Now surely the souls of those dead, outraged beasts must hover outside her door, waiting to do her harm.

Nia, nia! Her sins were many and great. She felt of the babe in her belly.

"My little one, I have marked you with my wrongs. But when you come, we will be in my *noss's* cabin. There we will live, among the beasts and the trees, and the gods will decide what is to be done about us."

She slipped out of the cabin, silent as a panther, to leave it forever.

She eased herself along the swamp trail, wishing she could rush away from it as fast as she had come to it. So fast had she come, as fast as the snow spinning down the trails, with her hand on her man's arm, feeling the warmth of his chest through his leather shirt.

She remembered the deer he had killed and left by her door, the marriage gift. *Ae,* she had fed it to him with quivering hands, eager to be done with the ceremony that would bind them together in the way of The People. She remembered sitting before him on the mare, with the stars close about and a pounding in her head like a drum. Thinking, "Now it is beginning."

Ae, she should not have gone off so fast from the things of her people. Even though the soft warmth of Jonathan's eyes made her flesh damp with sweat, though his voice was like the wind caressing her on summer nights, and his touch like fire. She should have put him from her mind and run and hidden herself in the cottonwoods when she saw his shadow across the door.

"I should have kept my eyes from his."

She must hurry back to her father's cabin and never remember how fast she had gone from it.

She trudged on through the snow. It was the earliest she could remember ever seeing it snow. Runners curled on the tip of every vine. The fox grapes and persimmons hung heavy. Corn stood unharvested in the fields. Indian summer was yet to come before the long cold snows set in. But on this day of Squaw Snow, the first brief cold of the season, it seemed that winter had come to the villages. They went by no calendar, but by the turnings of the year.

"It is a lucky thing to have a son born with the Squaw Snow, for great will be his wisdom."

So they said in the villages, but that could not mean this poor kicking lump in her belly, this helpless babe already cursed by the gods.

Down in the swamp, the big trees rose all about her. All tops and trunks they were, with no low branches for shelter from the driving snow. Red-tipped osiers pushed so tight against each other along the way, she had to stop and cast about her for the trail. Smaller paths led off from it, some made by trappers, some by hunters, some by creatures padding to their lairs, some by Jonathan himself in times past, when he was restless night-walking.

Of a sudden, the pains came so fast she could barely catch her breath. She went slower now, clutching at the trees as she passed them, pushing herself from one to the other. Her own mother, her *ninga,* had borne her on a windy trail beside a faraway river, but she had not been alone. Her man had been beside her to keep a warm fire going, to wipe the blood from her clenched fists and slip his hunting-knife under her pallet of hides and boughs to cut the pain.

Strange Rain bit her lips. Her time was so near that she was afraid to go on. A lonely, snowy trail was no place to coax a child into the world. It ought to have a warm cabin roof over its little head.

"It is wrong to bear a child like a thing of the woods, make it fight for its life from the very start. No, my babe will open its eyes to a warm clay hearth where a kettle squeaks on a wooden crane . . . if I can just reach my *noss.*"

Blindly she went on, stumbling and moaning, the weight of the babe pulling her down, her hands pulling her on. She went from blaze-mark to blaze-mark, and sometimes the world was white, and sometimes it was dark.

Then the trail narrowed. The trees were different, too. Surely if she'd ever been on this trail before, she'd remember it. She padded on in the silent world.

Once she thought she saw a man and staggered toward him, waving her arms and calling. But then she found it was only a tree broken and twisted by a storm, the light playing tricks over it, making it seem a mortal. Again she thought she saw a cabin. It even had smoke curling up from the chimney, and dogs, nose-to-tail, in the entry. But it blew away like fog, and there was nothing in its place but the snow dancing in the wind. A bush moved and she caught her breath. There was Odaw, wagging his droopy tail with the broken tip, his puppy's eyes glad with love. But no, Odaw was dead and gone to dust beneath the honeysuckle hedge at her *noss's* dooryard.

She was lost.

As sudden and still as the snow had come, it stopped. *Io,* any one of The People, all by his lonesome in the woods, would be safe enough. Even the smallest could track and read sign and tell you which way ran to the game-filled prairies, and which to the campfires. All but her. All the signs her *noss* had ever taught her had gone out of her head. Now, all she could call to mind were the tales told round the fires, of nights. Some were of the pitiful people who had got themselves lost and been found later half-chewed by those with the long tails, the panthers. Or found shot by the Morning Light people, or drowned and piled up in backwater till their bones fell apart like a tender cooked rabbit.

Now, at each movement along the trail, she jumped, scared she'd come up against yellow eyes that stalked in hunger. Night dogs and devil dogs would be bold this night. She knew how the little rabbits felt as they hunkered down in cover and sniffed the marten on their trail.

Then she saw moccasin prints before her. Someone else was out here, too. She felt better. Maybe someone had come looking for her. She went faster, her eyes on the marks. But then she saw they were made by her own moccasins, and she was walking in a hunter's circle.

The time went by. At first it had dragged, but now that dark was close, it began to pass her mockingly. "I'll beat you to the cabin," it seemed to say. "I'll be there before you!"

The night beasts were giving their calls when she stumbled on the chopped-off log. This made her feel better, for it showed that someone must be close by, a cabin, a trail that led somewhere. Weakly, she wandered around the log. She couldn't decide what direction to take away from it, and started off first one way and then another. She was terribly afraid to leave it. What if the way she chose went nowhere, and she couldn't find the log again? She drew close to it and felt safer, knowing a human hand had made that cut.

Around and around the chopped log she went, and suddenly it seemed she was watching herself go by. Yes, she saw the young half-burnt wood woman with the swollen-out stomach running around a black log. She was ashamed that one of The People should cry out like that. She frowned. The girl was no true Potawatome, Person of the Place of Fire, for listen to her cry and scream until her voice rang clear to the Great Lake and back.

"*Atawa! Atawa!*" the cry of despair rang out in the stillness.

She fell by the log and suddenly felt comforted, for she was sure it had been cut by Jonathan's hands. *Jonathan,* it said to her. *I belong to Jonathan.*

"And so do I," she thought. "So do I."

She pressed her face against the rough bark and cried, not only for the wrenching pain of her body, but for the pain of her heart.

"I would give up my gods for him. I would kill to save him. I would die in his place. What need have I of cottonwoods or the river or my own strip of sky? No, I need only Jonathan. I am but half a person without him."

She closed her eyes and trembled at the words running through her mind.

"I fear no gods. I fear no longer the look of those who would turn away from us because we are of different bloods. I fear not even for my babe, for Jonathan is my god, and he will not let the little one suffer any wrong. I was a woman made foolish. So it is in the villages sometimes, that when a woman is heavy with child strange thoughts come to her. It is only that. That which has brought me here to die in the snow far from my husband, with my little one fighting inside me."

Then she cried out to her gods, "No matter what path my feet would have taken, they would have led me to Jonathan."

The pains came harder. She propped herself up weakly against the log.

"I will not die sprawled out like a doe run down," she told herself. "I will die proudly, sitting up, watching the night coming on."

The light was gone now, and she knew that He-Who-Sees-Us had stepped into the west-running gorge. Where he turned his smoky eyes, a mist hung. When he sighed, the winds of night blew. And now the night hawks left his shoulders and rose, calling to the sky.

"*Ae*," she murmured, "they go to do his bidding, to tell the Hunter of Men who shall be visited this night. To tell the serpent under the waters who shall be born this night. Our lives are decided for us while we sleep!"

The old day-down prayer, taught her while she cuddled in her father's arms, came easily under the ghosty trees. And she thought she could hear it on the wind, being chanted by others of her blood.

"Oh, Kije Manitou, when you are hidden in the west, protect us from our enemies who would do us harm . . . who hunt us in the night when you are not present."

The women paused by the supper fires.

"Good Spirit, make known your wishes by sending us the god of sleep and dreams."

The hunter waited on the trail, fresh game on his back,

his bow and quiver held out for a blessing, to the fading light.

"Let the Spirit of Dreams tell us your will in the night, and we shall carry it out by day."

The dying ones borne out into the light by those they would leave behind, the dying ones facing their last light and whispering their last words, the prayers unfinished on their lips, "And if it should be that the time of some be closed, send them, Great Master of Life, to the great country of souls where they may greet their friends, where you are pleased to shine upon them with a bright and warm and constant flame. . . ."

The elder children calling sharp to the younger ones, the babes, taking away from them their playthings of bones and feathers and telling them the prayer in the dusk.

"Oh, Kije Manitou, sleep not long in the west, but return your people to light and life . . . to light and life . . . to light and life. . . ."

She stared out into the dark, waiting for the Hunter of Men. The cold crept up her legs and down her back. There had been no pains for a while, and she wondered if her little one were dead.

"No matter," she laid her hand on her belly, "we shall be together."

Pictures came before her eyes, long-dead people, long-lost things, long-forgotten places. She had heard it said in the villages that when pictures of things long past came reeling before your eyes, there was just time to sing your death song. She opened her lips.

"No, no. I will die a fat old woman with tall sons standing around me . . . ," she sang, over and over until the night beasts crept near, drawn by the loneliness of her voice.

Again she was a babe. She felt the gentle movement of her *ninga's* walk, and stared out from the cradle-board, and caught at the beaded fringe which swung before her eyes. She slept on a bed of moss, wakening to the dark green sky of the

81

forest, which had no sun or moon or stars of its own. She knelt by her *noss,* holding to her brother, and saw the earth sift over the hollow log that held her *ninga,* and put wood on the four fires and said the burial words, "Grieve not . . . your path is also ours."

Again she and her brother Wild Wind Running slipped from the wigiwam, the grass-mat hut, and listened gravely while their elders talked of wars ended and wars to come. They followed Night Dog on the trails, and marveled at the birds and beasts and learned to talk to them, like any children of The People. She saw the three of them going and coming on trails and rivers as numerous as beads in a wampum belt.

Then she saw the bleeding body of Wild Wind Running brought to them, and knew the sorrow of having a grave, not a brother.

Then suddenly she stopped and the death song failed in her throat, for what she saw now was no memory of things past, but a *tchibai,* a ghost. She struggled to get her feet under her, to pull herself up, to run from this terror which made a scream twist on her lips. But her stiff feet would not lift her.

The *tchibai* stood looking at her with green eyes, sad eyes. Its head was back, and she could see the knife-wound at the base of its throat. It came toward her slowly, not walking like a mortal man, but drifting like the mist. She pushed back from it in horror. Her tongue quivered, but no words came from her lips, only an animal sound, a steady whine and growl. There was nothing those of The People feared like a *tchibai.* Then a voice, sounding far off yet close around her, said, "Don't fear me, for I am not dead."

The scream burst out, and suddenly the stiff form was gone, snatched up as if it had been caught in a tree snare, and she was alone in the mist.

"*Micajah!*" she gasped. She looked down at her swollen belly. It was a boy within her. It was Micajah.

With the dead, she told herself, it is often so. The littlest

82

ones are spared the long walk, for they are too small to know the way, and the path has only a single coal to light it. Their spirits remain, they play together in the forest, in the fields. Their cries are heard as they chase the red-breasted robin. It is they who cause the stray corn plants to spring up. It is they for whom we leave bits of cooked food as gifts.

And the old ones, it is too long a trip for their feeble legs. They, too, remain in spirit, to be heard slamming their cabin doors, or seen carving on a hickory branch or hovering in the smoke of the supper fires.

Old and young were often buried on the path the women took to the stream. When the time was right, one of these souls would spring from its grave, and enter the woman and be reborn. It was the same with those whose lives had ended too quickly.

"Micajah . . . ," she whispered, in awe. "His feet did not pass over the pathway of souls. He does not wait restlessly, peering down from a star. No, his soul has waited, silent and sleeping, for my child to be born."

Suddenly, the soft girl-look went from her face. She could feel the dark blood of her ancestors humming through her head. They were stirring in the dust of their graves, called forth by this small descendant who needed their strength. Their wispy voices blew in her ears. Their bony hands pulled and plucked at her. She felt like a hawk rising above the clouds, saw the ground falling away from her, knew the feet she had thought dead were moving clumsily.

She crept on through the snowy night with a cunning lent her by the long buried. She shuffled from clump to tree, her quick eyes stripping each shadow until it gave up what it hid. Her nose snuffled at the woods smell, told her a curious fox trailed her, a panther had crossed her path ahead. Suddenly it seemed that her moccasins knew every hump of ground, stopped her before she reached animal lairs, led her around streams.

Close by she heard the night dogs, the hunger wolves give their howl, the curt barks that said a pack was hunting but

83

hadn't run on to game. She snarled at them. For every howl they gave, she sent back a snarl. She groped along the trail until she found a hefty stick, a club for any beast that might threaten her, or the life of her child. She was a squaw of The People defending her young, a bear-mother fighting for her cub. She trudged on, as fierce and strong as the north wind, talking to her child in low grunts, praying to gods only her ancestors knew, seeing the world as a beast-place, and herself as one of the beasts.

Then she heard a new sound, a stranger-sound. She crouched among the willows holding the club tight, her hands numb with cold. A soggy light glowed through the fog. With slitty eyes, she waited for this new beast. The snow was kicked up by its feet. Its big shoulders shredded the mist. And then she caught the scent of herbs, a familiar body smell. It was her mate's scent. The club dropped in the snow, for her ancestors left off their tugging and murmuring and returned to their sleep, knowing her safe.

"*Jonathan!*"

Io, it was shameful for a woman of The People to cry before another, but this other, he was her man. His kisses on her mouth hushed her sobs. His arms were hard and built a wall for her, shutting out the fearsome swamp. He said her name over and over, and there were other words, too, in her own tongue, love words. She was a mortal woman again, and had forgotten already the beast she had been.

She heard her own voice telling about the cottonwoods and the river and the strip of sky but how, wherever her man was, there she would spread her blanket, for he was her wigiwam and her fire. What a stupid one she had been! In the villages, they would beat such a one! She told him of the swamp and the twisted trails, the log and the pictures that came and went, the death song. But the story of the *tchibai*, that would have to wait, for this Morning Light Person could not know about dying and being born again.

"Once I was lost, too," he told her gently, "and all I wanted was to be a babe again in my ma's arms."

She knew he understood why she'd gone from him.

Again there was the warm bed in the cabin. There was the wind in the chimney where it belonged, not whipping at her among the creatures and the trees. There was the fire, Our Grandfather Fire, and the safe shadows of the corner logs. She was aware of the wooden floor with its fuzzy rugs, the cup of dittany held to her lips, and the bitter herbs Jonathan made her swallow to bring on her pains again.

As he bent over to help her with the last hard pains, he whispered, "There is no loneliness with me now. Your soul has come into my soul, and will never turn away." It was a love charm, and it pleased her.

Yet even after the birth was over, the bitter cold that had entered her body did not leave it. There were long nights of hard chills and heated rocks wrapped in buckskin to warm her bed. There were wild times of fever when she was again on the trail, and always Jonathan coming and going, feeding her, soothing her, covering her.

He-Who-Sees-Us cast his light into the cabin many times before she saw it. Then came a night when she awoke and was herself again. It was very still in the cabin, and she had dreamed she heard a child crying, and had come up from her blankets because she thought it was her little one. Then she fell back. No, no child of hers slept in this cabin. *Ae,* she had killed him, dragging him around in the cold and wet, and Jonathan hadn't the heart to tell her.

Suddenly she lifted her head and peered into the dark. Something new was in the cabin, a new smell. She crept from her bed and sniffed it out. It was something alive in the basket her own hands had woven for her child. She eased back the covers and saw, not one, but two babes sleeping there. She sniffed them over, her heart pounding, and knew the smell of her flesh and Jonathan's.

Ae, she sat back on her heels. Her child wasn't dead, and by a miracle of the gods, she had borne two instead of one! *Two,* such a rare thing among The People that special prayers and fasts were held at such a time.

85

She ran her hands over their tiny bodies. *Two! Ae,* the grave of Micajah was empty this night, for his soul was here in this boy who reached out in his sleep and grasped at her fingers. *Io,* each of them had back what once had been mourned as lost. She, Jonathan. He, his son.

Jonathan, awakened, was at her side. Then, seeing she was herself at last, he smiled and knelt down beside her. Together they looked at the babes.

"I went ahead and named them," he said. "I called him Nathan and her Tabitha."

That day they planted the afterbirth in a calabash, at the roots of a tiny redbud, after the way of The People. But before the day was out, Tabitha was spitting up her milk and looking sick.

"The Potawatomes," Strange Rain offered shyly, "they say that when a child is sick after being named, the name does not agree."

Jonathan smiled indulgently and said they would find something else to call the little one. So they changed her name to Tibby, and almost at once she was well.

6

YOUNG Seegwun, the god of spring, came down the trail with blossoms braided in his hair. He came through the dark woods and stood on the doorlog of the cabin that belonged to Peboon. Peboon, the old winter, began to shake with chills that would not stop. Icicles hung from his shaggy brows, and his tattered wild-bull robe no longer kept out the bitter air. He raised his faded eyes to Seegwun's shining black ones and knew that it was time. Sadly he went from his wigiwam, and his fire in its pit under the smoke-hole guttered out. In its ashes bloomed the white spring-beauty. Then Seegwun walked the country over, melted the snow from the ground, warmed the streams, and set the sap to rising in the monster trees. He came down the swamp trail and touched the redbud, Nathan's birth-tree, and made it bloom.

Every year Strange Rain sat on the doorlog in the first warm sun, cuddled her twins on her lap, and told them this story.

Tibby squeezed shut her greenish eyes and giggled until the dimple in her cheek showed. She loved the story because of the beautiful man-god with the flowers in his hair, and after she was old enough to have her say, she sat up at night and watched for him to come to the redbud.

But Nathan liked the tale because Seegwun made the world bright again, and with one whiff of the early bloodroot, sent the misery from people's eyes as completely as if old Peboon had never come down the forest trail with his snowshoes on his back.

"Is Seegwun a doctor like Pa?" he asked, for it seemed to him that Jonathan brought brightness, too.

Year in, year out, the blossoms flourished on the redbud, even down its trunk. They drifted across the warm spring nights and covered the leafy earth above Micajah.

A new fawn was seen in the swamp. The old hill-hooter that used to scare Tibby in her sleep no longer whooed on the elm. Night dogs that had been leaders of their packs when the twins were born now crept to their dens, old and blind. There were names no longer spoken with any thought of their owners answering. There were new faces to be got used to. Everything changed but the blossoms of the redbud, and they still came in their right time and in the same way. Jonathan would pull up his mare and sit looking at them, and the tired would go from his eyes. In a way, the leaves and blossoms were the only things you knew would be the same, come spring.

Like all young ones, the twins shared in doing chores as soon as they were able to learn them. There was water to be carried from the spring. There was wood to gather, corn to be planted and hoed. There were willow baskets to be woven, brooms to be made from rushes, and rush mats for the table.

As they grew older, they did harder things. Nathan learned to carve noggins and wooden trenchers. Tibby learned to work the grass-mat loom in the dooryard. But of all the things they did, their favorite was to gather nuts for buttons. Shagbark hickory, swamp oak, scarlet oak, hazelnut and buckeye trees had the best button-nuts. They punched holes clear through a nut and pulled whang through them. And, like his sister, Nathan liked the buckeyes best, not only because they were a rich glossy color, but because you could wish on them and they would fetch you luck.

There were games the twins learned, and toys they loved. There was Loose-Legs, Tibby's favorite, a wishing doll made from an apple, with rushes for legs. There were bark animals and duck decoys for Nathan, and the endless whistles to be made from twigs and bones and reeds. In the summer, they played hoop-and-javelin. In the winter they played snow-snake.

But as time passed, Nathan would be up and out of his pallet while night still hung on. He'd do his chores before the cabin stirred, so that he could be off with his pa. It got to be a common thing to see Jonathan riding down the trail on his new mare with Nathan perched on the saddle before him. Sometimes the two dogs trotted after them. Lannard had fetched the dogs for the twins. One was named Sin, because he was as black as, and the other By Hokey, because he was always hurling himself at folks who yelled, "By Hokey, get down!"

Many's the mortal's dying that Nathan watched with his pa. Lots of times he stood by, solemn-eyed, and patted a hurt man as Jonathan sewed him up. Sometimes he'd slip down from the saddle and hurry to the cabin where the sickness was to ask, grave-faced, if the new medicine had helped.

Tibby missed her twin at first, but Strange Rain told her their paths would always be different.

"Your brother must learn a man's way of life," she said, "and you, a woman's."

Strange Rain began to teach Tibby to cook. She showed her just when the elderberry blossom was ready to put into a Shawnee cake. She taught her how to make gravy with pounded nut-meats. She taught her to make a stew with wild rice, dried corn, wild onions, and fish. Strange Rain was a good cook, and many's the woman that learned some recipe from her.

Jonathan watched his young ones growing and laughed when folks asked was it the twins that made the grey streaks in his hair.

"No," he'd say, smiling. "Without them, my hair would be white."

The others, remembering his loneliness, and the emptiness of his cabin after Micajah's dying, felt good to see him happy now. His eyes were often on Nathan, studying him.

"It seems . . . how can it be that he is so much like Micajah?" he would say.

And his woman would smile in secret.

Seegwun came again and again. Nathan was seven now, thoughtful for a lad, and restless. When he sat down to the table to eat, the swamp beyond the cabin seemed to call to him, and he left his food and went out to it. When he got there, he didn't know why he had come, and he would search the trails and streams, as if he were looking for something. Sometimes he felt dazed and lost, as if he were wandering through a golden haze, lovely but blurred and bewildering.

Then one morn he opened his eyes and found the haze gone. For the first time in his memory, all things stood out sharp and clear. Light and shadow didn't run together. Edges were keen. It was as if his world had been covered with water, but now it had run off, and all the things that once had been wavy shapes bobbing past had real form.

"I can see," he said, in wonder.

Now everything called to him to look at it. He crouched down and studied the ground. There were things hidden in those grasses that he hadn't known anything about, little bugs that looked back at him with eyes like the tiniest of coals. Sometimes they said, "Keep your foot off'n me!" Sometimes they said, "How do." Even when he stood up straight, he could still see their movements as they hustled up and down digging out homes, hunting for food, fighting, kicking, dying.

He looked at the leaves. He'd pick one up and turn it in his fingers, as if it had come from some far-off land, some other world. These leaves, they were all colors, even purple like snow clouds. He'd press one against his face, sniffing it, tasting it, feeling it. It had ribs like a person, and a scent of its own, like a person. But once he threw it down, he could never find it again.

Now he noticed things about his ma that he had never seen until now. In the evenings, she sat close to his pa. Usually, her small brown hands were busy with some fancy beadwork, but her dark eyes would caress her man and smile.

Deep inside him, Nathan wanted all her smiles for himself, and the first pangs of jealousy gnawed at his small chest. He would crowd in between them and drop his head on Strange Rain's knee, and ask to hear the sleep-song again.

> "Papeuse in your willow basket,
>   Floating on the water,
>   Where the wild rice grows straight . . .
>   See how the rice covers you, hides you,
>   Keeping you from the hungry beasts."

Her rich warm voice filled the cabin and comforted his troubled heart, but the song failed to bring back the time when he had been a babe.

One morn when he woke, the late moon had laid long shadows over the dooryard. He could see the treetops down in the swamp, moving in the wind like feathered dancers. He could feel the wind-fingers pulling at him through the chinking in the cabin walls, wanting him to follow. He slipped down the ladder and over the doorlog, stealing away from the cabin alone for the first time. He felt strange, as though he were someone else. He ran to the stream and tried to see his face in the water, and know was he the same? But when he looked, he wasn't sure. His green eyes stared back at him like stranger-eyes, as if they knew things about him he didn't know.

He went back up the hill to his Birth Tree. Its leaves brushed his face and he felt comforted. He held the tree tight in his arms and wished to hear again his *ninga* singing the sleep song. He yearned to run back to the cabin and bar the door against the calling wind. But there was a deep pain pushing him from the tree, a real pain pushing him out of the womb of the cabin and into the hands of the wind and he had to go, just like a babe when it must draw its first breath or die.

He started down the hills slowly. Then the pain was gone, and he stepped from the moon-shadow of the cabin into the moon-shadow of the woods. He stopped on the swamp trail and looked back at the cabin. It seemed strangely alien, a little thing of piled-up logs in the middle of the vast woods.

"The cabin is not my whole world," he thought, surprised.

Day after day he returned to the swamp and the woods, as though he were under a spell. The wind had made it, he reckoned, and was charming him with it. *Atawa,* alas! This spell was so strong. It filled his head with thoughts he had never had, and made him know things he had never dreamed.

"I can touch the sky," he whispered. "I can hear the earth's heart beating. I can hear the gods walking."

When he went back to the cabin, of nights, to fill his small belly and to sleep, he saw his pa and his ma and Tibby as if they were strangers. He would sit cross-legged on the hard log bench and watch them through thick lashes which all but shut out the faces that didn't understand him any more. What did he have to say to them, a boy who could touch the sky, hear the earth's heartbeat and the gods' footfalls? True, he knew them all, but from a long distance now, as though he had been wandering far away, and for many years.

The spell gave him still another strange thought.

"I am of no human folks. My *noss* is the wind, and my *ninga* is the earth."

One dawn he stole out of the cabin carrying his other shirt, a ball of whang, some flint and punk, a piece of deer meat, a bag of meal, his knife and a blanket. On this day, he meant to see the world. Sin and By Hokey went with him. He tried to send them back, but they whined and trailed after him until he finally gave in.

He went north. Before long, he came to the Narrows, where the Salamonie met the Wabash. The water was running high. He stood on the bank and watched it. He felt no hankering to cross, but the wind kept pulling at him, and finally he had to follow.

He jumped in feet-first with his pack on his back, while the dogs howled from the bank for him to wait, then plunged in after him. There was a willow snag in the river and it hit him in his middle as the water cast him against it. He felt the breath go from him on a deep grunt. His teeth came together hard against the pain, against the tightness of his empty chest. The river jerked him downstream, doubled him like a dead crawfish.

He was whirled over and over. His hair washed across his face so that he couldn't see whenever his head was above water, and floated behind him like grass whenever he was below. Blood mingled with the water as his hands fought to catch on to roots and snags, and to give his battered body a rest. Sometimes he felt one of the dogs against him. Sometimes he glimpsed them on top of the water, and at other times he met them below.

"This river can't kill me," he choked, "because I'm a live-forever, and no mortal thing!"

He kicked and clawed at the water. His *noss,* the wind, brought willow branches low, so that his hands could grasp them. His *ninga,* the earth, arched her back under his feet. His gods ran to him and pulled him from the river. He sprawled face-down on the bank, shivering, hearing his breaths come as short and tremulous as a hooty-owl's call. For a long time he lay there, with the wet dogs fallen against him.

He wanted to sleep, but the wind kept pulling at him. Weakly he pushed himself up and stumbled into the woods ahead. The dogs dragged after him. He followed trails he'd never seen before, among shrubs and vines and stranger-trees. Hills reared up in front of him. He crossed a barrens and was in the deep forest.

After a while, he thought to stop and rest. Then, through the dark beast-trees he saw a light, a long stretched-out light.

When he reached it, he was in the biggest clearing he'd ever seen. Here no deadened trees stood with rings around their middles. Here were neither cabins nor villages, not even stumps. There was only grass, tall, *tall* grass that climbed high above his head. He'd heard tell of this . . . the Great Prairie that ran all the way to the Mississippi with nary a thing to stop it. He longed to be up above the grass and see the whole prairie laid out before him. After a while, he found a line of great boulders and clambered upon the highest of them. Then he saw it. Nothing but grass, rippling and flowing like water. Headed like wheat, it was, and colored blue. For a long time he stood there, watching the grass. For the first time he could see the wind, his *noss*. It had a shape; the grass showed it.

He lay across one of the boulders resting, and fell asleep. When he awoke, the red sun was in the sky. It was so big he marveled at it, but it hurt his eyes, so he buried his head in his arms again, shutting out the brightness. Here he idled away the morning and part of the afternoon, daydreaming or staring out over the rippling grass.

He would make camp here, he thought, stay through the night, perhaps for several days, and must therefore find wood for a fire. He gazed up at the great sky and thought surely, when dark came, it would be filled with stranger-stars. Often he watched the stars as they picked their way along, slowly, like a herd of deer grazing at night when the wind was with them. Sometimes one would fall, and he wondered what Hand could drop a star as easily as a hunter dropped a deer.

In midafternoon, he began to seek out wood. He crammed deer meat and soggy meal into his mouth as he went, but he wasn't really hungry, and gave the rest to the dogs. Then suddenly he stumbled on the bones.

He bent to touch them and then drew back, for he knew what bones they were, though he'd seen none like them before. They were the wild-bull bones of the great herd that had died in the year of the hard blizzard, six winters before his birth. Now seven more winters had passed and still they lay there, scattered and broken, but sheltered from the autumn grassfires by the string of boulders.

Atawa, alas! He touched them again. Often he had heard the story, how the wild bulls pushed through the snow, breaking it apart with their chests as it blew, stepping in long lines, single file, with the cows and calves at the center, and the old and wounded at the rear.

The herd was so big it stretched farther than a red-tailed hawk could see. He had heard how the Potawatome had crept up to it easily on their bear-paw snowshoes, and killed many to be eaten in a hunger time. And he had heard how the wolves followed after the bulls, their jaws brushing the legs of the last ones, but not killing them though their bellies growled like the gale. No, they had stayed in the deep path made by the herd till the storm was past, till there were only the bulls to fight and not the snow.

Atawa, alas! The great herd lay there, the herd that had lived in the vast woods, that had gone every Falling Leaf Moon to the Blue Licks, and returned every Grass Moon to the land of the Illini.

Dead. Ashes and bones. He stepped back from them. He himself, three winters old, had sat before his pa on the mare and looked on the last of the wild bulls. They had been fewer than the fingers on his two hands. He had seen them sheltering on the trace, another snow making them look like shaggy knobs, like a part of the land. Alas, they were all gone now!

He forgot the wood and went back to his boulder. He turned, faced the declining sun, and said his daydown prayer. But his prayer didn't make the bones go away. The herd came back before his eyes.

"The wind was their *noss* and the earth their *ninga*. They were live-forevers like me. How can they be . . . dead?"

But hadn't he seen Lannard and his pa bring down any game they wanted with their rifles? Hadn't he seen deer, squirrels, even his cousin, the bear, twisting in their last breath? Hadn't he squatted over them and crooned to them, to ease their pain? And when they were silent, their bodies never moved again. He crouched there, thinking, till his head touched his knees, and studied his moccasin toes.

"Everything that is alive sometime dies," he said at last. "I am alive, and I . . . can die."

His *noss* shifted and blew another way, no longer caressing his face. His *ninga's* heart stopped its beating. Even the sound in the prairie grass was only the grass nodding, and not the gods walking. It was all gone. He looked up at the sky. No mortal could ever touch it.

A new sick feeling came over him. It seemed that the feeling had a shape he could see. It broke through the grass and knelt beside him, a tall brave, dark and shadowy, with a face like all men.

"I am alone."

Slowly he got to his feet. His fingers shook as he put his pack together and called the dogs. He started down through the tall grass, following the trail he had made at dawn. He went back around the swamp and reached the woods. Dusk came on.

"I have seen the world, and it is a vast place."

His moccasins moved faster on the trails. He fled the prairie and the cold wind and the hard earth and the strange rustlings. Beside him ran still another brave who had the face of every man.

"I am afraid."

He heard the river ahead of him in the dimness, and came upon it so fast that he had to dig his toes into the ground to keep from falling in. He stared down at the massy swirl of waters.

"How did I ever cross?" he whispered.

He went up and down the bank, looking, trying to gather the courage to plunge in. His mouth was dry, his legs wobbly. Beside him went two braves, Alone and Fear. It was they who held him back. At last he huddled on the bank and put his face in his arms and cried.

Night beasts tiptoed out and looked at him. The moon rose up again. A hill-hooter cried. Tree frogs set up their calling. The dogs curled close and growled into the woods. Something crashed into the river on the farther side. He could hear it splashing but dared not look up lest it be death, the Hunter of Men, coming for him.

Then, out of the corner of one eye, he saw a mare's white feet stop near him, and the long legs of his pa clambering down. He saw boots coming toward him, knees that bent and crouched beside him.

"Where have you been, son?"

He lifted a face wretched with guilt.

"I didn't aim to worry you, Pa," he fetched out. "I just wanted to go by myself . . . to look for . . . I don't know what. . . ."

Jonathan leaned back and looked up at the stars beginning to shine along the river way.

"I know," was all he said.

Nathan fell into the bend of his pa's arm and looked up at his face. It was a gentler, handsomer face than any windface would ever be, this face of the *noss* whose blood was his blood and whose flesh was his flesh.

"Here the earth and sky are so far apart," Jonathan said. "But once . . . when I was seven . . . I stood tall on the earth and touched the sky."

Nathan caught his breath.

"And now that I have a son who is seven, I can touch it again." Jonathan smiled slowly. He held up his fingers and Nathan saw them sharp and clear against the moon. "See?" He added, "And now that you have touched the sky, my son, perhaps you will be content to stay on earth with us for a little while."

Nathan cried then, for not knowing before what he had learned this day, that he and his pa were the same . . . liveforevers caught inside mortal bodies that could die.

7

A YOUNG stranger-man came into the woods to trade that year, as strong and tall as the heartiest brave on the trails. There was no Indian look about him, though, for his hair was as yellow as the sun that never shone in this vast woods, and his eyes were the blue of chicory flowers.

Most folks took to him right off, but there were some who'd heard of him, and who turned their mouths down.

"An Injun lover, if you ask me!" Mrs. McCutcheon said. "And likely no better'n Scuddy! You'd think he'd hold himself higher'n them savages. But, no! He means to get some learnin and set himself up as an Injun lawyer! He says they're bein cheated . . . and by *us!*"

His name was Shawnessey, but the settlement knew him only as Shawn, and none knew him really well, except Jonathan and Nathan. To Nathan he was like a god, young and merry and wonder-wise. It wasn't long until Shawn, seeing the admiration in the boy's eyes, laid a comradely hand on his shoulder and asked, "How'd you like to be my taken-brother?"

It was an honor fit to choke a boy with pride. After that, whenever he came to the cabin, Nathan stayed close beside him.

Many's the time, long years afterward, when those days and nights came back to him along some lonesome stranger-trail. He smelled the dust deep in the cracks of the puncheon floor, the herbs on their bark strings, the meat on its trencher, clothes on their pegs, smoke from the embers, the soap smell of his pa's hands, the dried-flower smell of his ma's hair. All these things . . . they were a comfort to a boy. The dark braves, Alone and Fear, were not with him then. Shawn and Jonathan were with him, and their strong bodies stood hard between him and the ever-dangers beyond the dooryard.

The tales Shawn told them were like the tales told by Night Dog, his grandpap, of living and of the woods. Shawn's folks had been killed by Indians on the trail when he was a young one, and after that he wandered like a Solitary, slept in caves and hollow logs and under the timbers of burnt-out cabins.

Sometimes he did chores in the settlements for some food in his belly and a roof over his head. Once he worked for a miller, another time for a stump puller, and later for a stone-boat man. That was back in Pennsylvania. But when there was no work, he fought the dogs for scraps, and at night slipped into sheds where grain was stored, and ate it raw.

A woman found him sleeping in a ditch near a new settlement on the Ohio called Marietta. She had yellow hair like Shawn's, and he used to pretend she was his ma. He was past ten then. She wore fancy dresses and pinked her cheeks and lips with pokeberry juice. For nearly a year he did her chores and slept in her shed room.

"What happened to her?" Nathan asked.

"Somebody stabbed her. She called to me in the night and said for me to take the bit of money that was hid in the wall. She said, 'Shawnie, when you're older, don't hold anything against me. Love me anyway.' " His face went tight. "She was most like a ma to me," he said harshly.

He got work later at a trading post, and the trader taught him to read and write so he could help with the books. Then the trader got sick and went back East, but he left his two books and Shawn read them over and over.

"Many Tongues, a chief of the Delawares, found me and took me to live with him as his own boy. He was proud that I could read the talking-papers. He taught me to speak the tongues of the different tribes. Later, he was killed by a white man, and I came west. I thought a lot of him," he added, softly. "He was one of the few that helped me."

The way he'd lived, he said, was not uncommon to young ones left alone in the forest. And those that survived suffered a lot more than those that lay down and died of the hunger cramps.

"Most folks don't aim to be cruel," he explained. "There just isn't room or food for strays. That's why they sometimes drove me off, the way beasts drive off their sick animals because they're small and weak and can't do their share in the herd. They slow down the migration."

He went silent then, and just sat there in the light of the fire. Nathan stared at the face of his taken-brother, and suddenly it was a stranger-face that bore scars like the cut-marks of Indian knives. It came to him then that Shawn, also . . . and maybe all men . . . had to struggle against the two dark braves.

He could see the fear-mark cut when the hunger-wolves howled, the lonesome-mark of dark nights, the hurt-mark when the cabins shut him out, the struggle-mark that came of the fight to live, the weary-mark that longed for dying, and behind the eyes, held back by the tongue, thick in the throat . . . tears.

Shawn was the world come into his cabin. *Ae,* to have seen the face of the world!

The cut-marks of living were on that face of Shawn's, but the mask he wore over it hid them, just as the masks of the Shawnee False Faces protected them in the hard moons. It was a love-mask that Shawn wore, with smiles around the mouth and gentleness around the eyes, and sweetness over the whole of it.

"I will carve such a mask for myself," Nathan thought, "and it will hide and heal the scars I must bear."

Sometimes when Shawn rode away on his proud-stepping mare, Nathan climbed up in front of him and rode as far as Night Dog's cabin. His mother sent him there often now.

"My son, there are things you must learn of sign and trails and of the forest, while you are young."

Long before they reached his grandpap's doorlog, Nathan was homesick. His thoughts went back to the double cabin on its high hills, the light burning out of its windows at night, the smoke rising out of its chimney, the sound of his mother's and sister's skirts, and the smell of honeysuckle filling the dooryard. But when he felt the sickness crawling up his back like the rising of dog-hackles, he told himself, "Grandpap'll fetch me back any time I'm ready."

The farther he went, however, the more the woods called to him. Bright flitters dodged past him, the leaves threw sun-splashes in his eyes, the rivers hummed, the wind whistled in the swinging vines, the beasts and birds and bugs talked back and forth. By the time they reached his grandpap's cabin he had stopped his longing for home and was seeing Shawn as a near stranger who'd found him and fetched him here. He was anxious for him to cut short his easy talk with Night Dog and mount and leave before this new feeling left him.

Being at his grandpap's wasn't much like being at his pa's. He couldn't get used to having such a few chores to do. And it was strange to have no little ma and sister chattering at you to wash your face and keep your hands out of the supper kettle, and look at the mud on those moccasins. But it seemed stranger still to have so few white men coming and going on the trail. At home, they came all the time, as numerous as the honey bees that The People called the white man's flies.

They got up at daylight, though, just like at home. Day was made for man and night for beasts, his grandpap told him. Even Kije Manitou got up in the daytime, and who were they to do different from the Great God?

While the dew was still so heavy that the trails looked like the watery caves in the Salamonie banks, they took to the forest. Night Dog wanted to teach him sign while his young mind was as yielding as the wild rice shoots before the grain began to form.

He pointed out a narrow track in the soft dirt along the river. Nathan had to squat until his nose was nearly on it before he could make it out. He wondered how his grandpap could stand at full height and see it plain.

"What do you think made it?" Night Dog asked.

Nathan didn't know.

"Maybe someone dragged a stick . . . ," he could see from his grandpap's look that this was a mighty poor guess. He added, "Maybe a white-tailed buck scratched it with his antlers. . . ."

That mark, his grandpap told him, was the mark of a snake heading toward the river. But even if this snake laid hold of you and bit for all he was worth, no poison would ooze from his fangs. No, the worst you might get would be a few little cuts.

Nathan stared down at the faint track. That was a powerful lot for such a small sign to tell.

"How do you know?" he asked.

Now began the long days of reading sign. It was the most important thing that a boy here could ever learn. Every day, his life would hang on it, and the lives of his woman and his young ones when he was grown. In time to come, Nathan would learn sign, the ways of hunters, of beasts, and of the vast woods, and be sharper at it than any white man that ever came down the trail. But he was always to remember the first lesson best, because it was the first.

His grandpap knelt beside him and, with a clean feather, lifted blown dust from the track. Then he pointed with the quill end of the feather.

"See the little walls on either side? And how they lean toward the river? That shows which way he was going."

Nathan nodded.

Now here was an ant's trail, crossing the track. Down inside the walls, you could see drops of dew. And if you looked real close, you'd find the walls were starting to crumble. And there a June bug had flopped when he got turned on his back.

"This track was made two suns back. The snake was on the move early, to get out of the sun. The ant, up later, crossed the trail. Still later, toward the noon hush, the west wind sprang up, the way it does every day, and blew dust into it. Then, after sundown, the dew fell. Next, the June bug, flying at night, tumbled into it. Another sun came, and another wind, and another dew. Here on the bank, the track wasn't sheltered. If it had been in the deep woods, it would have stayed fresher and looked newer."

"But how do you know the snake has no poison?"

They crawled along beside the track and Night Dog showed him that it was nearly straight.

Snakes with no poison, he said, have to move fast because they run down their food, and this means that they have to go as straight as they can. He pointed to the faint bumpiness of the ground. The snake had touched only the high places; his body had not gone into the ridges at all. If he had been a poisonous snake, his track would have twisted every which way, hit the high and the low places, too. Poisonous snakes had no call for speed, but lay in wait for something to come along.

Nathan thought he had learned a lot, but that was only the beginning.

Next morn they went to hunt squirrels. They happened on a panther track beside a stream and saw where he had stepped carefully from rock to rock, dainty as a lady.

"Nothing a *meshebeshe* hates like getting his feet wet," Night Dog grinned. "This is a big male. See the round mark of his pug? And a young one, for there are no cracks on the pugs."

Nathan studied it, but to him it looked just like the foot-mark of a night dog.

"I . . . I can't tell them apart," he fetched out, shamed.

His grandpap set him down right there, and rhymed him a rhyme to show him the difference between the two.

"The smaller the pad, the bigger the toe,
The nails will show in the track.
The beast is a hunter who runs down his prey,
You'll hear him at night with his pack.

"The larger the pad, the smaller the toe,
No nails will show in the track.
The beast is a hunter who stalks his prey
And waits for a chance to attack."

They trailed the panther across the stream and down the other side. Even when his tracks petered out, Night Dog showed Nathan where a bit of reddish fur had torn off on a thornbush, and where the grass was bent and the moss flat. Try as he might, Nathan couldn't see half the things his grandpap saw, though he rubbed his eyes till they were sore, and stared hard whenever Night Dog pointed. They followed the sign till the sun was half across the sky of leaves. Then they found where the cat had rested. After a while, he'd slunk on a ways, then stretched out again. He'd done this three or four times. And when Night Dog crouched where the cat had been, he could see the beast had been watching something in an open glade of the woods.

"Deer feeding," he told Nathan, and scuffed at the pulled-down grass.

They went on, and found where the deer had broken and run. Night Dog paced off a piece of ground and scratched two lines, then counted the hoofmarks in between.

"A herd of about fifteen," he said.

They followed the deer sign. Farther on, they came on dried blood, low on mayflower leaves. Night Dog studied it, but it was too much of a puzzle even for him. They went on, guided by the blood on the leaves, and found where the panther had made his kill. They even found the kill, an old doe, half chewed out and covered with leaves as neatly as though some little body had patted them down with tiny hands.

Night Dog sat down with his back to a beech and lit his clay. For a long time, he sat thinking while Nathan waited in silence. The peewees were calling their lonesome daydown calls when he came up with the answer. The panther had something wrong with him, he said. He couldn't grab the deer by the neck and twist it around to bring it down, because something was wrong with his jaw. He had hamstrung the deer instead, a way of killing favored by night dogs, but not by panthers. The innards and hind quarters had been badly chewed, not in the usual neat way of cats. The panther was somewhere in this part of the forest, badly hurt.

Nathan moved closer to his grandpap. He stared at the quivering leaves, half afraid he'd see the beast, and remembered to shove his back hard against a tree, so nothing could jump him from behind.

"*Meshebeshe* must have a deep wound in his jaw. Maybe he was shot by a hunter, and that's why he kills his food so strangely."

Nathan didn't know whether it was the wind he heard walking in the woods, or the wounded cat.

"When a beast is hurt, he has to kill the best way he can," Night Dog said quietly. "And when he can't kill his usual prey, he turns to the easiest prey of all . . . humans."

Nathan looked at his grandpap sitting there so calmly and wished with all his heart that they were back in the cabin, any cabin. Hunting was more fearsome than he had dreamed.

"Maybe . . . maybe we ought to start back," he said. "Maybe pa's rode down to see me. . . ."

Night Dog didn't let on that he'd heard.

"That panther hasn't been back here for two or three suns. So he's either mighty hungry or mighty dead by now. Probably dead," he added, casting a glance at Nathan.

Ae, Nathan told himself comfortingly, the beast was dead. But back at the cabin later, when Night Dog sent him to the river for a calabash of water, he ran like a rabbit. Much of the water was sloshed out on the narrow footpath, for at every sound Nathan expected to see the panther's half-torn face poking at him from the weeds.

"Kije Manitou, guard me, protect me . . . ," he prayed as he ran.

For the next few days, however, he made a brave face as he trailed after Night Dog through the woods. He wasn't quite so scared now, for he had a bow in his hand.

In the second moon of the year, the Hunger Moon, Night Dog had split a hickory sapling and hung it in the smoke of his fire to season. Only after Seegwun had come did he take it down and begin to carve it into a bow. It was backed with sinew, and paint had been rubbed into its fanciful Pota- watome designs.

Together they chipped out arrowheads for the seasoned shafts of hickory. This arrowhead-making was no easy task, Nathan found, and he wished he could carry a curly-maple gun instead. But Night Dog shook his head.

"There might be a time," he said, "when you are without a rifle. Or, if you have a rifle, without balls or flint, or pow- der to strike the pan. You can do well anyway, though, if you know how to use what the Great God has put here for you. Before the Morning Light People came with their guns, we did not starve."

Night Dog took him to a cave along the river. There, wrapped in hide, were hundreds of pieces of flint.

"These were once used for trade," he said.

From the cache, they chose four oval pieces, four because it was a mystic number sure to bring luck. Nathan would have picked the ones with the prettiest colors, but his grand- pap showed him that some of them were already split, or weak on one side and would chip in the wrong direction.

An oval stone was laid on a puncheon. Then Night Dog took his chipping tool, which had a handle of wood and a precious piece of iron, like a long blunt needle, on its end. He held the tool at a slant against the edge of the flint and began to flake it off. He went around it again and again, and it began to take on shape. Each time it grew sharper and more pointed. When he thought it was right, he cut notches in the base; then the arrowhead was bound to the rubbed shafts with wet rawhide which was wrapped around and fastened through a loop at the end.

Nathan marveled at the arrows.

"Good for birds or small game," Night Dog warned him, "but nothing bigger." He told Nathan about the time of his first arrows, when he had tackled a she-bear with them. If his pa hadn't been close by, he'd have been dead this long time past.

When the noon hush set down, they tucked the squirrels they had shot into their belts and started back.

"Now show me how well you've learned your lessons of these weeks," Night Dog said. "I will go ahead, not by any trail, but through the woods. And you track me."

With two fat squirrels swinging from his belt, Nathan felt he could track an eagle to its nest.

"I'll catch you," he grinned.

He sat down and closed his eyes so he wouldn't see which way his grandpap went. Once he was tempted to peep.

"But tarnal!" he told himself. "Why peep when I can track so good?"

He waited a while, to make sure his grandpap had a good start, then began casting about for his sign. All the brag went out of him. It began to look as if he'd never get out of the glade. But then he found the broken grass-blades, still flat, and farther on, a broken twig hanging from a berry bush, and beyond that a heelprint by a stream. The trail wasn't half as easy to find as he had thought it would be.

He was hurrying to catch up now. Afterward, he reckoned that that was the reason he had paid no mind to other sign. A mountain jack scolded along a branch, but he didn't even raise his head. To one side he heard a twig snap, but he thought it was likely a curious fox. Crows cawed above him, four shrill caws and then a longer one. But still he wasn't as wary as he should have been. He went on slowly, touching

107

leaves and stones and bits of earth, but in the back of his mind, something was bothering him. It had to do with the crows. Then it came to him. They were giving the signal for great danger. He stopped of a sudden and straightened up. Later, he reckoned if he'd just kept on going, he might have been all right, for his grandpap passed this way and nothing happened. It was his quick move that did it.

Another squirrel chattered and peered behind him, and he whirled just in time to see the bushes fly apart and a panther with a bloodied face lunge at him. The lunge was off and the beast missed him. Nathan just stood there with his heart pounding as though it would strangle him.

His arrows might give him no help against this sick and wounded beast, but he could use his bow like a spear and try to stand his ground. He yelled and jabbed at it with his bow. The panther jumped out of his way, but its tail began to twitch and Nathan knew it would try another spring. Still, his bow might hold it off, for all beasts were afraid of horns and would back down from anything like them unless it was a beast cornered, or a beast that ran in packs and circled its prey.

He and the cat stared at each other and Nathan could see that this beast was scared, too. Likely it would charge and take him down. He felt sick and shaky inside. He thought he heard a whimper come from his lips, but his head was full of the grim aim, "I will go down with all my muscles knotted!"

He stood like a brave, and it flashed upon him, "Pa'll be proud I died on my feet like a man, and not on my pallet like a babe!"

There was a soft whistling thud, and the panther fell dead across the toes of his moccasins. His grandpap stepped through the bushes behind him. Never, no, never, Nathan thought, though he lived forever, would he be so glad to see a mortal! He blinked up at Night Dog and saw a pleased look in the great dark eyes.

"You remembered your lesson well, my son," his grandpap said gently. "I am proud that you bear your mother's totem."

Nathan leaned weakly on his bow.

"You must have stumbled on him where he was laid up for the day," Night Dog went on, as if he hadn't noticed the sick look on his grandboy's face. "He smelled the blood of the squirrels and came to see what he could pull down."

Nathan nodded, trying to speak. The whole world was covered with black spots, like gnats over a stream. Shame of shame, he had all but fainted!

That night, when they had eaten their fried squirrel and sweet potatoes and nut-meat gravy, they sat on the doorlog together, and Nathan thought of the day past. He had learned a sight more than sign and hunting this day. He had learned that the two dark braves, Alone and Fear, were not his enemies, but his brothers. They had stood beside him when he was charged by the panther, and it was they who had given him strength.

Ae, he thought, they will help you and watch over you when you come to know them, and there is no living without them.

8

OF MORNS, the late fall sun clambered up behind the cabin, pokey as an old woman puttering toward her buryhole. The days were turning short now.

Nathan stood in the dooryard of his grandpap's cabin and gloried in the skins pegged to the trees. Not even Lannard, he thought proudly, had ever had such a good summer's hunting! He sniffed the meat and fish hanging from their circle of poles in a cloud of rotten-birch smoke.

His grandpap sat on the ground sewing a little leather bag in which Nathan would carry his medicine rabbit. He had cut it out of a rabbit skin the day before, and his grandpap had been real pleased to see it.

"This ball of fur," said Night Dog, "will make your shots go straight all the rest of your hunting days. Others may find only empty trails and empty bellies. But the god of hunters has sent this gift to you as a sign that he will always hunt beside you."

Now that the lazy days had come, Nathan and Night Dog spent less time on the trails. The sky got up of morns, cool and blue. Down by the river, you could make out clouds like cobwebs. Mist hung on late, and came on early, about the

time the last peewee called. The mast was heavy, trees loaded
with nuts, winter-berry bushes that bent to the ground. Milk-
weed fluff filled the air.

Of nights, when the wind dropped, you could hear the
great cousin-bears wheeze, snuffling after extra food to cram
into their dragging bellies before the long sleep. The katydids shrilled, vowing frost would be here before the week was
out. Every time Nathan and his grandpap stepped into the
woods, they got stuck all over with beggars' lice and other
burrs. Of nights they lay on the river bank and said the geese
would be flying south by the next moon. The blackbirds had
long since whirred off.

Now they spent a lot of time in talk. Nathan had coaxed
his grandpap into telling him the tales of The People that
every babe in the villages knew. At first Night Dog had tried
to put him off until the snows came.

"The gods are on the trails as long as the days are warm,"
he said, "and if they hear us talking of them, they'll be
angry." But in the end, he could not refuse his little grandboy.

So, in the nighttime, they sat inside the cabin with the
door pulled shut, to close out the gods. Night Dog reeled off
tale after tale. At the beginning and at the end of each, he
would look into the fire and say, "So it ends. So it begins.
The hawk of our fate passes over. It bears the words of gods
and men to the end of the earth, and returns for more. For
words are life and to life, my son, there is no end." This was
the proper way to begin and end the tales, the way of the
villages.

"A man," said Night Dog, "lives the lives of seven beasts.
Perhaps you have heard this thing? Well, little son, listen
then and remember, and when I have been beneath my
grave-pole for many winters, it will come to you that I spoke
with a true heart.

"When you were born, you were treated like a little cub,
stared at and listened to as if your babbling held the wisdom
of our cousin-bear.

111

"But in your second year, you were like the chipmunk, digging in the dirt, stuffing all manner of things into your cheeks and carrying them off, even rocks.

"Now you are like a young panther running through the forest on quiet pads, screaming your gladness at all you see, puzzled by the beasts that leap out of your way, and by those that trail you and would do you harm. Now you hit at all things with careless paws, and snarl at those beyond your understanding. One minute, you wish to tumble and play, the next to be solemn and quiet, and the next to prowl through all the vast forest and find out its secrets.

"When you are a man, you will be like the young buck, careful with your antlers in velvet, bold when they come sharp and hard. Then you will thunder down the trails, giving the challenge cry, full of belief in your own cunning and knowledge. You will prance before the young does and dare the old bucks, and even sniff the panther's tracks with no quivering of fear.

"Then comes the time when you are like the wild bull who has a herd to protect. You are heavy with the problems of your herd, you lead it through the snow, breaking the trail, butting at the wolves which follow you. Your lot is hard, you search for the right path to the prairies of safety, and you are no longer sure that you are the proper leader, or strong enough, or wise enough.

"Then, when you grow old, you become like the hunger-wolf. You are selfish, no longer cunning or fleet of foot. New traps come into the forest, and you do not understand them. You grow wary and less brave, you steal the food of others and wish to den alone.

"And later, much later, you are like an old coon. Again you play like a child, unmindful of the world about you, forgetting all that has been, and all that you were."

They were both silent for a while. But the thing that had worried Nathan, ever since his grandpap had begun speaking of the path of life, came out.

"Is the path the same for us who are half-burnt wood men?"

Night Dog's eyes flared up. So already his little grandboy had learned that he was not like the others, but was made of two mixed bloods. He remembered when he himself had learned this. *Ae,* he thought, but the truth must come to us.

"Yes," he said slowly. "The path is the same . . . only harder."

"Is it a very bad thing to be a half-burnt wood person?" Nathan asked quietly.

"*Io,* no! It is a proud thing . . . *proud!*"

He slipped his arm around Nathan's shoulders and they sat listening to the fire and the autumn wind in the chimney.

"We alone," he said gently, "understand the song that the mourning dove sings in her sadness. We alone do not hide ourselves when the strange rain sweeps through the forest, that is neither white like squaw rain, nor dark like brave rain. We alone are free, for unless we wish it so, nothing binds us to others. But," he added, "we must walk forever with the shadows of two different people. Let us not tread on either shadow, but keep in step with them both."

Nathan was silent, but later he asked, "Is there a special totem for the half-burnt wood man?"

"From your own mother, you inherit the proud Delaware totem," Night Dog answered evasively.

"But is there no totem just for us?"

"It is time to sleep, little son. We will talk of this another night."

He turned his back upon Nathan and stayed busy for a long time, scraping the old ash out of his clay. But inside himself he was saying, "*Ae,* we have a totem . . . a heart torn as if panthers had fought over it. A heart chewed by the mad foxes set upon us by those of pure blood who revile us. A heart that would taste bitter in the mouth of a carrion-eating devil dog. A broken heart."

9

S NOW started with the Beaver Moon that the white men called November. It came down the north trail with Peboon, the god of winter, and like him it came to stay. The blizzard drove through the forest, and The People said its shrieks and bellowing were the *tchibais,* ghosts, of dead hunters, and the spirits of the wild bull herd killed in the winter of the great storm. Nathan thought of the bones on the great prairie, and wondered if they got up and danced to the sound of their own eerie voices.

The winter was a hard winter. The night dogs turned to hunger-wolves and came right up to the cabin and sniffed at its door. The two dogs Sin and By Hokey stayed inside and whimpered and barked at the beasts outside. Of nights, you could hear the nickering of the mare in the shed as the wild things prowled around and yipped that there was warm horse flesh inside. Of morns, when you stepped out into the door-yard, you could see footpads in the snow, the swinging mark left by the panther's tail, and the straight mark left by the night dog's tail.

The big deer stood on their hind legs to strip off the tree bark, and the smaller deer and the fawns died quickly. But you didn't come on their bodies. You saw only the bloody mess left by the other beasts, the ones that had followed behind them and waited. Then the snow let up for a while and the ice storm came, catching on the ground little squirrels that had gone down from their den-trees to forage. All night you could hear the winter birds crying as the wind beat against their trees, and the ice pulled their branches down. It began to look as if nothing would be left of the forest or its life.

In the Indian villages, beasts tore the heavy stones off the storage pits, and gorged on the smoked meat and flesh and dried corn and seeds. Both men and women sat up, of nights, to drive off the beasts with rattles, and some they shot had bellies full of stolen food. Even wee babes in their cradleboards were carried off sometimes, and only some beads and hunks of board would be found afterward.

They were desperately hungry in the villages. They said their hunger-prayers and did their dances, and then they slaughtered the precious horses. Still, by the time of March, the Crow Moon, their horn spoons were scraping bowls that held mostly water boiled with bark and a few grains of seed. Many's the Delaware you could hear hunting in the woods with his dogs. Many's the Shawnee that came to white men's cabins with the rough dark salt they treasured, hoping to trade it for food.

But the woodsies and settlers were no better off, and had nothing to give them in return. Even hunters like Lannard had gone begging for their babes' food. They dug ginseng to chew, to give their teeth something to work on, and like those in the villages, ate wild potatoes, wild onions, and cattail roots, and stretched them out with nut gravy.

One new-come family dug an Indian turnip, and ate it raw and died with the terrible cramps the poison brought on. The only thing plentiful was maple sugar, and they munched on it all the time. By the coming of the Grass Moon, April, folks were so weak from hunger they didn't look as if they could get up from their pallets to see if there were any beasts left to hunt. When you met them on the trails, with their buckskins hanging loose around their hams and their faces so thin and white, you knew what *wendigos* must look like.

In the villages, they worried that the wild bull ghosts which came with the blizzard might bring on pneumonia. But it was smallpox that came instead. It started at Fort Hamilton, to the south and east, and came right up the rivers with its chills, head pains, vomiting, fever, and ugly seeping blisters. It went into the villages, and in every lodge and wigiwam, someone died. It went into the cabins, and those who didn't die had pitted faces to remember the winter by.

Jonathan went to the places where the smallpox was, though there was little he could do for it. None of his boughten medicines would help. He had read an article in the *Medical Repository* about a man named Jenner who had found a means of keeping smallpox away by vaccination. But it did him little good to read the article, for he had none of the precious stuff that would stop the sickness.

He thought of the long distance that stretched between his cabin and the back-East settlements where they had new medicines and new thoughts and new doctors who would trade learning with him. He remembered the town where he had been born, the cobbled streets, and the quiet Yadkin river that never threw flatboats onto the rocks. He saw himself as he might have been, a doctor in a real office with a gold-painted sign hanging outside. He'd have been a man of renown by now, making his rounds in a carriage with a team of blacks, dropping in at a warm inn to drink hot buttered rum, wearing the white men's starchy clothes and polished boots.

He smiled and shuddered at the same time, and thanked the Lord for fetching him out here. If he hadn't come, he'd never have been free to walk a hundred miles just to clap his eyes on something that had got his wonder aroused. He'd never have known the woodsies, the settlers, the Indians. Likely, in time, he'd have taken for truth the common saying that they were just a lot of filthy drifters and savages who, it was hoped, would soon kill each other off.

When he saw the redbud blooming on the hills, saw his young ones whooping down the trail to meet him, his woman with her eyes as bright as the Hunter's Star, and when he sat as a friend in the cabins and in the villages, he felt himself complete. Then he knew that here in this vast wilderness was his true home, and no place else on earth would have satisfied him.

He reckoned that something had been nagging him always to come away from settled places. He remembered how, when he was a lad, he would stir in his blankets of nights, and sit up . . . listening. It wasn't a sound like the horn the woodsies talked about, that called men to far-off trails and streams. No, it was a roaring, a thundering, *a storm,* and the older he became, the wilder it blew. Later, in his books, he found the storm-feeling had belonged to men before him. There was the long-dead doctor Paracelsus who had talked about it.

"So I have traveled throughout the land and was a pilgrim all my life, alone and a stranger, feeling alien. Then Thou hast made me grow in Thine art, under the breath of the terrible storm within me."

He understood now the voice of that storm. It was telling him that sicknesses went from one end of the earth to the other, just as if they walked on feet, and the man who would understand them and slow their walk must follow where they led.

He thought about it as he made his rounds, as he whistled up and down the trails, and smiled at the little beasts that came out to see what it was that whistled. He tried not to be despondent because he had none of the stuff called vaccine, and dosed his patients as best he could with medicine from the forest. He gave them tea of mulberry bark for a purge, tea of wild rose hips to bring back strength, tea of cowslip flowers to lull restlessness. He made poultices of yarrow, and ointment of wild primrose to help soothe the blisters and heal the skin. And, when he saw his patients afterward, he felt they looked about as good as if they'd been tended by a back-East doctor in white gloves.

For a while, Jonathan didn't come back to his cabin at all, lest he bring the sickness with him, but stayed with some woodsy family down the trail. What meat he managed to scare up, he boiled or roasted, hoping to kill any breath of sickness that might be on it, then hung it in The Bucks for Nathan to fetch.

Nathan and Tibby, being such young ones, hardly knew what a bad year they were in. But their ma did, and she wished heavily that they were older. She needed someone to talk to, to help her study on what to do if one of them should be taken down, or if the food ran out altogether.

As the moon turned old, Tibby became fretful, disappointed because the cold stayed on, and the woods looked like fall instead of spring. Strange Rain kept her busy making baskets and bowls, saying, "Soon there'll be berries and meat to fill them." Tibby nodded and sat late over her work, as if the sooner it was done, the sooner would come the food to fill it. But Nathan knew this was the hard living Shawn had talked about. Once he said, "Shawn wouldn't just stand around the cabin and say *wait*! He'd find food somehow!"

At night, when he said his prayers, he spoke them tired-voiced, as if he didn't think there was any reason to mention them at all. Of days, he strung and restrung the new bow that his grandpap had made for him the winter past, and his mind kept running on ahead, to places his body couldn't go. Sometimes he'd be ready to start out, then he'd feel his ma's eyes on him, and remember that his pa said he was to stay off the trails, lest he get the sickness from the breath of a village or cabin.

"I *know* I could find game!" he flared once. "Leastways, I wouldn't just be standing here!"

His mother tried to please him with tales of The People, and he listened, polite, but she knew he was worried. She had caught him peeking under the over-turned wooden bowl that had all their food beneath. She knew he was thinking that, in good times, they wouldn't have fed this to the dogs. She knew he realized that it wasn't enough for the three of them, and before another day was out, they'd be boiling bark. She knew he felt responsible for them with Jonathan gone and maybe . . . she turned her eyes to the trail . . . maybe falling sick and never coming back.

She saw, every night, how her slight son stood on the doorlog and counted the medicine lights, the corpse candles, bobbing over the swamp. She saw how he'd turn back and look at their faces, especially the face of his twin, with her dark eyes circled like a coon's and her hard bones standing out as sharp as turkey claws. She saw how the fearing look would come into his eyes, as though he had seen Tibby's face in one of those lights. Being twins was a strong tie, stronger than the brother-and-sister tie, Strange Rain thought. It seemed that growing side by side in their ma's body had made them know each other's thoughts and feelings. She remembered the summer past when Nathan had been sick, and Tibby had sickened, too. Strange Rain looked at Nathan now and wondered if he could feel the hunger that was inside his little twin.

That night, as her children slept, Strange Rain went off by herself, taking the new clay bowl, the white feather, and the household god. She said a special sacrifice prayer that would tell her what to do about her young ones, how to keep their minds from fretting and their bellies from aching, till her man came home.

The next morning, she called Nathan at daybreak.

"Dress and come down."

When he slipped down the ladder, he saw that she had put all the food they had on the table, in his own trencher. He pulled up his stool and looked at it. Then he got up and took a piece of charred wood from the fireplace. He laid it on the table before him and rubbed some of its black on his hands and face, as a sign that he would fast this day.

But his ma shook her head.

"*Io,* no! Today you hunt and bring us fresh food, good

119

food. A hunter cannot leave his cabin with his stomach growling like a cousin-bear's."

He looked again at the food.

"Hunt?" he echoed, surprised. "Still I will fast," he said.

He stepped out into the clearing as the sun was poking up, lifted his bow and quiver to its light for a blessing, and spoke the morning prayer. Then, going back into the cabin, he took a bit of food from the trencher and threw it on the fire.

"Lead us in the way of food," he prayed.

"Bring a fat pigeon," his *ninga* called from the dooryard. "With a fat pigeon, I can do much."

As he went, he stroked his bow and made a song under his breath, so the Great God would know he was hunting and give him help.

> "The Hunter of Men walks through the forest,
> We hear the whistling of his hunger-arrows,
> We hear the whirring of his sickness-arrows,
> We get up looking into our graves.
> Even our shadows are thin and worn.
> Save our shadows . . .
> For without them, we perish."

He went west and crossed the Mississinewa river. From there he went south, toward a place where the villages were not so thick and the woods might not be hunted clean. He marked the sign along the way, but it was scarce and mostly old. He followed game trails, but there were precious few prints on them. He stopped by a salt-lick and waited in a hunters' tree, but nothing came. He found a grove of beeches and crouched near a den-tree, but not a squirrel poked out its head.

The day wore on.

"God of the Hunter, lead me," he prayed.

The noon hush came and went. He began to tire, and stopped often to rest. He had never known the woods to be so quiet. It was as still as if its birds and beasts had gone off to a far country in search of food, maybe where Night Dog or some of the woodsies were hunting now.

He went on, working south over game trails toward the Pwakanna, Pipe Creek. The sun was in the west. The shadows grew until the woods was like a dark cloud. It was getting hard to see. Still, he went on.

He reckoned it was time he looked for a place for the night. He remembered a glade that had a big hollow sycamore in it, as good a place as any. He came onto the glade in the fading light and there, standing by the sycamore, was one tired, scrawny little deer, separated from the herd and feeding by its lonesome.

He stopped still and stared at it, and instead of jumping and running, it stared back at him. His bow was ready, with an arrow nocked on the string. He swung the bow up and let the arrow fly. The deer stumbled as the arrow hit him in the short ribs. Then it ran. Nathan ran after it, slamming into trees, catching his feet on roots, ducking vines, not being careful or quiet or looking for sign as his grandpap had taught him.

Birds flew up and a crow called, and he doubled around, cutting through thick dead brush, hoping to head it off. Then all was quiet, and he didn't hear the running feet any more. He went on, slow and silent-footed, looking for the blood trail. When he came onto it, he was glad he had put a lightning-groove into his arrows, like The People of the far west. It not only made the blood flow faster, and laid a clear trail, but it slowed and weakened the game.

He came onto the deer standing stiff-legged, with its head low. It wasn't whistling now. Nathan shot it again, but the deer just staggered a step or two and never took his eyes off the dark leaf mold. Nathan shot his last two arrows, and finally the deer fell down.

The woods came still, as if all were watching. Nathan went up to the deer and poked it with the end of his bow. It stirred. He slipped out his knife to cut its throat, but when he knelt and lifted the blade, the small head raised up. Its large pointed eyes were as large as his *ninga's,* and as soft as his twin's. It was just as if they said, "Little brother, why have you done this to me?"

The knife dropped to the ground, and the hand that held it began to smooth the deer's poor head, and the tongue that had hankered to taste its meat was soothing it with soft words. As he crouched there, looking down at it, it did something which hurt him worse than anything in all his life. It cried, and it cried real tears. The tears ran down and mixed with the bloody foam that came out of its mouth. He stared back at it, shattered by its slow dying, and suffering for it. Then it reached out its soft nose like a puppy wanting to lick his hand. It looked at him with pity and forgiveness. Then it died.

For a long time he sat there holding its head on his knee and feeling sick. He went on talking to it. He tried to choke out the hunter's song of victory, but there was no pride in what he'd done. Of a truth, it wasn't the first animal he had ever killed, but none had died so pitifully.

The little deer had got through the whole hard winter, he kept thinking, the snow and ice . . . likely scraping with those little heart-shaped feet to keep its little body alive . . . maybe sick . . . running and hiding from the hunger-wolves . . . and now . . . and *now* . . . with spring coming on. . . .

He thought dully, "It'll never see it. I came along ahead of spring, ahead of the good time, the warm time, the food time. . . ."

He turned weak as he pulled out the arrows. Four arrows, to kill one tired little deer.

He looked back at its eyes, but they were peaceful now, as if they were seeing something way beyond him, way beyond its body.

Still he crouched there, stroking its short hair, feeling the chill come over it, like the ground cooling off at night.

"I never killed a deer before," he said to himself, and remembered that this should have been a bright time in his life. He should have sung the victory song. He should be looking forward to taking the deer home and hearing his folks praise him, and watching them eat his kill, but not touching any for himself. The last would be easy, he thought. He could never eat any of it.

He reached into his shirt and pulled out the little red strips of cloth to tie to the deer's hipbones when he hung them in a tree. He laid the ribbons under a rock and began to dress out the animal. He made the long cut down the middle, and its insides spilled onto the ground. But when they did, he saw that the little deer's heart was still beating. He watched it quivering and thrumping by his knees, counted its beats, and couldn't look away from it. After a long time, he got up and went off and was sick clear to his toes with retching, though he fetched up nothing more than a little sour water.

Not far off he heard the hunger wolves give their hunting howl with the short barks at the end, and he heard the night dogs leaping and crying behind them.

"No two ways about it," he said to the forest. "I've got to get it home."

He set his mouth and went back to it. He dressed it out, hard-faced, stopping ever so often to look up at the moon and wipe the sweat and tears from his face.

When he was done, he strapped the deer on his back with a tumpline, a carrying strap made of *shaganappi,* the green hide which the white men called "Indian iron." Though he thought he could have carried it without the *shaganappi* over his forehead and over the deer, for it was miserably small, and maybe weighed less than he did.

"Just wait," he said aloud. "Wait till they see what I've fetched."

But saying it did no good.

When he crossed the Mississinewa again, at its narrows, the blood from the little animal went out around him in the water. He could see it, even in the moonlight, and he thought the animal smell and blood smell and death smell would never leave room in his head for any sweet smells again.

It was almost dawn when he came, hallooing the cabin, and stepped into its light. His *ninga* and sister were up, looking worried that he hadn't come back before now. They ran to him when they heard his voice, and stopped with their mouths open when they saw his kill. Right off, his *ninga* took the raw liver and cut it into strips and gave one to each.

But Nathan turned away from his. "First kill," he mumbled, explaining.

"In time of hunger, it does not matter," she said gently, and pressed the liver on him. He went outside to sit on the chopping log where he was away from them and from the deer. He could smell its little body already turning on the spit, and hear his twin chattering happily as she basted it with bear's oil. He sat there, watching for the first light, with the raw cold liver in his hands. His belly ached from hunger, yet he couldn't force the liver into his mouth.

"I've killed before," he whispered, "and it didn't hurt like this."

He puzzled on it.

"It's like being the Hunter of Men," he thought. "It must be hard and hurtful hunting that he does . . . taking not only little beasts and birds, but folks too . . . who beg him, 'Please, I don't want to die' . . . folks who cry tears of pain. . . ."

He buried the liver, not wanting to touch it, though he knew this waste of food was a terrible sin, and went to his pallet, saying he was too tired to eat. He lay there in the dawn light, thinking of the little deer, the tears, the blood on the water, the Hunter of Men.

His grandpap was still long-hunting, but Lannard and Tinch and Rocreuse came back next day. They all had meat, and Lannard had killed a bear. When he saw the deer haunches smoking in the dooryard, and heard how it was that Nathan had fetched meat home, he clambered up the loft ladder, cursing its steep rungs.

"Right proud!" he began, squatting down beside Nathan. "Whar'd you fetch him down?"

"Down Pwakanna way."

Lannard's grey eyes gleamed. His own boy had no thought for the woods or its ways.

"Take you huntin with me today, if you're a-mind to."

Last moon, last week, any time before yesterday, Nathan would have given most anything to prowl the woods with a long-hunter like Lannard. . . .

"It cried tears," he said slowly, and was half-shamed, not knowing what a woodsy like Lannard might think of such talk. "It bled for me," he said then, to make sure Lannard understood.

Lannard's face softened, and he sat back on his haunches.

"The earth bleeds for us, when we hack at her with plows and harrows," he said finally. "Law of life. Sap comes up in a tree, and we cut the tree to draw out the sweetness, and it bleeds, too. Your own pa . . . he gives out of his heart, bleeds cause he loves the hurt and sick like his own body. Law of life." He twisted his mouth around, considering.

Nathan looked down.

"It doesn't seem right."

"Wal," Lannard rubbed his beard. "It's a thing to puzzle on . . . but that's the way it is."

Nathan was still, but he listened to the bird and beast sounds outside, and now he longed to feel the trails under his feet.

"C'mon," Lannard said. "That's the way it is, that's all."

Nathan rolled over and looked out of the fine new window glass.

"C'mon," Lannard nudged him gently with his moccasin, "They's trails and trails a-waitin. C'mon. . . ."

10

THE Great Bear, followed by the three brother-hunters and their little dog Jiyeh, had lumbered around his circle more times than Nathan could count.

"*Ae,* how many winters since I watched them from the prairie?" he wondered. "Six?" He added in wonder, "Am I fourteen now?"

It was hard to keep track, for the winters had blown by so quickly, and the dawdly days of childhood had vanished with them. His moccasins tramped stranger-trails, and always they followed either his grandpap or the woodsies. The babe-look was fading from his face. He had grown tall and lanky and now he pulled back his hair and tied it with a ribbon, as did his pa.

One day Lannard stopped him before a bear's den.

"When you hunt bear," he cautioned him, "always come up to the den from behind and work round to the front of it, slow. Fling a stone inside and wait. Your bear-cousin won't come flyin out. No, he's too smart for that. But after while, he'll tippy out and sniff the wind, and then sit down in front jest like a greybeard with his pipe. You can get close to him while he's dozy, and aim at the heart."

It was Rocreuse who taught him about deer, for, as the rest admitted, he was the best deer hunter in these parts.

"We can all get our plenty," Lannard said, "but Rocreuse makes a cleaner kill."

"When you stalk deer," Rocreuse told him, "lie flat and crawl on your belly when you have to move. You can sneak close up to him while he's grazin but watch his tail—when it flicks he's gettin ready to raise his head and look around. He's smart, but curious. When you're close, stand up when he's not lookin. He'll walk right up and stare at you. If you happen on several together and can't get a good look at them on account of the bushes, cry like a panther. One of them will look your way. Shake the bushes and they'll all step out in the open and blink at you. Choose the one you want and . . . *pfff!*" Rocreuse shrugged to show how easy it was.

They hunted by day, and talked of hunting by night. Rocreuse whittled a deer-call for Nathan from a split reed.

"When you blow on this," he said, "they'll come, for it's their distress call, the only natural sound to hear in the woods both day and night. But when you use the call, be keerful, for wildcat and panther will come too, hoping for an easy meal."

"Chipmunks make good eatin when snow lays on, in the spring, and it's hard to find meat," Tinch said. "Jest take a wild-oats straw and blow agin it. They'll come a-runnin and climb all over you."

They taught him how to build a proper hunter's fire, never up against a log, on leaf mold or pine needles.

"Iffen this old woods was ever to catch fire, it'd be the end of us!" Lannard said.

No, always clear the ground where you aimed to have your fire, or build it on a slab of rock. In winter, or when the weather was wet, whack off a strip of birch bark to use for a hearth. It was mighty strange about birch bark. You could make kettles of it, even cook in them if your fire was low enough. At the same time, it was the only wood that'd burn when all else was soaked with rain.

There weren't many boys of Nathan's age hereabout, which was one reason the woodsies took to him. Another was that most of them had sons they were half shamed to call their own. Rocreuse's son Gandy now, he not only didn't like the woods, he didn't like farming either.

"Looks like he's bound to end up livin in a regular settlement and wearin starched clothes," Rocreuse said gloomily.

The others shuddered.

"My boy Sammy is jest as bad, though," Lannard shook his head. "He'll likely take to tradin."

But there were some things the woodsies couldn't teach Nathan, and one was what made men become Solitaries. They were different from any other folks Nathan had ever seen. They roamed wild in this great woods wearing rags or nothing, grubbed up roots to eat, and ran off when they saw other folks around.

"Reckon some's got the crazies," said Lannard. "Others . . . well, I've heerd that some are learnt men who come out here to get lost, to forget the past . . . but learnt men."

"Like Pa or Shawn?"

"Yep, like them."

"Where'd they come from?"

"Out," Lannard waved his arm vaguely. "Out beyond the woods."

Beyond the woods, Nathan thought. Back at the double cabin, he set to pondering. *Ae,* he knew there was a beyond somewhere outside the woods, but he just hadn't studied on it much.

"I'll bet there are plenty of things," he said to himself. "The woods doesn't run from sea to sea. There's likely as many stranger-folks outside as are here, inside. But what's it like?"

He ran a tallow rag through his rifle and hung the gun above the door.

"Pa," he burst out, "tell me what's beyond these woods."

That night Jonathan told him things he'd never known, never even dreamed. Even Strange Rain and Tibby hitched their stools close and forgot their tasks.

There were seas, not one but many, and ships that sailed those seas. There were different countries where folks spoke in different tongues, just as The People did. There were places that had no trees . . . they all turned wide-eyed at that . . . places that were all sand, or maybe all ice and snow.

There were mountains that went straight up into the clouds. There were tribes of different colors, and some wore clothes and some wore nothing at all. Some ate locusts and some ate each other.

There were buildings bigger than the clearing with nothing in them but paintings, and when they asked what paintings were, he told them they were like the picture-writing of The People, only larger, and with more colors than you could believe.

There were buildings where young ones went to learn to read and write and study books. There were clocks as tall as men, thin dishes with flowers painted on them, glass lamps that held enough candles to make a whole cabin as bright as day. And there was a thing called a harpsichord that looked like a table, only when you sat down to it and touched it, music came out.

It was astonishing to hear what lay beyond the woods. Right through those summer nights, one after the other, they kept Jonathan talking. One night he took a book down from the mantel and said, "It's all in here, and more besides."

Nathan opened the book and studied the little black marks, but they made no sense to him. Strange Rain and Tibby came and looked over his shoulder, but they didn't see how the book could talk to anyone, for Strange Rain could write no more than her name.

"Pa," said Nathan, shamed. "You know I can't read."

"You can learn," Jonathan told him. "It's just like reading sign."

"No harder?"

"Easier."

He pulled his stool up to Nathan's and began showing him how all the little marks were different, and how they came together to make words and sounds. Nathan's eyes shone like a Spanish bit.

"Show me what they say!"

Jonathan took a white-poplar chip and a chunk of charred wood, and guided Nathan's hand so the boy could trace his own name.

That night Nathan forgot to bank the fire and had to come back from the medicine cabin to do it. The minute he heard Jonathan stir in the morn, he was up like a shot.

"Teach me some more words, Pa, before you leave. There's nothing really wrong with Mrs. McCutcheon, anyway."

After that, it seemed like every time Jonathan came up the trail, Nathan was waiting for him with the poplar chip on his knee, and the books beside him. All day he would sit and trace out words, and when Jonathan came home, he'd tell him what the words meant. Before long, Jonathan was printing simple sentences for him to learn during the day, and then he'd go over them with him at night.

One day Jonathan came lugging home a piece of slate, and showed Nathan how to roll pencils from clay and put them out in the sun to dry. Now Nathan could scribble to his heart's content, and when he was out of pencils, he could make more.

The day he learned to write Tibby's name he went straight to her at the soap kettle.

"That's your name," he said, but she hardly put her paddle down.

"You're sure that's how my name looks?" She peered at the letters traced across the slate. "I don't *feel* that's how my name looks!"

From that time on, Tibby had no use for learning.

"I'll learn women's work and leave readin and writin to them that wants it," she laughed, with a toss of her pretty head. "It don't amount to a hill of beans, fer as *I* can see!"

One day Lannard dropped by to ask if Nathan wanted to go hunting over by the Mississinewa and Nathan was tempted. It'd been more than a month since he'd done any real hunting, except poking out into the woods once in a while to get something for the supper kettle. But when Lannard saw what Nathan was up to, he didn't insist.

"I'm jest downright impressed," he said. "It's a fine thing that you're gettin proper learnin." He squatted down beside him and watched the clay pencil move over the slate. "My whole life long," he said, wistful-faced, "I been shamed that I never learned to spell out my name, nor even seen it writ."

Nathan wrote it out for him right then, and Lannard was as pleased as he could be. He fetched a poplar chip and had Nathan make his name with charred wood, and when Nathan handed it back to him, Lannard was as proud as if he'd been given a hundred fisher-foxes. He took the chip back to his own cabin and pegged it above the mantel for all to see.

"Won't no one have to wonder whose cabin they're in now," he bragged. "And won't no one say I can't spell out my name!"

Nathan's other long-hunting friends stopped by when they heard what he was doing, and soon almost every cabin around had its poplar chip over the mantel. But Lannard always reminded them that he got his first.

Lannard and Rocreuse and Tinch tried to learn to write a few simple words, and Nathan was willing to teach them. But in the end, they decided they were too old to cram any more into their heads.

"Them curlycues is liable to get us all mixed up when we're tryin to read sign," they said, and went off hunting without him.

"One of the best hunters around here," Rocreuse mourned, "and he has to go and take up learnin!"

"We mustn't look on it that way," Lannard told him. "The boy is gettin important things in his head."

But the others still complained.

"He's cuttin himself off from us," said Tinch sadly. "After while, he'll hold himself above us and hunt alone."

"You two ought to be ashamed," Lannard stormed. "*He* ain't like that, and he ain't goin to give up huntin. He's jest put it aside fer a while. The white part of him hankers for white learnin, but the Injun part of him will never get free of the woods."

They doubted that what Lannard said was true, and moped for the rest of the day, missing sign and shots. But Nathan proved Lannard's words when he caught up with them one day near Place of Thorns, on Sugar Tree Creek. They were proud to see him and anxious to know that he hadn't forgotten the ways of the woods. Tinch and Rocreuse kept fixing false sign to test him, but they couldn't fool him.

They found that his book learning hadn't changed him after all, and the four of them long-hunted together through the rest of that summer and autumn. But that winter, Nathan didn't run so many traps, and only went long-hunting once.

"Haven't got much time," he said. "I'm learning doctoring, too."

"Wal, I'm glad to know it," Lannard said. "We're allus goin to need us a good doctor, back here."

Shawn stopped by in the Hunger Moon, February, and was pleased to find that Nathan was getting the white man's learning.

"After I go to the Winnebago country, I'll have one more trading trip back East, and I'll fetch you some new books from there. Books are more plentiful in the East; lots cheaper, too."

"You trade that far north?" Lannard asked. "Clear up among the Winnebago?"

"Yep."

"They're a mite wild, ain't they?"

"Kind of," Shawn shrugged, "but I never had any real trouble with them. Anyway, it's my last trip up there. When I come back, I'll be a real-for-sure lawyer," he grinned. "Already got an office rented down at Harrodsburg."

"I'll be!" Lannard was awed.

"Harrodsburg?" Jonathan smiled. "Looks like you've turned into a settlement man."

"Well, I have to be where folks can find me. Anyway,

that'll give all of you a place to come and visit." He added, suddenly quiet-faced, "As long as it's safe to be on the trails."

His words brought to mind the stories of trouble they'd heard in both cabin and wigiwam. Seemed like everybody had cause to worry these days.

Many's the year there'd been peace in the Wabash valley, with the Miamis living like brothers among the white men, and holding to the treaties they'd made. There'd been no thought of trouble till other Indians, specially the two Shawnees, came among them.

It was told that the two Shawnees were twins, one of them with the name of Tecumseh. The other was named Lawlewasika, which meant Loud Voice, but folks called him The Prophet. His voice was so loud, you could hear him two miles away, and he was a scary thing to look on. Years back, he'd had his face slashed and one eye torn out in a drunken fight, and now he looked like the mask of a *wendigo*.

The Prophet didn't drink any more. Instead, he preached to the tribes, telling about a message that had been sent to him in a dream. The Indians must no longer live as brothers to the white men, but must drive them out. Then the gods would return their strength and give them back their lands.

The older Delawares shook their heads and murmured that this was not the path of peace. But the young braves listened with throbbing blood, hungry for glory and for the feel of a tomahawk in their hands. Hoarse cries of approval came from a hundred throats as Tecumseh shouted that the treaties were false and not to be kept.

"It's bound to lead to fighting," Shawn said seriously. "There's talk in the villages of raids on cabins and settlements. Already the forest is full of spies ready to carry word of women left alone, long-hunting parties easy to ambush, traders to be struck down for the guns they peddle."

"But we've seen no stranger-men on the trails," Nathan said.

"Such spies may be braves we've called friends for many a year. There's no saying who they are, and no knowing . . . as yet."

133

But when Shawn came again, in the Planting Moon of May, trouble with the Indians was still in the distance. It was like a summer storm that wouldn't break, an uneasiness in the air, a whisper that stirred the forest, a rumbling that never really stopped.

It was dark when Shawn came, and they were sitting at the puncheon table eating soup of dried meat and berries. Hardly had they finished their welcome, jumping up all excited and pleased, when he said, "I've got something to tell you. . . ." But before he could get it out, a stranger-voice hallooed the cabin, and when the door swung open, a dark man stood there with a buck deer across his shoulders. It seemed to Nathan that that buck must weigh as much as Shawn and Jonathan put together.

The man stood blinking in the light, then he came on in.

"I fetched us a deer," he grunted, slipping it off his back by the fire.

They stared at each other, for no white man ever lugged a whole deer into a cabin, and certainly not one that was blood all over and hadn't even been dressed out yet.

"This is Earthwild," Shawn grinned.

He was a craggy young man of the woods, and it struck you that if a shagbark hickory came alive and walked around like a man, it would be twin to Earthwild. He heeled-and-toed it, as silent as a Shawnee, but he carried his head low and his shoulders hunched, as if shamed to be so tall.

He nodded to them all, but when his eyes fell on Strange Rain he spoke to her in the tongue of The People, then hefted up the deer again and carried it outside.

Strange Rain, who knew a little of the language of the Winnebago, was surprised to hear him apologize for bringing into her cabin a deer that hadn't had the sacrifice words said over it, or the head and hipbones tied with ribbons and left in a tree.

"I'll take keer of it right now," Earthwild called back in the white man's tongue.

"Some of that hunch," Shawn began, "comes from working the forge, at the smithy's in Harrodsburg. But most of it comes from a bygone time in his life."

They turned back to him.

"Reckon he's a lot like me," Shawn went on. "The woods just spit him out on a riverbank years back with nothing, not even a human name. When I found him, he was a slave in the Winnebago camp, and they swore they'd just stumbled on him, a boy roaming wild and naked, there along the Yellow river."

Shawn had traded for him, and Earthwild cost him plenty. The young buck who'd owned him used him as a horse when he went hunting, and sometimes he hunted as far south as the Paint river in the Illini prairies. He would whip Earthwild if he stumbled, or if he gasped for breath, or slowed down to a walk.

Shawn had haggled over the price because of whip scars on Earthwild's body, for he knew his Indians, and if they thought him too eager to trade, they wouldn't give the boy up at any price. But poor Earthwild didn't understand, and had come near to crying for fear Shawn would go off and leave him.

In the end, he brought more than a good mud-and-plunger horse. When they started to leave the village, he'd crouched down so Shawn could climb on his back, and was puzzled when Shawn shook his head and motioned that they'd walk off side by side.

"Found out later he thought I might be going to sell him to other Indians."

Shawn took him back to Harrodsburg as some folks fetch home wild and motherless cubs to raise.

"It's jest like Shawn," the folks down there pulled their mouths tight, "to come draggin back a dumb beast-boy and turn him loose with civilized people! Why didn't he leave him whar he found him?"

But Earthwild gentled. He got over his snappish ways, and quit snarling at the other whites when they crowded around him on the streets. He no longer dodged every time somebody lifted a hand, and he quit wolfing his food from a bowl.

"He'll do anything I ask," said Shawn gently, "on account of being so glad he doesn't have to act the horse any more."

When he learned, he spoke the white man's tongue with a slow accent.

"The way he came by his name was odd," Shawn went on. "The Winnebago had given him a calling-name no white man could wrap his tongue around. The nearest I could come to it was 'Earthwild.' Fits him, though, even if he did get it just by chance."

"He seems real nice," said Tibby suddenly.

Shawn smiled and nodded, for most folks took to Earthwild when they got to know him. Men admired his strength, women his kindly ways, and girls couldn't forget his rough good looks.

Tibby's eyes were soft, her cheeks pink with excitement. She got up and ladled soup into a bowl and went out to Earthwild. Inside the cabin they could hear her merry voice rattling on, and his slow one answering.

Shawn and Earthwild left next morn. All trailed down to The Bucks with them. Strange Rain gathered new greens as they went, and Tibby skipped beside her like a young fawn, looking up now and then to see if the blue beast-eyes of Earthwild were turned on her.

In the shade of The Bucks they squatted down and talked a while longer, about game and the settlements, and the many stranger-Indians seen on the trails these days. Earthwild had little to say, but Tibby chattered to him all the time, and when she picked a little wild flower, he took it gently from her hand and pulled it through a leather loop of his hunting shirt. They all put off leaving as long as they could, even lying back on the soft moss with no sign they'd heard when Shawn said they must go.

"I don't know when to tell you to look for me again," he said slowly. "I get mighty lonesome for all of you, but we're so far apart in miles. . . ."

They said good-bye, but Nathan lingered.

"I figure to hunt down by Grandpap's," he said. "I'll walk with you for a little."

They went down the trail in silence, listening from habit to the bird and beast calls, and squinting at little pieces of sky just as if they hadn't seen a good big piece of it in the clearing.

"Looky thar!" said Earthwild, shy. "Through that button-wood, see it? Ain't that the bluest patch ever?"

Shawn and Nathan stopped and looked where he pointed.

"Sometimes," Earthwild went on, "when there's clouds, it seems like you can almost make out shellbark roofs up there, and folks movin around."

They stood staring upward, rubbing the backs of their necks when they began to ache, shifting when the leaves moved in the wind so as not to lose the patch of blue, forgetting to swear at the mosquitoes. A hawk drifted over the patch of sky and shrilled at them.

"Bet we look like a bunch of sillies, cranin and stretchin to peek through a hole in the leaves," Shawn laughed. "Wonder if someday we'll be up there in heaven, strainin to look through that hole again and see the earth we've left behind?"

"Can you ever be anybody's horse up there?" Earthwild asked.

"I don't reckon so."

"By damn, to live in that whole big blue sky and never be anybody's horse . . . what more could you want?"

"Life," Shawn told him.

They went on silently, and it wasn't till Nathan stopped where the trail to Silver Heels village crossed, that they spoke again.

"Mind you take good care of yourselves," Shawn said. "There's strange doings in the air these days."

Nathan nodded. The feeling of unrest dogged them all, the worst they'd ever known. Braves had been seen in vast numbers, slinking west to the Tippecanoe river where the Shawnee twins had built them a village of their own. Prophetstown, it was called, and white men had come to think of it as the Indian capital.

Any brave was welcome in Prophetstown no matter what his tribe, just as long as he followed the Shawnee brothers.

Lannard brought word that as many as a thousand warriors gathered there, not only to listen to the preaching and pray to their gods, but to practise with bow and tomahawk and war club. Some came from far-distant villages. Stranger-Indians were seen every day now, and not even Night Dog could speak their tongues. Old villages were deserted, and the prayer drums called all the time. It was a scary thing.

"It's all that Tecumseh and his wild brother," Shawn said. "Nobody knows what they'll bring down on us before they're through!"

They leaned against the trees, running their hands up and down their rifles, chewing at fresh leaves. They stared down the trail Nathan would take, as though it had a great difference from the one they would take, and finally they parted.

Nathan watched the two go off, his yellow-haired taken-brother, walking slowly as if he were going some place he didn't want to go, and big dark Earthwild shuffling beside him like a woods shadow. He traced their movements for a long time after the monster butts of the trees hid them, for the birds and beasts told of their passing. When the woods was quiet again, he knew they were really gone.

He looked down at the spongy earth where Shawn had stood. His deep footprints were still there, but a sugar-tree seed had fallen into one of them already. He picked it up and looked at it, and was a long way down the trail before he noticed that he was still carrying it between his thumb and forefinger. But when he thought to throw it away, he dropped it into his pouch of shot instead, as if it were something he wanted to keep, he didn't know why.

He was thinking of this so hard that when he ran into Lannard and Tinch and Rocreuse, he didn't even notice how tight their faces were, or think it odd that they didn't ask him to go with them. He only nodded absently when Lannard said, "Tell your pa that Scuddy's back."

11

NIGHT Dog stared down at the dead beast. The monster trees stared, too. The wind blew its breath in his face in little puffs, like an enemy laughing. There was a sharp smell around him that seemed fetched from the fir-tree land where his ma and pa were resting in their lonesome bury-holes. In that moment, he thought he saw foggy ghost-shapes, *tchibais,* drifting toward him.

Ae, in that moment he tasted on his lips the smoke of long-dead medicine fires. He felt his people and his gods very near, and fancied he heard their shocked whispers, *"Who will now bear the name of Night Dog?"* For they could no longer keep him from harm. By the killing of this beast, he had given up his life!

He knelt and laid his rifle gently on the mossy ground. He reached out to touch the night dog, the beast of his guardian totem. It was beyond belief that he had killed it!

"But it was a squirrel!" he whispered hoarsely. "I saw it! A squirrel. Surely the medicine of some evil god had changed it to a wolf!" His eyes read the sign that told him the wolf had lunged at the squirrel and taken his shot instead, yet the body there was that of a night dog, a very dead night dog.

"Atawa!" he said slowly. "Kije Manitou knows I did not mean to kill my own blood, my guardian who watches over me in the lonely night, on the danger-trails when my enemies would hunt me out! I did not mean to kill my hope! Kije Manitou, you know . . . you *know* I would not do this!"

He sat a while in stunned silence, then lifted up his voice again.

"You remember the time when I and my woman of the Delawares were surrounded on the north lakes by a pack of hungry night dogs? *Ae,* you remember! She, being big with child and fearful, she begged me to shoot into the pack, to kill just one so the rest would turn. You remember that I would not. Think back! I would not, for I was pledged to be brothers to them, as they were pledged to be brothers to me, to protect my living body on this earth, and my little heart-soul when I died.

"*Ae,* I would have let myself and my woman be killed. I would have let the boy babe be killed, and the unborn child, before I would have lifted my hand against my guardians! That night . . . we passed it with our death songs on our lips, the boy crying, the girl stirring in her mother's womb. Had it not been for the hunters coming on us. . . ." He cried out, "Surely, Great Spirit, you cannot punish me for this! It was an accident! Time and again, you have seen me loose my brothers from traps, even leave my kill to feed them when the hunting was hard." He closed his eyes and prayed desperately, *"Make my brother live again!"*

After a time, he opened his eyes and looked at the night dog. He poked at the ragged bullet hole, pulled grass to stuff in it, tried to get the wolf back on its feet. But he could not make it live, and his gods would not hear him.

"*Ae,* old brother, greyed at the muzzle, with broken teeth, so starved that your bones are like bent arrow shafts beneath my hands . . . *ae!"* he wept. He sat holding it across his lap, stroking it, singing sleep songs to it, asking its forgiveness. Finally, he scooped out a grave and put up a pole marker. The beaded bands from his leggings he tied on the marker, and carved the wolf symbol on it, upside down.

Then he went back to his cabin.

"*Ae,* my own death is coming," he murmured. "My punishment for killing my totem."

Once he had known a young brave of the Ottawas who had been made a war chief, but when he killed a *carcajou,* wolverine, which was the totem of his tribe, he was driven from the village. The snows were heavy, and the hunger-wolves close, and the warrior had been unarmed and naked when he went from the fires of his people. They did not even watch him walk away, lest he might shiver and they would see, lest he fall on the crusted snow and they step forward to help him, lest the wolves find him before he was out of sight, and they would lift their bows, forgetting. When Night Dog himself had begged for the warrior's life, since he also was young, he had been put in a wigiwam and a guard set over him.

In the spring thaws, when they hunted with their dogs, they found the warrior's bones split and scattered where the wild beasts had dragged them. But the tribe would not even gather these bones for burial. No, they let the dogs fight over them, and did not even utter his name, for the great evil he had done threatened all. When Night Dog bent to touch the bones, they pushed him aside and said, "Behold, those are only the bones of a deer!"

Night Dog had wondered then about the small soul that lived in a man's heart. Would the heart-soul of this warrior ever be reborn, and would it ever find the sacred Pathway? And the big soul, the one that was a man's shadow and stayed on earth to guard the body it had once walked with . . . how could it guard all those scattered bits and pieces of bones?

When he reached his cabin, he took down his medicine bag, a new clay bowl to carry embers in, a white wing to fan the sacred fire, and clean wooden tongs to lift the embers onto the willow boughs. Then he climbed back down the river bluff to make a prayer and read the smoke.

But the prayer fire and the household god and the sacred things from his medicine bag . . . none of them gave him strength or courage, nor did they banish his fear. He crouched, murmuring over and over, "*Wa-ho-ho,*" as one did

141

when speaking to a god. He prayed in anguish, "Let it not be as I think! Protect me!"

After a while, he noticed he was praying so loud that the bird and beast sounds had stopped. He heard his words, he heard the silence, and he knew only the woods was listening, not the gods. The smoke fell and blew back in his face, sign that his prayer was refused.

"*Atawa,* my hope is gone, and when a man is without hope, he is dead!"

He sat back.

"I am here, but soon I shall not be here any more. Death was always so far away. It would never happen . . . except to others. Even when I first knew that I could not live forever, that I could die, I didn't believe it. Who of us does?"

He jumped up suddenly and kicked dirt over the fire, not even bothering to gather the unburnt wood and bury it, or cast the ashes on the water as The People required. No, he even left behind his medicine bag and the wing and the bowl and tongs.

The hill had grown very steep since he came down it. By the time he reached his doorlog, he was very tired. He tried to think calmly, but he must have become someone else, for surely this frightened person of little faith could not be Night Dog. He slipped his hand inside his shirt and felt the throbbing of his heart. Perhaps the little soul was trying to get free.

He got up and stripped off his buckskins and looked at his body. It was not an aged body. It had not a wrinkle, it was still hard and round and strong. He peered into the calabash of water. His eyes were still as bright as the sun on leaves, and his hair the color of walnut hulls in their second year.

"The gods will understand," he said at last. "I am not an old man. I am not used up. I am not going to die." It made him feel better for a little while.

"Someday," he said aloud, "when I am very old and my hair is white, and my face as wrinkled as an ancient buckeye, then, *then* I will die. It will come on me slowly, so slowly that I will not even know it. It will be like the change of a season, slipping upon me in the night. I will be ready then, tired of this world, this woods, this life. Then I will welcome the Hunter of Men. But that time is not yet."

But soon the fear returned and he shivered and pulled his clothes on quickly. *Ae,* but that was a cold wind for the Grass Moon!

He had been so careless with his life, prowling unknown trails, drifting down streams no man followed, trading with tribes who kept their hands on their knives, facing a world where a half-burnt wood man seemed to have no belonging. He chilled. The man who had done these things had had a brave heart, had been rash, no, *young* . . . a fool! *Atawa,* he thought aghast, I might not have lived till now.

The day wore on, the noon hush lifted. The sun swung across the woods on vines. The green light began to go. The grey came down. The blue shadows turned to black. Ghost flame would be spinning in the swampy places of the woods. Deer would be jumping up on pointed feet. The hungry hunters would be coming out of their lairs.

He began to believe that he was to die this night. He got up and went back down the hill and gathered up the sacred things. He buried the wood left from the fire and threw the ashes on the river. He lingered along the bank watching the night come on. He waited till the whole woods was singing and the river shone dully, like the head of his trade tomahawk. Then he went back to his cabin.

He began to get his household in order. He sorted out the things he wanted buried with him, the seed necklace his woman had worn, the straw toy his girl had played with, the old buckeye his boy had carried, the first arrowhead Nathan had made. These odds and ends would have no meaning to anyone but him.

The medicine bag with its secret charms, his sharp bone knife, his rifle and pouch of shot, his golden earrings, his good moccasins, his warm wild-bull robe, the *parfleche* got in trade . . . these things he would leave for Nathan.

143

It was strange to think that they would soon go on without him. They would still feel the sun in spring and hear the katydids tell of frost and know the cold winter winds. They would be carried by other hands, warmed against another's body, seen by another's eyes, hear another's spoken thoughts and prayers.

Ae, he was an old warrior who balked at dying, yet the Hunter of Men would come, and he would have to go, for that was the way the gods had arranged it from the beginning. He was not the only mortal to die, but few found life as precious as it had been to him. Even with the hard times, the sad times, the hurtful times, life in any way was better than no life at all.

"*Ae,*" he whispered, looking around his warm cabin, "it was good."

Hooty owls were calling when he sat before the fire to eat his stew. He was dressed in his best buckskins and beads, as a warrior should be when planning to make the journey on the starry Pathway of Souls. He sat on a fur rug, having moved into the shadows all his furniture, all things that reminded him he was part white. He had adopted many white ways while he lived, but he would die an Indian.

But not alone! Yearning surged through him. To die with another's eyes above you! *Ae,* yes, to be comforted by your *noss* when you went out of this world, as you were comforted by your *ninga* when you came into it!

"How lonely," he murmured, "to have no one's hand in yours."

He began making up his death song.

"I fear nothing but the brittle bones and broken teeth of old age," he sang, tapping his wooden spoon against his bowl. "Mighty and great in life was I . . . and I was honored. Now, behold . . . I am aged and wretched. . . ."

But when that was done he turned his back to the fire, so that he faced his shadow soul, and put his hand over his breast to hold on to his little heart-soul.

"Stay yet awhile with me," he murmured to them.

He was sitting on the doorlog with his head tilted, smiling at the cry of the ancient toad that lived beneath his doorstep, when Nathan came.

"*Ae*, Kije Manitou!" he thought, his heart filled with gratitude. "You have sent him that I need not be alone, that we may once more sit beneath the stars together!"

He brought a bowl of stew for his grandboy and watched him eat it hungrily. They didn't talk much. His grandpap was thoughtful tonight, Nathan said to himself. There was a distant look in his eyes and as he pulled at his pipe, he hummed the words of Frenchy songs sung on the far-north rivers.

"*Je vois les rapides . . . ,*" he sang, then broke off. "My *noss*, he had blue eyes, and my *ŋinga* black ones. They were always above me . . . around me . . . warm. My name then was Little Quivering Pine. Their soul-shadows were long, even in the thick of the pines. *Je vois les rapides . . . ,*" he sang again.

Nathan felt strange, as if his grandpap weren't talking to him at all, but to the wind or shadows or sky. Or to the gods.

"As a boy, I was very small," Night Dog went on. "I was not a good fighter. When my mother made me stand in the icy waters of the lake as a test, I cried like a babe. I was weak and a shame to my proud Potawatome *ninga!* But my French *noss*, he understood. He would hold me and warm me and tell me of his own father's fine stone house, and how they had many horses and many men dressed in bright colors, and he said he had seen white men cry, and it was no shame. As a boy, I was afraid of the dark, the woods, the beasts. It is hard to grow up . . . and have so much to overcome."

Nathan was touched by the words. He had never thought of his grandpap as weak or afraid or needing his folks. He looked out of the tail of his eye and nodded and murmured, "*Ae*," for didn't he know?

"My son Wild Wind Running was never afraid like me. He was a fine boy, strong, brave, quick . . . like you, like

Micajah." He rose suddenly. "Come inside, my son. There is a thing I must tell you."

They had just stepped over the doorlog when a startled voice broke in upon them.

"Nathan! You *here?*"

Lannard and Tinch had come up so quietly that neither Night Dog nor Nathan had heard them, though both had tensed, their hands on their knives, seeing new shadows suddenly.

Right off, they knew something was wrong. The two woodsies stood with their jaw muscles jerking their beards, their eyes wide and fierce.

"Let's git inside!" said Tinch.

Their faces softened somewhat when they saw the familiar cabin, the mugs on the table, the milkweed-down pallets, the stew kettle on its wooden crane, the broken-design blanket on the wall, the furry rug; and they seemed puzzled that everything could be the same.

Suddenly there was a soft sound of feet beyond the door. Tinch crossed to the cat-and-clay and kicked out the fire till only a few embers glowed. Lannard reached out and hauled the heavy door shut. Now the cabin was dark, save for the faint red light, and a little starlight that sifted in through the chinks and the oiled-skin window.

"What is it, Brother?" Night Dog asked.

"Hesh!" Lannard whispered.

Their moccasins scuffed softly as they waited just inside the door. The floor smelled pungent from the mosses and ferns their feet had come through. Lannard's finger pulled at his hunting knife. Tinch raised his gun to the crook of his arm and checked its priming. Then they heard a scratching sound, as if someone fumbled at the latchstring, nails scraping the wood.

"Cain't be Jonathan," Tinch whispered to Lannard. "Simonton ain't had time to get to him yet."

"Who's thar?" Lannard called harshly.

"Me, you tarnal fool!" Rocreuse's voice came back at them in a half whisper.

"*You!* Git away!"

"I won't let you stand up to a bunch of drunken woodsies by yourself!" Rocreuse flared.

"Wal . . . I dunno," Tinch's voice was uncertain.

He and Lannard looked at each other in the dimness.

"God's sake, Lannard!" Rocreuse burst out. "Lemme in! I come on ahead . . . don't that prove nothing?"

Slowly Lannard pushed the door open and Rocreuse slipped in. When he saw the skinning knife in Lannard's hand, he shoved it away from his chest.

"Don't be a fool," he said, hurt.

This time it was he who turned and shut the door, even lifting its heavy bar into place.

"They're comin by the trail, but it'll be some little time afore they get here. Carson's doin all he can to slow 'em down."

"What in tarnal . . . ?" Nathan began.

Lannard prodded Nathan and Night Dog.

"Grab your rifles and come on. We'll talk on the way. We can travel fast, and without a light. We'll be outen their reach by the time the moon clears the trees. Then later, when them woodsies is sobered up. . . ."

"Woodsies?" Nathan said. "Good God, Lannard, they wouldn't turn on *you!* Why, they look to you. . . ."

"Listen!" whispered Tinch.

They moved to the door and pressed their ears against it. They could make out a voice or two carried on the wind, sometimes a word, sometimes rough laughter.

"They're comin faster than I had reckoned," Rocreuse said.

"Brother," Night Dog began, "if it is my help you need. . . ."

Rocreuse faced him.

"Tain't us needs help, it's you! They're comin to kill you!"

"*What!*" Nathan burst out. They didn't have to have a light in the cabin to know how wild his face had turned.

"It's that damn Scuddy!" cried Tinch. "We run him outen this country once. I wish to God we'd kilt him while we had the chance!"

"The woodsies . . . they've found out they're spied on by a man from Tecumseh, and they set on Scuddy, sure it was him. But he saved himself by promisin to take 'em to the real spy. 'I'm a white man,' he said. You're lookin fer an Injun, or a part-Injun.' They're drunk, and they don't know him like we do. . . ."

He broke off. The voices were louder now, and closer. Torch lights glimmered far down the trail.

"Let's get outen here before we all get killed!" cried Tinch.

They could hear Nathan fumbling in his pouch for shot. Night Dog turned to the back of the cabin.

"If you're figurin on sayin you won't come with us, lemme tell you something!" Lannard flared. "We ain't leavin without you . . . not even if we all got to die here!"

"But . . . ," began Night Dog.

"Ain't nobody goin to kill any kin of mine without a fight!" Rocreuse stormed. Then, as if shamed by his outburst, he added, "I might jest want to kill you myself, someday!"

In the faint light, he and Night Dog looked at each other, and in this moment they *were* brothers.

"Come *on!*" snapped Lannard then.

"All right," said Night Dog slowly. "We go now."

They opened the door slowly, holding their hands over the squeaky hinge. They peered out, blinking into the starlight of the clearing. The drunken men were close now, but their path had taken them into a dip where their lights were hidden, their voices muffled. Feet padded by on another trail, but they were beast feet. The ancient toad had stopped his calling.

"God's sake, *come on!*" cried Nathan desperately.

Their feet scraped over the doorlog, their shoulders brushed the wood of the door frame, their breathing was hushed, their eyes and ears turned to the shouting down the trail. Each of them stooped quickly, rubbed dirt over the barrel of his rifle and over the whiteness of his face and hands.

Lannard and Rocreuse went first, with Nathan and Night

Dog following after, and Tinch last. The woods swallowed them up. The night sounds made a cover for them. They moved silently, their feet feeling out the trail, their hands feeling out the branches and leaves ahead of them.

A storm was muttering in the distance. They could hear the wind stirring the roof of leaves. They could hear the sighs and moans of the old widow-makers as they waited for the blast, shaking their brittle bones. It was harder to hear now because of the murmuring wind. Wet leaves, blown loose, stuck to the soft hide of their clothes.

"Rain'll make it easier to blind our trail," Lannard said hopefully.

They went on, hunched forward, sniffing the wind, stopping to listen, their shaggy heads like beast-heads, their feet lifting and falling with the cunning of beast feet, their voices coming in hoarse whispers.

"*Hurry!* We got no time. . . ."

"Watch out! There's a hole. . . ."

"Keep your gun away from me. Tarnal!"

"Keerful, keerful here! It's slippery. Must be a spring."

Suddenly Night Dog stopped.

"I cannot," he said softly. "I have never run from any man. It is better to die now, while I am prepared."

Nathan reached out quickly, but his grandpap had gone, and not even Lannard had felt him slip past.

"Never mind," said Tinch. "We ain't goin on without him."

"Whar'd he go?" Lannard whispered.

"Back to the cabin, course!" Rocreuse burst out.

"But *why?*"

"He aimed to stay all along, I think. Came this far jest to get us away. . . ."

Nathan stared into the dark, held his breath to pick up any sound it might cover, sniffed the air like a hound. Tracking in the dark was hard, few men could do it, but if they managed to follow the way he went, they'd reach the cabin almost as fast as he would.

"On the right!" he whispered. "He's just crossed that patch of nettles. I can smell them, crushed under his feet."

They followed the boy swiftly, silently.

"Straight ahead here," Tinch offered, after a while. "You can smell the pipe smoke on his clothes. Kinnikinnick."

"We'll ketch up with him yet!" Lannard panted.

They ran, shoving against each other in the dark, made clumsy by haste, careless with their guns, forgetting to hold branches for the man behind, swearing, gasping, grunting. They came out into the clearing and saw what looked like Night Dog's shadow running ahead of them. He had almost reached the cabin door.

Rocreuse got to the door just as Night Dog slipped through it. He got his knee inside and they struggled, pushing and heaving against each other.

"Fool!" Rocreuse gasped.

"Go back!" Night Dog panted. "Let me face them alone. You do not understand. The Hunter of Men has called me this day. . . ."

Lannard grabbed the edge of the door and they yanked it open and got inside, all but Nathan. They pushed him back and shut the door in his face.

"Git outen here!" Lannard snapped through the crack. "They may be after you, too!"

"No!" said Nathan, calm-faced. His half-moon eyes looked straight at the crack where he could see Lannard's grey ones. "I stay!"

"I said *git!*"

"I'm no boy, taking orders! I'm near grown! I. . . ."

"Nathan, *hurry!*" Rocreuse's voice came out to him. "I'm your godfather! If I tell you, you must go!"

The woodsies were less than half a mile away. Their voices were loud now, thick with rum and hate. Their torches seemed to light up the woods.

"*No!*" He pounded on the door, wrenched at it with his fingers. Little pieces of wood fell away. He sobbed wildly, "He's *my grandpap!*"

Night Dog's voice came through the door.

"Obey, little son. What have you learned? You shame me!"

His fingertips came against the door crack and Nathan pressed his own fingers against them. His grandpap's fingers were warm and alive. But they pushed him away.

"Go, little son. *Go quickly!*"

Then it was quiet inside the cabin and the warm fingertips were gone. Nathan pressed his ear against the door. He could hear someone breathing, someone else whispering. The wind rustled the leaves. The moon darted in and out of fast-moving clouds, throwing a white light into the clearing. The voices of the woodsies were closer.

"I will face them myself," he thought suddenly.

He turned. Now he could see the men on the trail. Long shadows danced toward him under the moon. Sometimes it was a tree shadow, sometimes it was a man-shadow more twisted and monster-looking than the trees. He heard Lannard call out in a low voice, "Nathan, be you gone yet?"

He didn't answer, but slipped his gun up on his shoulder, holding it by the barrel. Then he walked out from the cabin to meet the drunken men.

When he stepped into the torchlight, they halted and fell back a little, taken by surprise. He could tell none of them had looked for him to be here. They stared, mouths open, eyes rolling toward each other.

"Evenin," he greeted them calmly.

They nodded uncertainly, made a murmurous sound that had no words.

"Huntin?" he asked.

Scuddy pushed forward with a grin that showed his broken teeth.

"*Yep!*"

"Mind if I go with you?"

They glanced at each other.

"I don't think this is arything for boys," one said.

"I don't see why not," Scuddy said. "He's as welcome as can be, fer as I'm concerned!" He looked carefully at Nathan in the light of his torch and added, "Danged if you ain't the picture of Micajah! I could almost think it was him. 'Ceptin I see you got some Injun blood."

"Leave him be, Scuddy!" Carson said. "He ain't got no part in this."

The rest muttered vaguely and shook their heads.

"I'll tell you what we're after, boy," Scuddy went on, ignoring them. "We're after your grandpap. We're fixin to kill us a dirty Injun spy!"

Nathan stared at him coldly.

"Who started all this spy talk?" he asked.

"Him. Scuddy," Carson said.

"Makes you wonder who really *is* the spy, don't it?" said Nathan, hard-faced.

Scuddy turned on him, snarling like a beast.

"Don't you tell no lies on me, boy!"

Carson drew Nathan away from the path, pulling him sharply.

"Don't say no more, Nathan," he muttered. "They're so blind-mean drunk, they'd jest as soon it would be you as your grandpap!"

Scuddy started forward.

"Come on, boys! Let's burn the cabin!"

Nathan twisted away and made a grab for the torch, but Scuddy was running across the clearing. Then the others were running at his heels, shoving, yelling, trying to hurl torches on the cabin roof, wild as a Potawatome raiding party.

Nathan was struck aside and went sprawling to the ground. A heavy foot came down on his ankle with shattering pain. He reached for his gun, but somebody scooped it up out of the dirt and carried it along. He rolled over and tried to drag himself on his elbows, but Carson slipped back, hefted him to his shoulder, and hurried him into the cover of the woods. Afterward, he thought it was when he was lifted up that he lost consciousness. He remembered only that he had had his mouth open to tell Carson he was carrying him the wrong way.

12

THE yelling had stopped when he opened his eyes, but he knew the cabin was burning. He could hear the crackle of flames and the cries of little birds and beasts as they fled the blaze. Once he tried to move, but the agonizing pain in his ankle covered him with sickness and sweat.

Then he heard someone coming, Carson maybe, or Lannard. No, the feet were quiet, sneaky. He slipped his knife out of its loop and lay still, aware of all around him, the fire, the shadows, the sway of a bush on the left, the snap of a twig, a pebble rolling, a squish of the soft earth.

"Think I couldn't find you, boy?"

It was Scuddy.

He sprang suddenly and was on top of Nathan. His trade tomahawk was red in the light. Nathan fought to push it away.

"You look *jest* like him . . . Micajah!" Scuddy panted. "God, how I hated him! He hit me in the mouth with his rifle butt once. . . . I always wished it could a-been me that kilt him! But it'll be jest as much pleasure to finish you. . . ."

They struggled, rolled, fought to get a grip, to sink knife or tomahawk. Nathan was pinned down, faint and weak from his blinding pain. The tomahawk came down and he pulled himself aside, and it missed him by inches. He came up with his knife and slashed Scuddy under the chin, but only deep enough for the blood to run down into his eyes. Scuddy raised the tomahawk again, but it never fell, for just then he went limp all over and collapsed, a terrible groan mixed with the blood in his mouth. Then he was jerked to one side and thrown into some bushes. Nathan saw Tinch standing over him.

"Never could stand that varmint," Tinch spat, and wiped off his knife.

Nathan was crying, struggling to rise.

"Help me!" he gasped. "Grandpap. . . ."

"Ain't no need now," Tinch told him gently.

A great stillness came over Nathan. He could not bear to even think of the word, and yet he had to say it.

"Dead?"

"Yep. He . . . he never felt the bullet, it was so quick." Tinch added clumsily, "We . . . we done all we could."

It started to rain then, and he craned around to look at the fire crackling and fading.

"Old cabin went fast," he muttered.

Nathan was numb.

"Rocreuse . . . he fought like a panther. They turned on him, too. . . ."

Carson and Lannard came, carrying Rocreuse. He was blood all over, and so pasty-faced that their eyes said they didn't think he'd live. He murmured and mumbled, but mostly in Frenchy talk, and his eyes were glazed, as though he looked in instead of out.

"Hope we ain't lost two good men," Lannard said quietly. He jerked his beard toward Scuddy's body. "Who done that?"

"I did," said Tinch. "Knifed him."

"Um." Lannard moved over and knelt down by Nathan. "While we was waitin, your grandpap said, 'Whatever may come, I say this of my life: Hear me, it was good.' "

Nathan began to cry in awkward sobs. They looked away

154

from him. Then Lannard reached out and rumpled his hair and wiped the blood off his forehead with one sleeve.

"I'd druther it'd been me," he muttered.

Simonton came up then, the only one of the men who'd sided with Carson. They sat in silence while the rain spattered the leaves with woods-smelling dampness and finally the moon came out again. Then they heard the hoofbeats of Jonathan's horse on the trail.

Lannard went out to meet him, but Nathan lay still. He could hear their voices going up and down, hear his pa asking how many men and who? And he wanted to leap up and cry out in bitterness and fury, "White men! It was your own all-white folks that killed him!"

Then he saw that Jonathan's face was ashen above him, that his big hands opened and closed, opened and closed. He reached out and touched him and said gently, "Pa . . . I'm not hurt bad."

They made litters for Nathan and Rocreuse. Lannard and Tinch and Carson and Simonton carried them.

"Leastways," Lannard said softly, "I ain't carryin you home dead, like I carried Micajah."

Jonathan put the bodies of Night Dog and Scuddy over his saddle and walked, leading the mare, who tried to throw them off more than once because of the death smell.

Now and then Rocreuse roused and muttered.

"If he lives till the sun's high, he'll at least get through the day," Jonathan said.

"Wisht I knew some of them Frenchy prayers he says," Tinch mumbled. "I guess the Good Lord wouldn't know a prayer was meant fer him, less it was in Frenchy."

They ate jerked meat and dewberries and waited. They saw that Rocreuse still breathed, and they went slowly on to Jonathan's cabin.

They buried Night Dog in the graveyard on the hill. They threw Scuddy in on top of the coffin without even a covering, in the way of The People, for he was a murderer.

A hunter from Manjinikia's village stopped by when he heard the news.

"Night Dog had a brave heart," he said, "but Scuddy . . . if one of your people had not killed him, one of ours would have!"

In a few days, Nathan was up again and could hobble around, for his ankle was not broken despite its pain. There was a stronger tie between him and his godfather now, and they spent many hours talking of Night Dog. Sometimes they looked over the things in the *parfleche,* which Lannard had saved from the fire, and together they wondered what was in the medicine bag. But Nathan could not open it until he had made his warrior's fast, and then no eyes but his own would ever know.

As soon as Rocreuse was able to go home, Nathan took his grandpap's rifle and stepped out over the doorlog. The shock and grief of Night Dog's death were still with him. When the woodsies and settlers had come to the cabin sober-faced and spoke falteringly of that night, words stuck in his throat. All had told how sorry they were, had cursed the rum, the unrest caused by Tecumseh, the lies of Scuddy, and expected Nathan to say he understood. But he didn't understand. All he knew was that their words did not bring back his grandpap, put songs into his throat again, let him dance to the drumbeat, hunt along the streams.

He was distressed by the sorrow of his mother, the tender pity of little Tibby, the grave concern of his father, and what had flared up in his heart. For whenever he met white men coming or going on the trails, he hated them.

"Don't look for me," he said quietly. "I don't know when I'm coming back. I've got things to settle in my mind . . . away from here."

He went down to Asanzang Town, the Miami village where he and his grandpap had always been welcome. But the welcome was not the same now, for there were stranger-Indians in Asanzang Town, and they slanted their eyes away from him, not seeing him, till his Miami friend White Loon called out to him, "You have come," and Nathan answered, "Yes, I have come." It was only when he gave the proper answer that the stranger-Indians knew he belonged there, and let their eyes turn to him.

He walked down through the village, and without looking directly at any of the stranger-people, he saw them all. There were Wyandots, their ruddy color and full lips as marked as their long tunics and woven sashes. They sat silent-faced beside their fires, listening to the wild Shawnees whose talk was suddenly solemn and intense. Kickapoos talked with Winnebagoes. Ottawas wearing vests and puckered moccasins ate with Miamis, from the same pot.

Strangest of all, there were no traders here, and no sign that there had ever been any, save for a broken keg of rum on the riverbank. The women were sewing designs on their men's buckskins, patterns made from shell beads, stone, nuts, corn, teeth, and claws. Men were chipping heads for axes and knives and tomahawks. Some trade cloth was burning in the council fire.

"Brother," he said to White Loon, "what has happened here?"

"We do as The Prophet has told us. We return to our old ways." More he would not say.

Nathan stayed with Far Thunder, a young Shawnee war chief who had often come to his grandpap's cabin. For many days they hunted together, sometimes riding out as far as the Illini prairies, where they could look to the south toward the Spanish settlements. For many nights they talked, and sometimes of Night Dog.

"Do you not know," Far Thunder asked, "that any of The People might have killed him in the same way? *Ae*, being drunk and thinking he was a spy for their enemy, they might have done the same." Another time, seeing the homesickness in Nathan's eyes when they skirted a white settlement, he said, "Do not stay in the wigiwam if you long for the cabin."

Grass Moon passed. Planting Moon came, then Rose Moon and Heat Moon. Still Nathan stayed on. It was in the third sleep of Heat Moon that Far Thunder took him to the council lodge.

"Dancing Light, brother of my father, has been killed at the settlement Vincennes," Far Thunder said slowly to the men there. "Who will ride with me to avenge his death and cast a lock of his hair on the battlefield?"

"I, Standing Stone." A Potawatome chief stood.

"And I, White-Cold-from-the-Sky," a new-come Shawnee called out.

"And I, too," said another.

None of the Miamis pledged to ride, for they were of Little Turtle's clan.

"No," they said, "for it is sworn we will be friends with the Morning Light People. We cannot."

But many Shawnees and many stranger-Indians gave their pledge, each jabbing his knife into the dirt of the lodge floor as a sign that they were joined. Finally Nathan was the only one unpledged. All eyes turned to him.

"And you, Brother?" Far Thunder asked.

Nathan looked back at him silently. His hand rested on the little crooked knife hanging in his belt loop, yet he did not cast it down.

"*Ae,* will you not pledge too?" Standing Rock asked. "Your blood is as ours. You bring the kill to our village. You dance to our drum. You pray to our god. Why not you?"

Far Thunder drew a line in the dirt and each man took back his knife, for now they would vote with their knives as to whether this half-burnt wood lad should be allowed to come with them.

White-Cold-from-the-Sky rose. He was near to sixty winters old and when he spoke the men listened to him, for his age had made him wise.

"Let him prove himself," White-Cold-from-the-Sky said. "He is not yet a warrior. He has not yet made his fast. But he has come to our village. If he would stay with us, then let him ride with us."

158

He sat down again and the others nodded at his words. Now they talked about Nathan with their heads turned away from him. Sometimes one would get up and come over to look him squarely in the face. Sometimes one would ask him what was his born-into totem. He knew they would soon cast their knives.

He stood up. And suddenly the wigiwam seemed filled with the scent and sight and sound of white men's things, starched aprons, hard boots stomping over a puncheon floor, rough Eastern voices and soft Southern ones, the fiddle singing, the smell of tobacco that was not kinnikinnick, a blue-painted mantel above the fire.

"Brothers," he said quietly, "my heart is like this lodge. There is a line drawn down the center of it. One half is smeared with white clay. The other half, with red clay. My heart-soul casts its knife to one side and then the other . . . but my heart will never change. Always it will be divided. I cannot ride with you. But I will never ride against you."

They looked at one another.

"In LeGris Town, the half-burnt wood men do not talk so. They stand on one side or the other. They stand on *our* side," Standing Stone said.

"You have told me that you spoke against the Morning Light People," Far Thunder said.

"So I spoke."

"Then?"

Nathan faced them.

"Brothers, I tell you this: The path I follow is mine alone. Sometimes it may run with yours. Sometimes it may run with the white men. How it runs is my concern. My feet alone will take this path. I harm no man, nor will I fight for any, save him whose need of me is very great."

He stood in silence while they looked back at him. They saw, not the gangling breed-boy who had entered their camp a few moons ago, but a tall young warrior who spoke to them with no sign of fear or reluctance. *Ae,* they nodded, his tongue

159

was quick and straight. His hands were strong and skilled, knowing the work of hunting and of healing, and he would never lift them willingly against another man.

"It is finished then," Far Thunder said, and stooped to wipe out the line in the earth. The others nodded. Nathan left and went back to Far Thunder's lodge to get his belongings.

"Where do you go?" White Moth, the young chief's sister had stepped in beside him.

"I go . . . home," Nathan told her simply.

At the edge of the village, Far Thunder caught up with him. He slipped a gold bracelet off his wrist.

"To remember me," he said, "for I go on a long journey. And yet . . . it is not as hard as yours." He took his knife and cut off a lock of his hair and handed it to Nathan. "To carry on to the field of battle for me, after I am dead, for I have no proper son or kin to do this for me."

His words brought between them the chill shape of a *tchibai,* which Nathan tried to destroy with bold words.

"But we will meet again," he said. "We will meet many times before the Hunter of Men has claimed you. *Ae,* your years are long yet. . . ."

"All good go with you," Far Thunder said quickly. "I will think of you . . . but your cabin will be far away."

He turned and walked back toward the fires.

It was evening now, and for a moment Nathan stood still, looking after his friend, hearing the familiar sounds of the village, knowing the stark loneliness of parting. Indian talk went up and down, like the wind scraping branches together. He heard children's shouts, dogs barking, horses blowing. When he came here again, it would sound the same and look the same, but it would never be the same. The blood tie that ran between him and The People had been weakened by his refusal to ride with them. He knew they would never welcome him as warmly as before, would never look on him as openly as before. The words on their lips would be guarded, their wampum belts hidden lest he read and know their messages. Something was gone that would never belong to him again, and already one part of him longed for its return.

Then he turned toward the double cabin on the hill, toward those who lived in it and those who came to it. He hefted up his pack and slung his rifle on his shoulder. Soon he was hurrying along, thinking of his pa's deep joy, the sweet welcome of Strange Rain, the chattery delight of his pretty sister. Presently he stepped from the deep-grooved Indian trail and took the white man's.

Far Thunder stood looking after him.

"Forgive me, Brother," the young chief said. "I had no wish to make you choose in front of all, for I knew your heart, and your answer was plain to me long before you gave it. But I had to send you home. I had my vow to keep, and the time is short. *Ae,*" he stared up at the nighthawks flying high, "will his *noss* know that I have kept my word, that I have given back a life for a life, a son for a son?"

He turned again toward the village. In memory he saw his beloved brother, burned and dying, there in Jonathan's dooryard, and close by the little boy that had been himself.

"*Ae,*" he said, "I have kept my word. And even if the *noss* of Nathan never knows it, our Grandmother, the Moon Woman, knows . . . and I."

13

MONTHS later, Nathan hunted again along the Silver Heels trail. His feet followed the familiar path to his grandpap's cabin and he pretended, when he came in sight of it, that Night Dog would be there, sitting on the doorlog. But when he reached the last bend in the trail and saw the place where the cabin had stood, he was heart torn.

Vines had sprung up through the dirt floor and wild plants were blooming where the table had stood. The cat-and-clay had crumbled until nothing was left of it but a piece as high as his knee. Honeysuckle, wild as the woods, tumbled against it. The walls lay in charred and blackened ruins.

He walked through the ashes. Once in a while, he'd squat down and poke them with his fingers. He found a horn button, a flint arrowhead, and his grandpap's crooked knife. Nothing else was left to show that any mortal had ever lived there. It seemed like a stranger-place.

"*Ae*, it is quiet!"

When he started away, he turned back and called as he had called in his childhood, "Grandpap? *Grandpap?*" He knew no answer to that name would ever come again, but the calling was something he had to do.

Days later, he came by Asanzang Town and found it nearly as quiet as the burnt-out cabin. Many of the wigiwams and lodges were closed. There were no horses by the river. Only a few women and young ones were in the fields. There were no men at all.

He found White Moth at her brother's wigiwam and when he asked her where Far Thunder had gone, she said, "Away. You must go, too."

He glanced around the empty village with only one cooking fire burning in its center.

"Where are your men?" he asked.

"Hunting."

"All? Even Cripple Foot?"

"*Ae!*"

"Where are your women?"

"In the fields."

"I saw only a few. Where are the rest?"

She shrugged as though the answer was not known to her.

"I never thought my sister would speak to me with a lying tongue," said Nathan.

She turned to him quickly.

"Only go!" she said huskily.

"Am I an enemy, that you would send me away with an empty belly?"

She hurriedly put smoked meat and berries in a small calabash and gave it to him.

"Eat them on the trail."

He raised his brows.

"You send me from the warmth of your fire?"

"Go!" she said harshly. Then her eyes softened, and she moved closer to him and whispered, "Now no village is safe for you, nor for anyone who has the blood of the Morning Light People."

"Little sister . . . ," he began, but she pushed him firmly through the doorway.

"Only *go!* There is soon to be trouble! The Prophet

preaches against all white men. He talks of peace, but he cries out for war. It will come."

"War?" Nathan smiled and shook his head. "Little sister, you have been bewitched. Neither the Miamis nor the Delawares will hear such talk . . . not while Little Turtle lives. As for the Wyandots, Two-Clouds-of-Equal-Size will see that they do not listen. And Black Hoof, your own chief, he brought your people here when they lost their hands in the southern war . . . is he not as powerful as Tecumseh? He will not let the Shawnees follow the war path."

She looked at him.

"Two-Clouds-of-Equal-Size has been murdered. By Tecumseh."

"When?" he cried.

"Four sleeps ago."

Nathan caught his breath. Then the rumors were true that the Three Fires were burning again, that the Potawatomes and Ottawas and Ojibways were reunited.

"Is it true then that the Wyandots went to the Miami villages on the Mississinewa and shamed them into joining the New Fires that Tecumseh has kindled?"

"I cannot say."

"Tell me."

"*Ae*," she said softly, at last. "It is true. They have all gone to Prophetstown. They have sent for the Weas and the Sacs and the Foxes, the Winnebagoes and Kickapoos. And Tecumseh has gone south to bring back the Creeks, for they are his mother's people and will fight with him."

Nathan stood in troubled silence. The war talk must be true then, for it would take a great and fierce purpose to bring together all these old enemies.

"*Ae*," she said sadly, "The People no longer listen to their true leaders, but only to The Prophet and Tecumseh."

Suddenly she stepped back inside the wigiwam and pulled the skin door-flap shut.

"Wait!" cried Nathan. "You have not told me . . . where is my brother? Where is Far Thunder?"

"Did you not hear me?" she asked slowly. "I said *all* follow the Shawnee twins."

But though Nathan waited, and called to her again, she would say no more of her brother, save that he had gone to Prophetstown and she would soon follow him there.

That night Nathan camped along Deer Creek, and the next day he hunted on the Mississinewa river. The villages he passed were as quiet and empty as Asanzang Town, and twice he stepped off the trail to let files of Delawares pass. They carried packs of household goods on their backs, and even their dogs were with them.

Toward sundown he ran into Lannard and Tinch.

"We been warned to stay outen the villages," Lannard muttered. "Have you?"

He nodded.

"Looks like it's really comin then," Lannard said.

Now both woodsies and settlers were on their guard. News sifted down the trail that The Prophet had asked the Ojibways, the Ottawas, and the Potawatomes to burn all the cabins and kill all the settlers along the Ohio, as far east as Cincinnati. But attacks along the Ohio never came. They came instead along the borders, up and down the Wabash, and west to where the Illini lived. Isolated cabins were burned, their people killed or captured, their dumb beasts slaughtered or driven off.

Winter was early that year and none minded, for Indian trouble seldom came when the snow was on. They plowed with their guns in one hand the following spring, and no man hunted far from his cabin. Then the border attacks stopped. Many Indians were again seen in their villages and in their fields. The woodsies and settlers began to feel that the danger was past. Often they ran into traders and Indian fighters on their way to join General Harrison's army. The woodsies couldn't decide about joining the army. Lannard decided it for them.

"When it comes, if it comes, thar won't be any army here, whar we stand now. Thar won't be a soul to look after our women and our young ones, our cabins, and what precious-little belongings we got. Nope, when it comes, I'll fight it out right here!"

The only one to disagree with him was Abe McCutcheon, who ran off one night. His ma stayed alone in her cabin. "Ain't no Injun goin to scare me away from what's mine!" she stormed. And Lucy, Lannard's oldest girl, who'd stayed single in the hopes of Abe asking her to wed, cried for three days.

Fall time came, and the rains set in. Word came that there'd been a battle between the Indians and General Harrison's men, at Prophetstown, on the Tippecanoe river, but none knew for sure. Word was always coming that there'd been a fight somewhere, and mostly the word was wrong. So when a settler from Harrodsburg told them that Shawn had joined the army, and Earthwild too, they didn't put much store in it.

But the night Earthwild came, wearing a soldier jacket with a red collar and a gold pin, they believed it. He stepped in out of the cold, windy November dusk and they saw that he was by himself.

"Where's Shawn?" they asked him right off. And when he tried to tell them, and couldn't fetch out a word, they knew. They sank down in front of the fire and stared at him and tried to think it wasn't true, it just couldn't be.

"That's why I'm here," choked Earthwild, "because he's . . . he's dead. Shawn and me, we didn't have ary folks, 'ceptin you. I figured he'd want me to tell you afore you heard it from some stranger-man. Anyway, I didn't know whar else to go."

He and Shawn had been together at Prophetstown, at the battle of the Tippecanoe.

"I'll tell you," he said. "I'll tell you. But first . . . there's somethin else. It's been over a year since we came here last, but I reckon you know he made himself a lawyer. Yep, and he was a good one, too. But folks wouldn't come to him. Called him an Injun lover."

He cast his eyes down.

"He sent upriver to get his furniture, real boughten furniture. Desk and three chairs. Morn after morn, we'd walk down there together. Me, I'd take myself to work at the smithy's, and Shawn would go to his office room. When I started home at evenin, he'd still be sittin there, sittin and starin at them three empty chairs. Few white folks ever came, and *not one Injun!* Not even when they needed help. Laws were made for white men, they told him, and they wanted nothin to do with his lawyerin."

Jonathan looked up and spoke.

"I was afraid for him."

"It near broke his heart, I reckon. The night . . . the night he closed up the office room for good, he leaned thar against the door and looked like somethin was dyin. He said, real quiet, 'Earthwild, don't you ever act the fool, the way I've done.' "

Nathan looked away.

"Next morn, he went to join up with Harrison. I went, too. What should I do down at Harrodsburg without Shawn?"

They were all quiet. Slowly, Strange Rain got up and began pouring tea and rum into their wooden mugs. Earthwild watched her. Seemed like it rested his mind to have nothing more to think about than a woman pouring tea and rum.

Shawn got to be an officer, a fine-looking officer in a plumed hat and white leggings and blue coat. He was a major and rode a big grey.

"Seemed like he perked up some, in the army, was even sort of gay-larkin for a while. But I don't think he ever forgot that office room."

Late in October they went north with Harrison to Prophetstown, and there wasn't a man among them who didn't know the Indians there were ready to attack. But when they reached the village, after marching nine days, three chiefs came out with a white flag, saying the Prophet asked that Harrison camp for the night and hold council with him in the morning.

The men wanted to attack right then and there, but Harrison didn't want bloodshed if it could be helped. So they made night camp on a high triangle of ground, the only dry place, with marsh and willows all around it. There wasn't time enough or wood enough to build any breastworks, so they just slept on their arms and hoped nothing would happen.

"On toward daybreak, I opened my eyes and saw that Shawn was already awake. It was rainin a mite, dark and nasty cold. All of a sudden, the sentry near us heard a noise in the grass, grass higher'n a man's head, and called out, 'Who's thar?' For a minute, it was still. Then the answer came back as bold as brass, '*Potawatome!*'

"Then they were swarmin all over our camp. You never seen such a shameful, mixed-up mess! Men were runnin up and down, half asleep, stumblin right into Injuns. Nobody knew where they ought to be . . . 'ceptin Shawn. He was right on his feet givin orders to his men. Trouble was, so many of our officers went down right away. Owens . . . Spencer . . . Warrick. We were dodgin rifle balls, and there were arrows and fire goin every which way!

"One man, name of Warnock, a rifleman, had talked all the way up there about how he'd had a dream, that folks in his family always had before they died. You know . . . a token-dream. Now he kept runnin back and forth yellin, 'I told you! I told you!' He was killed at the start of the battle.

"Fires were burnin all around and made it easy for the Injuns to see us, so we put them out. We was fightin like she-bears. It was hard to know you weren't killin one of your own men. All of a sudden, I saw Shawn go by on his big grey and I heard him yell a charge to his men. Eight of his dragoons followed him. I was with Snelling's men, and I didn't belong with Shawn, but I left my place in the line and ran up and grabbed hold of his stirrup. Others were there, too, that didn't belong, men whose officers were dead, who were jest lookin for somebody to follow. Then, too, thar was something about Shawn . . . like we all thought we'd get out alive if we jest stuck close to him.

"I looked up and seen his face shinin with sweat and rain. I grabbed hold of his boot and wanted to hang back . . . not for me, but for him. I had a feelin I was goin to lose him . . . I jest *knew* it! He looked down at me and asked, 'Be you afraid, Earthwild?' real gentle-like. I shook my head and he said, 'Get back to your rifles, then.' But I wouldn't leave him.

"Thar was so much I wanted to say . . . and no time. I wanted to yell, 'Shawn, *don't go! You're* all I got in this whole wide world!' He looked down and grinned before the grey lunged forward, her heels kickin up mud. Then the Injuns hit us from a clump of trees. The first shot knocked Shawn clean out of his saddle, but one boot caught in the stirrup. The grey went on, draggin him.

"I yelled and ran after, wild for Shawn. . . ."

He paused and stared into the fire, and they all turned their heads and looked into it, as if the battle would be there for them to see, for wasn't that what Earthwild was seeing?

"The mare went right through the middle of those Injuns. You could hear them yell and scream, tryin to get outen her way. Somewhere I'd lost my gun, but I had a foot-long skin-nin knife, and I had a grip on that. Then I was in that pack of Injuns, too, yellin and howlin and cussin, worse'n any savage there! I felt blood spurt up in my face and saw an Injun's mouth as I slashed it, blood washin off the half-moon painted on his cheek, blood stickin in his hair. But all I wanted to see was Shawn and that grey.

"I finally found them. The grey was standin there quiet, like she knew she had dragged him to his death and was ter-rible sorry. I grabbed Shawn and lifted him up in my arms and eased his poor foot outen the stirrup. He looked at me, and I could see every word he was sayin . . . in his eyes. He was sayin, *'Don't let me die!'* Then he died."

He was silent, and for a while the only human sound in the cabin was their breathing. Then Tibby began to whimper and laid her head down on the table, crying. The others watched her, fighting back their own tears.

"Next day," Earthwild went on quietly, "I buried him on a hill under a big tree. One of the officers showed me how to cut his initials in the bark. I covered his grave good with leaves, so no Injun'd find it.

"I shot the mare," he added. "She was a fine horse and I'd like to have kept her. But I shot her. I did it so she'd never have to lug anybody on her back again. I was a horse once, and I know."

His voice dropped to a whisper.

"Did you know . . . that his first name was Jason?"

Outside it began to sleet, and the thin brittle sound on the windows made them shiver, for they could not help thinking of Shawn in his lonesome buryhole. Tibby sobbed into her apron. Nathan went over and sat down beside Earthwild. Jonathan stood up suddenly and went outside.

After a while, Strange Rain rose and began dishing up the stew.

14

War came to the whole country that year, a second war with England. Lannard brought word of it one hot June night, on his way back from trading at Fort Wayne.

"Won't be no Indians callin this the Rose Moon now," he said. "Nope, it'll be marked on their countin-sticks as the War Moon."

One good thing, though, there was no need to worry about Prophetstown any more. The day after the battle on the Tippecanoe, Harrison and his men had gone into the great village and found it empty. They had burned every cabin, every wigiwam; destroyed all the grain, all the crops, all the livestock. The powerful Indian capital was now only ashes and blackened earth.

The defeat of the Indians had put an end to all they had in mind, and a near-end to The Prophet. Angry warriors who had listened to his promises of victory tried to kill him, and he had to take to his heels to save himself. Folks said he was hiding in the wild country around Asanzang Creek, with a few other Shawnees.

When Tecumseh returned from the southern nations, he

was enraged to hear about the battle, since he'd ordered his brother to keep peace while he was away. He tried to gather the tribes again, with a big council over at Osage Town, the mixed Miami-and-Delaware village on the Mississinewa river. When he asked them to unite, the Miamis, who had never broken their treaties, said they would unite in peace, but not in war. After that, Tecumseh spoke out for peace, but now everything was changed. The war between the United States and England meant that many Indians would go over to the British.

Lannard took a long swig of rum.

"We'll be fightin agin redcoats and red men both," he said grimly.

Rocreuse and Tinch reached the clearing about daybreak. They'd got word of the war at LeGris Town, and left for the woods right off.

"Some Shawnee run into the village and rammed a red pole in the ground, jest like they do in them Southern villages when it's war. We didn't waste no time gettin out!"

Mixed with their fear, though, there was a kind of relief, for now there would be no more wondering whether it was safe to enter an Indian village or go on a long-hunt. At least the war had started, and when there was a starting of something, there'd be an ending, too.

"When war comes," Tinch said, "somebody shoots at you and you shoot back at him, and thar's no need to fret ary longer about treaty lines, or treaty words, or the proper way to act in a Winnebago village. Thar's only one thing to worry about, and that's killin before you're kilt."

They talked the rest of the night, hushing sometimes to listen to the songs the wind fetched from the Mississinewa village on the west. North, they could see great fires roaring into the sky, fires that said medicine was being made at Wipitcaki-ungi, * and they could hear the heavy drums from Manjini-kia.

The days passed. Warrior feet cut deep grooves in the

* Huntington, Indiana.

woods trails. Bowls, with lines marked through their centers, were hung outside the villages to show that the braves had gone to war, but would return to drink from the peace side of the bowl. Squares made of logs were found with their openings toward the white settlements. Braves had slept in them with their faces turned homeward, so their gods would know they wished to come back. Muddy sticks and grass were seen near swamps and streams, where war parties had carefully wiped their moccasins, according to the war custom.

Earthwild did not go back to the army he had deserted after Tippecanoe.

"I wasn't the only one that left!" he said. "Leastways, *I* left *after* the battle!" He added bitterly, "Them white men never done nothing for me. If it was up to them, I'd probably still be a slave in that Injun village, carryin my master!"

At first, not much happened. A couple of fields in crop were burned, and had to be replanted. A man was shot longhunting. Some oxen were killed and two horses were stolen, farther south.

The first trouble close to home was at the Simonton cabin. Simonton went out to dig ginseng one day, and while he was gone a brave came to the cabin and shoved his way in. The Simonton boy, now in his twenties, was still crippled in the legs, but his arms and chest were powerful. He grabbed the Indian, threw him down on the floor and called for his ma to bring the ax.

"Crack his skull!" he yelled, as the brave struggled above him with a knife.

She slammed the ax down on the Indian's head and then fainted. By the time she opened her eyes again, the boy had dragged himself around, cleaned the blood off the floor, and pulled the brave out behind the chopping block.

Little Turtle died the following month and his Miami followers split, some for peace and some for war. The month after that, his white taken-son, Blacksnake, was killed at a massacre up at Fort Dearborn * on Lake Michigan. He had

* Chicago.

gone there to bring the garrison back to Fort Wayne, but his Potawatome escort turned on him, and his Miamis deserted him. All said none would have dared to harm him if his foster pa had been alive.

After the massacre, things got worse. In September, the Hunting Moon, stranger-Indians attacked a southern settlement called Pigeon Roost. Most of the folks there were of a single Kentucky family, and most of them were killed, twenty-four in all, and sixteen of them young ones. That same day, Indians attacked Fort Harrison * on the Wabash river, and the day after that, Fort Wayne—Indians in the service of the British.

"Tarnal!" Lannard said. "Ef the Injuns hadn't lost both of them battles, we'd be overrun by redcoats now!"

Folks were so restless and edgy, sometimes it seemed as if the whole Indiana Territory had come down with the crazies. Woodsies, with lifelong friends in the villages, went out and joined the army. Even the Miamis, always so peaceful and honest-hearted, took up ambush and attack. Prophetstown was being built up again; Tinch and Rocreuse swore they had counted as many as forty huts and cabins there. Men hunted warily in the forests, not knowing if they'd ever see their cabins again, while women, left behind, called the young ones in and kept a weapon handy.

All thought it was Indians retreating from Fort Wayne who attacked Mrs. McCutcheon's cabin. Her outside dogs set up a wild barking one night and she heard owl calls, so she crouched by her door to listen, with her ax in her hand.

Soon someone hammered on the door and called out in broken English, and when she didn't answer, began chopping a hole in the wood. It got to be a fair-sized hole, and a couple of Indians poked their heads through it. She smashed them flat with the ax.

Then she heard a scrambling on the roof and knew that others were trying to come down the chimney, so she snatched her precious featherbed and dragged it into the

* Terre Haute, Indiana.

fire. The terrible smoke blinded the two Indians on the roof and both fell down into the cabin. She killed them as she had killed the first ones, and turned just in time to see another crawling through the hole in the door. Desperately she swung the ax and killed him, too. Then she seized her cabin knife and cut off their heads.

"Jest to make sure they was dead," she explained.

She dragged the bodies outside and set fire to them.

"That's why I've come to live with you for a spell," she told Jonathan afterward. "I ain't afeerd to stay by my lonesome . . . but I got to wait till that burnt-Injun smell is gone."

Jonathan was thankful that she said nothing about her experience in front of Strange Rain. These were sad and troubled days for his wife.

It was a great relief to the settlers and woodsies when Harrison came with his men and burned the Miami villages along the Elkhart river to the north, and the other villages on the Wabash forks. The new Prophetstown was destroyed, and the big Kickapoo village of a hundred and sixty huts and cabins. Wipitcakiungi * was burned also, with the corn in the fields and storage pits, a fire that could be seen from Jonathan's cabin. Only Little Turtle's house on the Eel river was spared, for he had always been a faithful friend to the white men.

Nathan was gone most of the time, running traps, hunting, scouting out Indian sign for those who needed him. He'd turned sixteen that fall. He was tall and lean now, looking older than his years, and the daughters of Indian women who had once hankered after his pa now hankered after him, for he had his pa's good looks and pleasant ways. He followed the trails unafraid while woodsies and settlers stayed in their cabins. Among stranger-Indians he could pass for a hunter from the mixed town of LeGris, and among the Indians who knew him, he felt no fear.

"But, mind you!" Lannard warned. "Blacksnake felt safe

* Huntington, Indiana.

175

among *his* Injuns, too, but his Miamis run when he needed them, and the Potawatomes that was s'posed to protect him tore his heart out while he was alive, and et it afterward. Don't be too dumb-brutely bold!"

Rocreuse laughed.

"If *he* was taken, some little squaw would save him!"

"I'm not afraid of The People," Nathan said. "Remember that Blacksnake wore a soldier's uniform and took back his white name. He'd turned into William Wells, captain in the army. If I stripped off my clothes and hung myself over with beads and bells, and smeared war paint on my face, some woodsy would kill *me!*"

"That brings up somethin else!" Lannard went on. "Ef you run on to some stranger-whites, they're likely to take a shot at you, on account of the brown color of your skin. Try not to run into ary one of them in the bright of day, but only in the deep shadders, or nights when they cain't see you well enough to know what you are!"

"And what am I, Lannard?" Nathan asked, turning his eyes away. "On whose side do I stand?"

"You stand on ours, the side that's right!"

"You're sure we're right?"

"Wal . . . we're right to be agin the British!"

"*Ae!* But against The People? All of them? Many were our friends."

"Cain't be helped," Lannard shook his head. "When a new race comes into a country, the old one has to fight 'em, or give in. That's what war is." Then he added, aghast, "You wouldn't fight agin us, no matter what . . . you wouldn't turn agin *us!*"

Nathan was slow to answer.

"Let's hope," he said finally, "that we never have to find out."

Sometimes he met war parties on the trail and often he saw, behind the paint on their faces, boys he had hunted and traded with, but no words passed between them. Sometimes he met warriors with white captives, but they wouldn't give their captives up to him, no matter how many brooches and hides he offered. All he took away with him was the memory of the way the eyes of those whites had followed him.

His trapping and scouting took him far from home; sometimes he wondered if he'd forget how the double cabin looked, before he saw it again. He ate, slept, and lived with the wild things, and knew what is was like to be a Solitary.

He was on his way home during the Long Night Moon of winter, when he made his camp just south of the burnt out Prophetstown. It was bitter cold, but he dared not light a fire, for he was just off a war trail that many stranger-Indians walked. He huddled in his furry cape and stomped his feet, trying to keep them warm.

It was because he was so bone-weary, he reckoned afterward, that he never heard the Wyandot creep up behind him. When he did start up, sensing danger, he felt thongs on his wrists and knew he was a prisoner. He jerked forward, throwing the Wyandot to the ground, but there was little he could do with his hands bound to his back, and when he felt a knife at his throat, he stopped struggling. The Wyandot grabbed his hair and pulled his head back to get a good look at him in the moonlight.

"Delaware!" Nathan burst out.

The Wyandot snorted.

"Morning Light People, half-breed!" he said, and pulled Nathan to his feet, peering at him closely. "Scout? Spy?" He nodded, grinning. "British pay much!"

He made a pack of the things Nathan had taken in trade at Vincennes, even jamming into it Nathan's rifle, knives, tomahawk, pouch of powder and shot, and a bag of jerky. He hefted the pack on his back, then cut a loop of whang, tying one end of it to Nathan's belt and the other to his sash.

"Go! *Go!*" he motioned.

They went up the Wabash in an oak-bark boat. Before dawn they reached a village, where the old man tied Nathan to a tree. He then went off to the village. When he came back, the pack was a lot thinner, and the old man was belching and smelled of bear meat. They went on in the boat, leaving the Wabash behind them and turning up the Tippecanoe. For another day they followed this river, and then they left their boat and went into the woods.

At first Nathan thought he'd be able to get away from this Wyandot, but he was an old man and no tricks were new to him. At night he tied his captive, spread-eagled and staked to the ground with a loop around his throat, so that if he moved he would strangle himself. By day Nathan's hands were bound to his back, and the Wyandot held on to the whang loop around his neck.

They moved at a steady pace from morn till night, with only a slight rest at the noon hush.

The Wyandot ate the bag of jerky. After that, neither of them had anything to eat. One day the Wyandot killed a small rabbit and gave Nathan the liver, but the rest he kept for himself. The next day the Wyandot kicked up several rabbits, but all of his shots went wild. Then they were out of the thick-game country.

"Rifle!" The old man spat on the gun. "White man's foolishness!"

The next day the Wyandot caught a bird and ate it all.

"The Delaware can live on air and water!" Nathan told him proudly, when the old man offered him the feathers.

North and east they stayed, and the forest thinned out. Flat prairies lay before them. Snow started one night and didn't stop for three days.

"Let's see if the Delaware can walk on snow!" the Wyandot jeered, slipping his toes into the straps of long Ojibway snowshoes.

Now a biting cold set in. The Wyandot took Nathan's robe and threw it over his own which was torn and tattered, and he took Nathan's fur hat and mittens, too. The boy clenched his teeth to keep them from chattering. He had never known such cold, for between him and the whole outdoors were only a linsey-woolsey shirt under his hunting shirt, breeches and leggings and fur-lined moccasins.

He set his mouth and squinted his eyes against the snow-flakes and stumbled on. Where were they going? Canada? He'd heard Tecumseh was in Canada now, and that the British had made him a brigadier general commanding all the Indian forces of the West.

Soon the snow was as high as his knees, and he couldn't walk in it. His heart hammered from the effort. Time and again, he fell and the Wyandot pulled him up, swearing and kicking at him.

"Broken Knee not leave you behind!" he burst out in garbled Shawnee, for that was the only tongue they had in common. "Young war chiefs say Broken Knee too old to fight. *Hah!* Let them see me bring in scout! Let them beg me forgive them, that they told me to stay with the women and children!"

The hunting got worse. Most birds and beasts were holed up, waiting for the storm to break. Once Nathan and the Wyandot boiled bark and drank the broth. Another time they found bones, broke and seared them in the fire to kill the vermin inside, then boiled them, ground them between stones, and ate that mixed with a little melted snow.

"I good man," Broken Knee said. "Strong man. Like Delaware. Live on air and water, too."

Now the world they walked in was grey, like thick mist. They couldn't see more than a few yards beyond. They were far from all villages, too, for no man could live in this part of the prairie, and The People said only *wendigos* or *tchibais* ever walked this ground.

"If I were such a wise old warrior as you," Nathan flared, "I would have taken a better trail!"

"Words of a half-breed!" the old man sneered.

But they were both weakening from the lack of food, and the bitter cold that could burn pounds off a man when it held on. Every step was harder, and often one or the other of them fell. Nathan choked against the whang loop and finally Broken Knee took it off.

"Where you run to?" he cried, laughing.

The sun moved above the clouds, and they moved beneath them.

Nathan would squint ahead at Broken Knee and think, "Soon now, he'll go down and won't get up." But the Wyandot seemed to know his thoughts, for twice he turned and shouted above the wind, "I, like Delaware! I go on and on!"

The night they were caught on the frozen lake, it looked as if he had been mistaken. The flat of the ice gave them no shelter at all, and snow slashed their faces like knife blades. Nathan's feet had been numb for a long time, but now they began to hurt and he feared they were frozen. His ears burned as if a poker had been laid on them. Finally, he was able to talk Broken Knee into cutting the whang that bound his wrists.

"They will pay you nothing for a scout whose fingers have frozen and dropped off!" he shouted. "Such a scout could not write the marks that make a paper talk and tell where the American soldiers are hiding!" When he saw Broken Knee hesitate, he added, "They will cut off *your* fingers, too, for being so stupid!"

When his hands were free, he pulled the sewn-on cape of his shirt up around his ears and tied it there with his belt, then slid his hands under his shirt. That made him a little warmer.

The snow was very thick and the cold agonizing. They had to stop often to rest. Nathan saw that the old man was tiring very fast now. Sometimes he would shake his head and stare around him as if he were in a daze.

"Great in war was I," he blurted out once, "and wore the split feather. Now, I ride at the head of no men, and am grateful to have found one captive." His mind was confused and wandering.

"Broken Knee!" Nathan shouted against the wind. "You must know this lake! What is the shortest way off of it?"

But the old Wyandot only shook his head and tottered on, looking vaguely in one direction and then another.

It had been dark for hours when they heard the guttural

howl that meant hunger wolves were hunting. They stood very still. The wind was in their favor, blowing their scent away from the beasts. But it brought the howls so close, the wolves seemed just beyond the fringe of snow around them, though both men knew they were still miles off.

"If they scent us, they'll get us!" cried Nathan. "Let me have my rifle!"

"No use!" Broken Knee called back. "No powder!"

"Better move, then! Feel the wind? It's shifting!"

They trudged on, turning wary when they saw a dark shape ahead of them on the ice. But it was only a log frozen in the lake. The Wyandot chopped a hole in it, and with both of them working the flint and steel, they managed to get a fire started. They stood with their backs to the wind and sheltered the fire with the furry cape, but they were so cold they could feel no warmth in the blaze. The wind blew toward them again, and they heard the hunger wolves much closer.

"They've got our scent!" Nathan shouted.

Broken Knee nodded solemnly and gave him back his knife.

Still they lingered by the fire as long as they dared. Finally they started on again. Once Nathan stopped and looked back at the log gleaming in the dark. It was a cozy sight, and he might never see fire again.

"Our Grandfather Fire," he thought longingly.

They tried to go faster now, for the wind had turned again. But they were walking against it, and it seemed that for every step they took, they were blown back two.

"Cabin close," Broken Knee gasped, and pulled Nathan off to the right. Nathan thought the old man's mind was wandering again, but peered into the blowing snow anyway. "There!" Broken Knee shouted positively. They went on. Sometimes Broken Knee would stop and cast about him for some sign to tell him he was right, but there was nothing to see but snow and dimness.

The wind grew stronger, and they had to hold on to each

other to stand up. Nathan felt his strength going. He stumbled more and more, unable to feel what was beneath his feet. Suddenly they both fell down and lay there.

After a time Broken Knee roused and shouted again about the cabin, but Nathan didn't believe him. He tugged at Nathan desperately, but couldn't get him up. Then he knelt down and began working with Nathan's feet, rubbing and twisting them, trying to get some feeling back into them.

Nathan lifted his head.

"No use!" he shouted. "Go on!" The hunger wolves howled closer. "I can't do it!"

Broken Knee shook his head.

"Not leave scout!" he yelled, stubbornly. "Scout all I got! British pay me!"

He pulled Nathan up and over his back, and managed to take a few steps before he sank down. Then he didn't say any more. He just lay there on the ice, staring out ahead, looking for the cabin.

Now the hunger wolves were giving short barks that meant they knew the men were up ahead. Soon they'd catch up and start the Surround. Nathan lay there thinking numbly. Faces swam in and out of the snowy fog around him, Tibby, Strange Rain, his pa . . . they'd never know what became of him! If only Tinch or Lannard or Rocreuse were with him now! He wouldn't mind so much being killed in any other way. But a pack of hunger wolves, that was a hideous way to die.

He stirred. The long piece of whang that tied him to Broken Knee's sash was still fastened. He drew his knife and cut it. If they were going to fight the wolves, they couldn't risk getting tangled. He jabbed at Broken Knee, but the old man's eyes were closed. He yanked Broken Knee's cape off and threw it toward the wolf sounds. That would slow them down, for they would eat anything, fur, wood, boots, anything. He staggered up and began dragging the old Wyandot along with him.

It seemed they went on for miles this way. Snow blew into

his face; the cold was freezing him. Behind, he could hear the hunger wolves snapping and snarling over the cape. There was little time now. He tried to go faster, but he was too weak. He stopped, let go of his burden, and turned in the direction of the beasts.

Broken Knee roused just then.

"*Cabin!*" he insisted, thickly.

"No! We must save our strength to make a stand!" Nathan yelled in his ear, but Broken Knee shook his head.

He started on, half-crawling, half-dragging himself, for his snowshoes made crawling hard. Nathan hesitated, then followed, leaning down to shout at him.

"Fool! Together we can fight! Apart we'll both die!"

"I think we die anyway," Broken Knee said. "But let us die moving."

The fog thickened in Nathan's head. He pulled the old man up and together they dragged themselves along, looking at each other, nodding, grunting, like some stranger-beasts.

Suddenly Nathan stopped, swayed on his feet.

"I . . . can't do it . . . ," he mumbled.

"What kind of Delaware are you?" Broken Knee shouted. "Good Delaware do it!"

They staggered on and then, suddenly, Nathan quit wanting to stop, to lie down, to rest. He became a warrior with endless strength, wanting to go on and on and on. He began to feel warm. He began to hum the harvest song of The People. "*Hi ya!*" he shouted, ever so often, and grinned at Broken Knee.

Then he saw something black ahead of them, just off the ice, and clutched his knife tight.

"The Surround . . . ," he began, but it was the cabin. The old man saw it, too. They tried to run.

"It's real!" Nathan kept babbling. "It's real!"

They scrabbled in the snow around the door, clawing it away so that the door could swing out. But it was frozen shut. Broken Knee hacked at its bottom edge with his tomahawk, and Nathan pried at it with his knife. They worked with desperate strength, for now the hunger wolves were so close they could hear them panting as they ran.

"God, where *are* You?" Nathan burst out. "Can't You see us?"

Slowly the door came open, and they fell inside and yanked it shut. Then they lay on the floor together, gasping and sobbing.

15

AFTER a while Nathan opened his eyes and squinted into the dimness of the cabin. It was empty. Not even a table stood in its middle. There was a hole in the roof big enough for a man to fall through, and snow had drifted down from it. But it did have a cat-and-clay, with wood in a corner. And a loft above broke some of the wind coming down through the roof hole.

The Wyandot began to giggle. He thought he was out on the prairie where the sun was hot on his back, and strawberries grew thick and sweet. Nathan shook him, but could get no sense out of him at all. Finally he crawled to the hearth and worked the flint and steel. A little fire started up and, quickly, he chipped pieces off the log walls and threw them on it. He brought wood from the pile in one corner and slowly fed it to the fire. Then he turned back to Broken Knee, but the old man was babbling wild.

He chipped more bark off the walls, chewed it up and spit it into Broken Knee's mouth. It seemed to revive him a little. But as the fire burned higher and Nathan could see better, he knew the reason he had seemed strengthened was because the Wyandot was dying. The Hunter of Men was very close, closer even than the hunger wolves.

They were circling the cabin now and trying to jump its walls, for the man-scent came out very strong through the roof hole. Before long, they began tearing at the chinking. Nathan knew they could rip a hole right through the cabin, given enough time. There was a pole pegged to the wall that had been part of the framework of a bed, and he jerked it loose. When he heard a wolf chewing, he'd bang on the wall, and once he rammed the pole right through the chinking and into the mouth of a beast on the other side. He could hear its teeth crunching as it seized the wood.

Now it was only a matter of time until one would scramble up the drifted snow and jump into the cabin from above.

He drew his knife and stumbled back to Broken Knee. He shook him and tried to make him understand about the hunger wolf. But Broken Knee was dead. Whatever was coming now, he had to face it alone.

A noise on the roof brought him to his feet, for it told him one of the beasts was up there. He hauled himself painfully into the loft by his arms, then reached back for his pole. He shoved the wolf off the roof. He heard it yelping as it fell. But soon there'd be another, and another.

"I'll die when I can't push that last one off!"

He rolled over on his belly and looked down into the cabin. His eyes fell on Broken Knee. He looked at him for a long time. He let himself down into the cabin. Then he pulled off the Wyandot's clothes with shaking hands.

"Brother," he said, "you know in your heart-soul there is nothing else I can do."

He stared at the poor naked body a moment longer. Then he cut the whang that still trailed from his belt and tied the old man's wrists together with it. He slipped his head in between them and hitched the body over his back and crawled to the loft hole, not daring to open the door. Twice he fell before he got the body into the loft. Below he could hear the wolves snarling at the scent of men so near. Still he hesitated. Then his eyes went cold and he hefted the Wyandot onto the roof and gave him a push. He heard the body going down the bark shingles, and heard the wolves yelp, and heard their snarls as they fought over the dead Indian.

He let himself back down into the cabin and lay on the floor on his face. The desperate rush of strength that had supported him was gone. He retched, shivered, then retched again. After a while he heard the wolves moving away, as one would seize the body and steal it, and then the others would catch up and steal it back. He heard them farther and farther off, and finally he didn't hear them any more.

He was lying there staring at the drops of water on the floor that were tears from his eyes when he heard a snarl above him. He glanced up and saw, in the loft, one of the biggest hunger wolves he had ever seen. It was looking down at him, and the light made its eyes glitter.

He rolled as it jumped, and the strength of desperation flooded him again. His skinning knife plunged in and out of the wolf's ragged coat as he held it in his left arm, so tight he could feel its ribs cracking. It snarled and its fangs tore at him, and he snarled back at it. For a moment, he was a beast instead of a mortal man, and strange sounds came from his throat. Then it was over and the wolf was dead and he was smeared with its blood.

He lay gasping beside it. Now he saw that it was a white wolf, and likely that was why it had been alone, for it had hung back from the pack. When the others went on, it had stayed behind.

"*Ae*," he murmured, "a night dog, the totem of my grand-pap. His hope . . . now my hope, too, for it is food."

He slit open its belly and tore out the liver. It tasted strong and bitter.

"A white wolf that can run in no pack . . . he is like me, half-burnt wood creature. *Ae*, my grandfather watches over me from the Country of Souls."

He took snow from the floor and rubbed it on his clothes and hands, along with dirt, to try to kill the blood smell that might fetch the others back. He hacked a trench with his knife and bled the wolf into it, then covered the trench.

187

When he was through, he fell back in a daze. He dragged himself near the fire and shut his eyes. He was shaking and sick, and he could not get the thought of Broken Knee out of his mind. He longed for sleep, but a deep sleep would not come to him. Time and again he woke and started up, thinking the hunger wolves had come back and were ripping their way into the cabin. More than once he found himself with his back jammed against the wall and his knife in his hand, but the sound was only the wind. Sometimes he dreamed he heard Broken Knee outside trying to clamber up the snowbank, heard his voice calling, "I am Delaware," and heard his frozen fingers scrabbling at the latchstring.

Ae, but he was hot!

He knew he must have a fever, and was aware of a throbbing pain in his feet. Numbly, he pulled off his moccasins, catching his fingers in the ankle thongs. The skin of his feet had broken and was seeping fluid. He looked at them and said to himself that if they grew worse, he might as well let the hunger wolves have him.

He crawled around the cabin and stripped more bark off the walls. He rummaged in the pack that Broken Knee had carried and found the clay bowl. He melted snow in it and put the bark to boil. Then he tore up his linsey-woolsey shirt and put it in with the bark.

He fell back into his restless dreams. Now and then he'd rouse and remember the strips of cloth, and then he'd take some out to cool and wrap around his feet.

"I've got to get home!" he whispered. He stared into the night darkness of the cabin and then shouted, "I've got to get home!" He slept again, but when he woke he was saying, "Got to get home . . . got to get home. . . ." It sounded like a warrior chant in some stranger-tongue.

"Southwest," he mumbled feverishly. "I can do it. I've got to do it . . . *got to*. . . ."

The days passed, but when his body began to mend and he felt a little stronger, he found his mind didn't run on a straight line any more. No, it got onto things that weren't related or important, like how to make a burl noggin, the face of a woman he'd seen in a settlement once, and how far was it from his pa's cabin to his grandpap's?

But he knew what it was that made his mind wander. It was the woods-sickness that came on a man when he was alone in the deep of the forest, scared and dead tired. All of a sudden the boldest man was raving, bolting this way and that, talking to trees as if they were men. If he came on a yellow panther, likely he'd try to pet it, taking it for some tame kitty from the settlements. Should he see his own face peering up at him from some stream, he'd run and scratch himself out a hiding hole in the leaf mold, behind some rotted tree. He might even die there, and his kin would never know what had happened to him. Only the beasts would know, and they'd howl that the woods had snatched another. Only the burying beetle would lay away his remains.

"Broken Knee!" he cried out suddenly, for it was another mortal that Nathan needed now. When the woods-sickness got a grip on a man, he felt so far away from other mortals that soon they were like a dream he had dreamed and not real any more. Nothing was real but the woods or the prairies or wherever he was struck down. He forgot all the real things he had ever known. That's why, in this back country, more important than food, than water, than rest, was the company of another mortal. Though it might be somebody as stupid as a sheep, he would keep the sickness from you by just being there, with eyes that blinked and a voice that talked back. No beast, no growing tree, not even God could do this for you, unless you had the faith of a Black Robe or a *jussakkid,* medicine man. Only a mortal could do this for you.

Night after night, Nathan woke and propped himself up against the wall and fought the twisted thinking until grey light began to come.

"Keep moving . . . remembering," he told himself thickly.

He skinned out the wolf and roasted it in the cat-and-clay, catching the fat drippings in the bowl. He pegged the hide to the floor with pegs whittled from the firewood.

"Keep moving . . . remembering. . . ."

In the days that came, he ate the wolf meat, kept himself stirring around during the day, tried to sleep the whole night through. He talked out loud about everything he was doing to keep his mind straight. He went over his memories time and again, and sometimes spoke to his pa or Lannard or the others, telling them about his plans.

At first he couldn't do much, for he was still weak and his feet pained him constantly. But he mixed dirt from the floor with wood chips and melted snow, and mended the cabin chinking. He made a mud lid for the clay bowl, so he could carry some fire with him when he left. He sewed his torn clothes with whang and patched his moccasins. Lacking fur, he powdered pieces of bark and put this in his mittens and moccasins to keep him warm when he went out.

Every day he made himself put on the snowshoes and step outside. The first few days, he went out only to scrape the snow down from the roof, for the night winds piled it high. But later, he began walking out from the cabin and studying the land about him.

It was spotted with deep woods and open prairies. He cast about for tracks in the snow, to see what animals came and went this way, but there were precious few tracks with the snow so heavy. He watched the weather sign, and clouds and sun and wind. He noted the trees, made tea from sassafras bark and birch twigs. And he made waterproof bowls from birch bark, to eat and drink from, and even to cook in if he kept his fire low enough.

As he grew stronger, he dug in the snow with a broken puncheon he had shaved down with his crooked knife. He found rose bushes with the hips still on them and gathered them, for they would hearten a man's blood. He found hickory nuts a-plenty from a shagbark stand. He boiled these and pressed them into cakes. Some he ate, and some he saved to take with him on his long walk home.

He ranged farther and farther from the cabin, and found blazes on the trees. None were white men's. They told him the tale of this country better than anything else. Here was a gash on oak bark that meant hunting was never good here. Farther to the west, he found a red painted arrow sunken in the ground, with only its tail feathers showing above the snow. War trail, it meant, and he looked back to see if his cabin could be seen from there, but only the smoke-smell gave it away, for there were hills between.

North aways, he found two sticks in the ground. They were lashed together to make an X-shape, and had a long pole laid across them. Cliff ahead, they meant, and it was a sign for fast-riding horsemen, so there must be a village ahead, with hunters and warriors a-plenty coming and going in peacetime. He finally found the mark of the village trail half-buried in the snow, a tall upright stick with a little one leaning against it and pointing north. The tall stick told him the village was far away. For two nights, he climbed on his roof and looked north, but he never saw a signal fire, so he reckoned the village must be many miles distant.

The hide dried, and he laid it on a piece of wood set at a slant, and began fleshing it out with a sharpened bone. After he had cleaned it of all fat and flesh, he buried it in the wood ashes under the floor, to loosen the hair.

Then he set about making a toboggan. When he left, he would carry all the wood he could, for after a day or two on the trail, he'd be too tired to do more than rest, come night.

From the loft he took the narrowest puncheon and chopped off one end, so that it was only about five feet long. He shaved it down with his crooked knife until it was no thicker than his thumb. Then he dug out holes along the sides. It was a crude toboggan, for its front was flat instead of curved, but he thought it would carry his things.

He took the wolf hide from its pit and scraped off the hair

with a pointed bone. Then he sank his hunting-knife in the floor, almost to the hilt. He pulled the hide against it so that he cut off the strips he would tie his cargo to.

The night came when he had done all that he could. The snow had stopped and there was a bright moon, but the wind was still howling. He put down his bowl of tea and watched the moonlight filter through the chinking. He listened to the wind in the chimney, and it was a lonesome sound. It rattled against the cabin, and the fire snapped back at it. The shadows of the loft were very black, and they moved their edges and quivered a little as the fire moved. He had never been so lonesome.

He didn't care any more that the food he ate made his stomach twist. He didn't care that his feet and legs hurt every minute. He didn't even care that he was caught up in a war that had tossed him to the edge of the wilderness-world, in this cabin. All he cared about was his sudden desperate need for someone who cared about him.

It was true that down there on the Salamonie he had folks that cared about him. But they didn't care *first* about him, and second about another. His ma and his pa, they belonged to each other, and what mattered most to them was what happened to each other. He knew that Tibby, close as she was to him, was still closer to Earthwild now. And the others, they each had someone, too. But there was no one person who cared first about him, no one whose whole life would be miserable-long if he never came back, no one who didn't have somebody else to turn to and say, "I loved Nathan, but thank God, it wasn't you!"

It would be powerful sweet to know that if he went to the door and looked out, there would be another pair of eyes looking for him, maybe even toward him, no matter how many rivers and hills and night beasts stood between them. It would be powerful sweet to know the kind of love that had no blood ties to it, that a woman gave a man.

He closed his eyes and tried to put the longing from him, and after a while, he slept. He was having the dream again, that Broken Knee was fumbling at the latchstring, when he awoke. But this time something was really jiggling the string. He took his knife and stepped softly to the door. At first he thought it might be a sound made by the wind, but then it sobbed and sounded like a panther cub, only no panther would be wandering this frozen wilderness. He half-crouched, listening with eyes narrowed. No, it must be something out there in the night that wasn't the wind and wasn't a beast. Maybe a stranger-Indian, or worse, the *tchibai* of Broken Knee.

He braced himself to spring, pushed out the door, and saw little fingers reach around its edge and try to pull. He shoved the door out then, and looked at what had been doing the scratching and sobbing. A little gal-child!

He was too astonished to move, or even speak.

She stood there in the bright moonlight, a small girl of perhaps ten or eleven. She was wrapped in rags of cloth and hide, with only a little robe of twisted rabbit fur around her shoulders. Even through her tears, he could see that her eyes were dark blue, the color of dragonfly wings. She looked at him with fear in her face, but no sound came from her lips.

"Here," he said awkwardly. "*Here.* . . ."

He reached out his hand to her. Her fingers were icy cold. Gently he pulled her inside and barred the door behind her. She went to the fire and stiffly sat down on the robe he used as a pallet. He stood by, staring at her.

"Where in tarnal. . . ?" he began, and said no more. He was staggered.

He squatted down beside her. He noticed that her moccasins were new and had small holes cut in the bottom. So she was dear to someone, for moccasins were made like that so the Evil Ones would think the children poor and not steal them.

"Um . . . let me see you."

He leaned down and stared straight into her face. He couldn't tell if she was white, or a half-burnt wood person like himself. But one thing was sure, she was no pureblood of The People.

"Where . . . where are your folks?" he asked, but she only looked back at him. *"Folks!"* he said louder. He thought a minute. *"Niccon,* friend," he said in Potawatome, and pointed to himself. He told her the same in Shawnee and Miami and Delaware, but none of the words seemed to mean anything to her.

"Where," he pointed to the door and made a great circle with his arm, "did you," he pointed to her, "come," he made his fingers walk across the floor, "from?"

She shook her head and mumbled something in a stranger tongue.

"Well," he muttered, "you had to come from *somewhere!* You weren't born half-grown outside my door!"

He saw her eying the bowl of broth and gave it to her. Then he pulled on Broken Knee's tunic and long, pointed snowshoes.

"I'm going out," he said. "You stay here."

But when he opened the door, she started up.

"No! Stay there!" At his gesture, she sank down.

The moon was so bright he didn't have to light shellbark to see what was outside. She must have stood for a long time outside his door, for her footprints in the snow showed how she had hesitated, started away, come back. He followed them to the lake, but there the wind had blown them away. He cast about in circles and finally found the person she'd been with, a squaw of the Winnebago. She was lying on the lake, curled tight in her last sleep. There was no sign of another mortal anywhere.

What had brought this woman and this child to this lake on this night? He shook his head.

He half-carried, half-dragged the woman to a thick stand of beech, and wedged her up into the branches as high as he could. She was small and light and easy to lift, though the effort made him weak. But it was the only burial he could give her, even if he had been strong and well, for there could be no digging a buryhole in this frozen ground. He wanted her out of sight, for he thought it might be hard on the child to see her again.

He took the woman's robe and snowshoes and went back to the cabin. The little girl turned her eyes away when she caught sight of what he carried. She sat leaning against the cat-and-clay, and wouldn't give up to sleep.

Nathan drank his tea and watched her out of the corners of his eyes. She was wary as a squirrel, and even the snapping of the fire made her jump. Where the robe fell away from her arm, he could see whip marks. So she had been beaten. And on her throat was a burned place that looked as if a coal had been held there. Then she must have been a slave, whatever her blood. But the new moccasins with holes in them? He frowned. The dead squaw must have made them for her, he decided, maybe adopted her; no, more likely stolen her. That would explain why they had picked such a time to travel.

He rolled up in the woman's robe and closed his eyes and pretended to sleep. But he hadn't missed seeing that the other skinning knife was gone from its place by the door. Seeing his dark reddish hair and green eyes, she must have taken him for a white man. He wondered what she'd heard of white men that made her hide a knife in her robe.

He lay quiet and watchful, but she didn't make a move toward him and later, when he opened his eyes, he saw that she was asleep.

"Poor babe," he whispered. He looked at her a moment longer and then added, "You're not the mortal I was wishing for, but I'm glad you're here just the same. It's not so lonely any more."

In the morn, she was still asleep, and he moved around quietly, getting things ready for his journey.

"I reckon I'll have to take her with me," he said to himself.

He cut down saplings for extra wood. He left half of what he cut in the cabin, in case someone else came after he was gone, and needed the fire to save his life. Two saplings he kept out to use as staves. He packed the toboggan that day, leaving a place in the middle for the child, where the load would protect her from the cold.

When she woke, he tried to explain to her that they were going on a far journey. But he didn't think she understood any of what he said, even though he signed out a lot of it with his hands.

The next morn, after they had eaten their last meal in the cabin, he picked up the woman's robe to wrap the girl in, but she broke away from him and ran outside. He ran after her, calling, but no matter how he called or coaxed or wheedled, she wouldn't come back. Finally, he stepped into the cabin and stood there and waited. She lasted longer, out there in the cold, than he had thought possible. But when he saw the latchstring wiggling and the door pull out, he didn't look up. After a while, she slipped in and crept to the fire, and knelt down to warm herself.

He thought he knew what was worrying her. She didn't know whose cabin she was in, whether she was slave or free, where he was taking her, to the British or the Americans or The People. He tried to think of some way to make her understand that he wouldn't harm her. The only thing he really knew about her was that she had lived in a village. How could he explain to her that he was going to take her to Fort Wayne, where someone might know of her folks or, if not, someone might want to adopt her?

He rumpled his hair. How would he ever get her as far as Fort Wayne? The way she mistrusted him, she'd run off at the first chance, and he wasn't going to strap her to the toboggan, for that might scare her clear out of her little head.

"Fort Wayne?" he asked.

She shrugged and looked back at the fire.

"Fort Defiance . . . Fort Harrison . . . Fort Recovery . . . Vincennes?"

She kept her back to him.

"Well, where *did* you come from?" he burst out. "You must have heard of *some* of those places!"

She whirled, her eyes wide. It was plain that, if she knew nothing else, she knew the sound of an angry voice. He calmed, and was sorry he'd lost his temper.

Suddenly he picked up the robe and when she saw what he was going to do, she jumped to her feet. But he was too quick for her. He got it around her and carried her outside to a tall stand of birch by the lake. She fought and kicked and screamed at him, but he held her tight with his left arm, and when he set her down, he knelt behind her. He put his right hand on her head, then hesitated. He hoped she'd seen an adoption ceremony before and would understand.

"Father," he said to the sun, "hear me! I swear now to be this girl's father forever, to protect her in time of need, to keep from her all who would do her harm, to teach her the True Path. So do I swear this before you, Kije Manitou."

She had quieted, and he thought she understood the meaning of his hand on her head. He got up and let her go, but she stood still and waited. *Ae,* she understood. She was waiting for the rest. Hurriedly he pulled a piece of birch bark and cast it down in the snow.

"With this bark, I cast away her old self and her old name. Now I take out all her blood be it white, or of The People, and make it the same as mine. I give her the name. . . ," he glanced down at her, remembering how she had followed his fire, and added, "Firelight."

He ripped off another piece of bark and, with his crooked knife, scratched her name. Then he handed it to her. With his right thumb, he rubbed his cheek and her own.

"The same," he told her. "The same blood, the same kin. Now you are my. . . ," he stumbled on the word, it was so absurd, "my daughter."

She looked at him solemnly, and then she went to the toboggan and climbed in. He stood watching her, shamed. It was a hurtful trick he'd played, letting her think he had adopted her, for the oath was not binding without a chief to witness it. Still, it had to be done for the sake of the poor, scared babe. He followed her back to the toboggan.

"You ought to know," he muttered, "that I'm not old enough to be your pa."

He started into the cabin, but she said something, and he turned back. She was holding the skinning knife out to him.

"Oh. Well, you can keep it," he smiled.

He went inside the cabin and, with charcoal, wrote on the cat-and-clay: *Have been a captive of the Wyandot, Broken Knee. Am starting for the Salamonie on foot. Nathan Raoul. December 1812.* He thought a moment, and added: *Son of Dr. Jonathan Raoul.*

If he didn't make it home, maybe someday somebody who could read would see it and send word to his ma and pa—a trader, soldier, even one of the Black Robe priests.

He went out to the toboggan, slung the traces over his shoulders, and smiled at the quiet little girl.

"Firelight," he said, "we are going home."

16

THERE was a crust on the snow that made the going fairly easy the first day. They made good time. That night, Nathan found a sheltered place in a ravine. He cut a narrow trench in the ground and they built their fire in it. He and Firelight sat with their legs across the trench and the robes pulled around both of them, but he dared not fall into a deep sleep, lest the fire go out. He didn't get much rest.

The second day he was as tired when they started as when they stopped the night before. His feet were beginning to hurt more, and the next day they were so much worse that he could walk only a few steps at a time. He leaned heavily on the staves now. The fourth day they made no time at all, and when the sun went down, he could look back and see the hill where they'd been that morn. Common sense told him they would never reach Fort Wayne, and yet he *knew* they would. He built their fire, and long after Firelight fell asleep, he sat thinking. He heard wolves this night, off to the west, but the wind stayed steady, and the beasts didn't scent them.

The fifth day, he didn't try to go on. He built a shelter against a fallen log and threw his robe over the top of it for a roof. He piled brush around it and snow over it, so that it looked like another snow dune. They lay by their fire all that day, and he felt the fever coming back. That evening he looked out and saw a long file of The People and their captives moving along a ridge to the east. Firelight saw them too, and began to cry. For the first time she moved close to him and blurted out words in her stranger-tongue.

The next day he was better, and able to make a half a day's walk before they had to camp.

But the fuel gave out and they wasted another half day searching for fallen deadwood, and cutting saplings when they could find nothing else.

After that, he lost count of the time they were on the trail. The days came and went, and each seemed worse than the one before. He prayed to his gods as he went along, and sometimes he heard himself praying very loud but making no sense, and he knew the fever was on him again.

He remembered stooping down by Firelight and saying, "If something should happen . . . if I should fall down and not get up again, as your *niccon* did, then you keep going the way we're going now. . . ."

But it was no use. Even if she could understand his words, she was a girl. A boy might be able to get there, a boy might not be too afraid. But a girl! He remembered taking up the traces again, he remembered falling in the snow, and then coming to, with Firelight tugging at him and crying.

It was either the day after that, or the one after that, when they came in sight of the village. If they were where he hoped, this village was on Cedar Creek, almost due north of Fort Wayne. He approached it cautiously, but no dogs growled at their coming. No smoke came up from wood laid for the supper fires. There were no stones on the storage pits, which meant that the pits were empty of food.

He left Firelight and slipped into the village alone, but he found nothing.

They camped that night in a cave the river had cut. The weather began to warm, and they stayed on another day, for he was very weak. The day after that, it was warmer still, and he took his staves and went down the river trail. In a canebrake, he found what he was looking for, a left-behind bark boat.

They abandoned the toboggan then, and took only the bowl of fire, their last bit of meat, and his pack. They drifted south the whole of that day. Sometimes they would run onto a place where a stretch of ice hadn't melted. Then Nathan would bring the boat to the edge, climb out, and work it along the bank till they reached open water again.

About sundown, they ran onto another stream, and the sight of it filled his eyes with thankful tears. He knew it was Bean Blossom river, and that it would take them to Fort Wayne. The moon was rising when they drifted past an unknown village where only one fire burned, and an old man with a rag around his head and beads around his waist was singing a Frenchy song.

During the night, they ran onto more ice. Nathan reckoned it was because he was so tired that his feet lost their sureness, for when he was trying to drag the boat around the ice, he slipped and fell into the frigid water. He was out of it quick enough, and back to the boat, tugging it across the frozen shore. But when they were floating again, he began to shiver hard. Finally, he lay down in the bottom of the boat and pulled his robe over him. But he could not stop the shaking of his body, and he was worried when he heard how his breaths rasped in his chest.

"Never mind," he gasped to Firelight. "Never mind. Someone'll find you. . . ."

Then he didn't think about anything more, for he didn't know anything more.

Firelight crept close to him. She pulled her own robe over him and tried to warm him with her own thin body, but this didn't seem to ease him any, and his face had the look she had seen in the face of her friend who had died on the lake. Her mother's face, too, had had that look when their onetime friends and neighbors, the Winnebago, had attacked, declaring their hunting lands had been violated. Her mother had been killed, and she herself had been made a slave in the Winnebago village. None would adopt her, for her eyes were blue, and the medicine man said blue eyes meant evil blood. They had taken from her her pretty name, and called her only *Wowashi*, Worker.

"*Zonta?*" she tugged at the tall, red-haired youth. "Trusted One?"

But he didn't stir, and she was very frightened. This man, he had made the ceremony she had often watched longingly when a child was adopted by a warrior. He had put his hand on her head and said the words, then he had thrown away the bark that was her old self and given her a new piece of bark, with the symbols of her new self carved on. The symbols spoke her new name, and proved she was now a child of his blood.

She began to sob. If he went back to his ancestors, who would care what happened to her? She could never return to the village of Yellow Hawk, up on the top of Lake Micisagiengan * for there she would be put to death as a runaway. And she could never go back to Crooked Face, her home village, for she had been a captive, and captives were disowned.

This one, he fed her, he kept her warm, talked softly, smiled at her, and he had never beaten her. Even when things were very hard for him and he was sick, he had not left her behind. And that day, back in the small wooden lodge, when he had been angry, he had not clubbed her to death as she had expected.

"Trusted One . . . ," she shook him again, but he twisted and mumbled in his fever dreams, and his breathing was hard and slow. She lay down and pressed her face against his shoulders and prayed for him.

Darkness fell. Sometimes when she raised up, she would see night beasts along the river, watching them as they drifted past. Small deer stood with their antlers lifted, and

* Lake Michigan.

dipped their heads to the boat. Raccoons, thick with winter fur, stopped their fishing to sit up and stare at them. Wary panthers leaped away from the banks, but gazed out at them from the brush, and a small, sad-eyed fox followed them. Rabbits froze when they saw the boat, and she called out to them not to be afraid. Night dogs howled in the deep of the woods, and she knew they sensed her young father's dying, and were mourning for him.

Owls, hunters in the night, swept low. Cold branches shook down leaves that had clung to them through half the winter, leaves that fell over the boat with a soft rustling sound, some of them on Nathan's quiet form. The forest talked and whispered, saying good-bye to him.

They were a small dark boat in a big dark world. The four winds warred above them, the stars fought in their pathways, the evil serpent stirred in his cave.

She thought she heard singing far, far off, very high in the sky behind them. It was a woman singing a wind song, a melancholy tune like the wind blowing across the lonesome prairies. She listened, and said to herself that it was more than a wind song. It was a death song.

She smoothed Nathan's hair, sobbing quietly, and put his rifle in his hand. She pulled his shirt straight and arranged the fringe of his cape so that it fell gently over his shoulders. His heartbeat was a slow drum.

They floated, lost the current, gently touched the bank, broke free and floated again.

"*No!*" she cried out suddenly. He must not die! But the look on his face told her he was going away from her.

She cried herself to sleep lying against him. Much later she was roused by men's voices, and by the carrion smell of the Morning Light People. She felt someone lift her up, and when she opened her eyes, she saw white men lifting Nathan.

She fought them and struck them and called them terrible names in her slave tongue and in her own tongue, trying to make them so angry that they would kill her and Trusted One, and not torture them. Ahead she could see the big log lodge with high walls around it, where the Morning Light People tortured their captives, starving them with burned food, giving them the fire drink that made them mad, and worse still, shutting them up in cages. None of The People could live in a cage. It was worse than the fire at the stake, or the green hide strapped around you in the sun, or the double line of squaws beating you with sticks and hoes!

But not all her kicking and biting and screaming could stop them, and the white warriors laughed and said Fort Wayne had never seen the likes of her. When they laid down Trusted One, though, she tore loose and ran to him and pulled the knife from his belt and stood them off . . . for a moment, at least.

Before Nathan was well again, it was Crow Moon, and the flowers of fur, the pussy willows, were grey on their stalks. The Hunter's Star got up later now, and the bats came out of their caves.

When Nathan was able to go for walks, Firelight walked with him like a small, living crutch, for he was still weak and his steps uncertain. As they went up and down the paths, Tibby or her ma would turn from their work to watch them. It did their hearts good to see him up, for it had been a long time since Jonathan and Earthwild had fetched him back from Fort Wayne, with the pale little girl who spoke a stranger-tongue.

She had been taken to the family with pity and tenderness. Under Jonathan's fatherly care, she grew strong and rosy, learned to smile, even to laugh. She clung to Strange Rain like a cub to its *ninga,* and looked with admiring fondness at Nathan's pretty, grownup twin. They braided her thick dark hair that had a white-man curl to it, and the clothes they sewed for her made her proud because they were like the ones worn by Tibby. Now that the starved, wizened look was gone from her, she looked older, and Strange Rain said she was at least twelve, for she had come into maidenhood.

During the time he was laid up, Nathan taught her English, and lately she had been learning to read. She was quick at learning, a lot quicker than his own sister, and Tibby was jealous.

"Likely someone has taught her afore!" she sniffed.

By the time the hummingbirds came back, Nathan was again on the trails, trapping, long-hunting, sometimes with the woodsies, sometimes by himself. But he didn't stay away so long now. Things were different since he came home.

For one thing, he had Firelight, and she had grown so dear to him that he would never let her go to any other folks, as he had thought at first. "*Ae,* what am I doing with a daughter?" he would ask himself wryly, when he caught sight of his face in some stream.

When he was away, he was filled with anxiety for her, for the others had not learned her broken speech as well as he, and he feared she could not make them understand if she was ill, or needed something. Too, she worried when he stayed a long time in the forest, thinking he had come to harm. He would know her eyes were watching the trail for him, and would turn back.

But the thing he found most different was the feeling toward The People.

It was while he was gone that the troops had ridden down the Mississinewa river and burned the Miami villages, something the woodsies talked about with a savage elation in their eyes and heat in their voices. When they spoke of the Miamis these days, it was in the way that the Circuit Rider spoke of the devil, and Nathan was stunned. These Indians had always been their friends, had traded honestly with them, had given food and shelter to many of them, had fetched herbs to them when they ailed, had stood up for them when the Shawnees wanted their blood, had saved many a woodsy's life.

But now they were to be hated because a war had flared, and spread up and down the rivers.

Once he started out for the Mississinewa villages, but then he turned back, for he didn't want to see their suffering.

Not yet, not until he understood this ghastly thing that had come into the woods, this *tchibai* with the heart and spirit of Scuddy.

Hatred.

It had caused old enemies among the woodsies and the settlers to unite as if they were kin, all turned against The People. And it seemed that the worse the white men treated the Miamis, the more they hated them, instead of hating the tribes who had done the real harm, the Shawnees and Potawatomes. Even newcomers who had shown no real interest in the land were caught up in this hatred, shiftless white men who drifted aimlessly as hunters, dragged at plowing, or showed little care for trapping. It was as if all had found something to follow at last, the way a lost hunter would line up trees to lead him out.

There was less modesty among the womenfolk now, and the men were rougher than ever. All ate more, drank more, talked wild. They were like an old warrior chanting his death song, a quick, frantic death song because the flames were high.

"The way of war," said Lannard. "It makes varmints of folks. Always has."

Even Tibby took to talking out of turn when Indians were mentioned. More often than not, she sided with the white men, forgetting her mixed blood. Nathan was ashamed for her, and set down on her hard, when they were alone.

It seemed everyone felt a need to speak out. People stood on stumps in the settlement streets and spoke against the Indians or drink or the devil, anything they could think of. Settlers turned on the Praying Indians who lived in the white missions, getting them drunk, tormenting them, even burning them alive in their log churches. Woodsies stoned to death friendly Indians who were only carrying messages to the troops. Murder, once rare, became rather common. Lies came from every tongue. Theft was an everyday thing.

Nathan began to think that, outside of his own folks and a few of the woodsies, the whole place had gone crazy.

He turned from it and went to the Mississinewa villages, but he found the craziness had spread there, too. The squaws, without men, took any man. The children were sent on the trails to beg. The prayers were no longer said. The People had become a part of the earth, for they had nothing left.

He began to wonder if any people would survive and be as they had once been. Would any of them ever be human, mortal beings again, or would they stay the wild, foam-mouthed beasts they had become?

One thing he was sure of . . . the woods would survive. Since people had first entered it, it had tried to get rid of them and had failed, but what it couldn't do, they themselves were doing. They were destroying each other, and if it didn't stop, there'd be nothing left but trees.

He came home saddened, quiet, full of a stranger-feeling that had come to him on the trail. As he stepped over the doorlog, he stopped and looked back, for it seemed the sensitive side of his Indian nature couldn't look ahead any more. No, he didn't see the years reeling themselves off, and the seasons changing, and his ma and pa and twin beside him, safe and close. He shook his head. There was a word white men put to such a feeling. Token. "Some untoward thing is going to happen," they'd say. "I've had a token."

But Tibby took it out of his mind, for she was waiting for him with her eyes bright.

"Me and Earthwild," she said shyly, "we're getting married."

17

FROM then on, the double cabin was a noisy place. As soon as the word went up and down the trails the women came, war or no war, and set to getting ready for the wedding. It took hours frantic with sewing and cooking and planning to bring such a frolic off, and weeks went by before everything was done.

The day of the wedding, the women were there before sunup.

"Loll all you can!" they called up to Tibby, as she lay abed in the loft. "It's the last time you'll ever get the chance!"

This last morn of work had them all so flustered that spats started over how many fistfuls of sage to sprinkle over the sides of meat. They were worn out from planning and working and bending over kettles and squatting on the hearth, but what else could they do? Strange Rain was a sweet and good woman, they said among themselves, *extra* sweet and good for an Indian. But it took a bunch of all-white women to know how things should be done, and to see that the bride was dressed proper. They owed this much to Jonathan, they told each other, this much and more!

They dressed Tibby in the middle of the cabin floor, their

rough hands kindly. The dress was in two pieces. Instead of having just a skirt that went over her short gown, it had a top, too. The top matched the skirt and the whole thing went over a petticoat. Tibby fidgeted. She didn't care much for this thing called a petticoat, for it gave her a too bunchy feeling. A sash of long white ribbon went round the waist of the dress and hung clear down the back, and she didn't care for that either. The women kept telling her to watch that she didn't catch it on something, and to be careful how she sat on it, and to remember how much Jonathan had paid the peddler for it.

Strange Rain combed Tibby's hair till you could hear it snap, and wound it into a bun at the back of her neck. It didn't feel right to have her hair pinned up instead of loose on her shoulders, and what was worse, she had to hold her head stiff while the women fastened flowers into the bun. When she thought they were finished and started to walk away, she stepped right on Sally Carson, who was putting the last stitches in the hem of the wedding dress for luck. The last things she put on were her cowhide shoes, and she nearly forgot them, she was so flustered.

They all stood back and looked at her then, and she wanted to peek in the looking glass, but they snatched it away from her and cast their eyes up toward the loft boards in horror.

"Don't you know that'll bring you the worst kind of luck?" Sally cried.

She teetered into the entry between the two cabins. Earth-wild wasn't anywhere in sight, but her pa was close by. He came over and paraded her around, and said wasn't she the pretty one? She clung to his hand like a babe, for she felt scared and unlike herself, with everyone staring at her and talking to her as if she were stranger-company and not home-folks.

Strange Rain came to her then, and took her hand, and talked about her own wedding day. She and Jonathan had first been wed in the Delaware way, and then in a building where a man with spectacles read off words from a book. That wasn't what she wanted to say, though. No, she wanted to say that Tibby had been a sweet, dear daughter and the cabin would be lonesome without her. But such words were hard to say, unhappy and tearful for such a happy time, so she did not say them, but held Tibby's hand as if she would never let it go.

Tibby looked around the dooryard. It was filled with flowers the women had set out, some fetched from their own dooryards. A gourd vine was halfway up the cabin wall, and morning glories had climbed clear to the roof. Calabashes planted full of calico flowers decorated the table where the Good Book of the Circuit Rider would rest, and where she and Earthwild would stand. Of a sudden, it seemed too nice a place to leave.

She cast her eyes at the people gathered there, the women fussing over the new-made table of halved logs that waited in the shade of a catalpa tree heavy with blossoms. She smiled at the young ones screaming at their games and zipping in and out of the sunlight. She listened to the easy, friendly talk. She sniffed the smells of roasting meats, woods flowers, pipe smoke, earth, buckskins, starched calico, gunpowder, and sweat. And it came to her that her pa's cabin was always the place where folks did their getting together. She reckoned this cabin had known more pain, tears, laughter, funning, and serious talk than any place else in the whole wide world.

It set her to thinking. What would her own cabin be like, and where? Whatever made her think she loved that clumsy Earthwild? Though up to this moment, she'd felt she could face an Indian attack by his side. What had made her want to go away? When she was sick, who would stay by her side and hold her hand and tell her not to fret? When he was out in the forest long-hunting, who would chat away the hours with her?

All at once, it was the most dismal day she'd ever seen. Her shoes pinched her toes, the wind was blowing her hair, she knew her dress was going to burst a seam, and anyway, she didn't want to get married, she was too scared.

"Pa . . . ," she quavered suddenly, but Mrs. McCutcheon

gave her a sharp look and shoved a jug of whiskey into her hand. She stood there and felt tears in her throat, and long afterward, when she was a married woman, she laughed on that a lot.

Seeing her with the jug in her hand, everyone perked up. You could see they'd started listening for the riders on the trail.

The younger men had taken Earthwild down to The Bucks, where he gathered twigs and they all drew, to see who would ride for the whiskey. It was Nathan and Lannard's boy Sammy who got the two lucky twigs.

Back in the clearing, folks could hear the horses coming, and the men began to chuckle. For days they'd been laying bets on who would be the two to ride, and now the betting men gave out yells fit to make your ears pop. "Sammy, I got two skins on you!" one howled.

Nathan broke out of the swamp first, hunched forward on the mare, with Sammy right behind him. They reached the bride at the same time, and for a minute, you couldn't tell who was going to get the jug. Tibby was holding it out to Nathan, for she wanted her twin to carry it, but Sammy cut him off with his horse. They shoved each other around so furiously that they nearly trampled the bride. But it was Nathan who leaned from the saddle and snatched the jug from her hand. He wheeled the mare, and they could hear him yipping and yelling all the way back, as he rode to meet the others, passing the Circuit Rider on the way.

All in the dooryard sat down to talk and pass the time, for they knew the young men wouldn't be in a hurry. They had to bring the jug back dry as a bone, and there were a lot of flushed faces and silly sniggering when at last they stumbled into the clearing. Abe McCutcheon, who never drank, was carried back as limp as a soggy leaf, with mud stains on his uniform from falling down. The Circuit Rider gave him a stony look and said they would now have the wedding. It was plain that he thought the sooner they ate, the better for everybody.

But when it came to the actual saying of the words, Earth-wild gave them all a bad moment. When the Circuit Rider asked him his name, he couldn't remember it.

"I had one, all right," he scratched his head. "I know I had one, but it was such a long time ago, and after that they gave me that crazy Injun name, and now . . . I forget."

"Well," said the Circuit Rider flatly, "you cain't git married with no last name!"

Finally it was decided that he should take Shawn's name, for they had been like brothers. So Tibby became Mrs. Earth-wild Shawnessey.

Afterward she was handed a Tear Handkerchief made for her by Auntie Gentry. All stood back and gave her plenty of room to cry and when she slowed down, they coaxed her on, many chiming in to help.

"My insides is goin to outgroan you women if we don't eat!" Lannard snapped. "Ain't you tormented yourselves enough fer one day?"

The tears stopped then, and all agreed it had been a good cry. Tibby had taken to it like an old hand, and they reckoned she had shed tears enough to fetch her a lot of luck.

They went about hustling food to the table. Logs had been rolled up to sit on, stools and benches fetched from the cabin. Young ones were set to shoo the flies away, but they did more tasting than shooing. There was a God's plenty to choose from, and everyone got a little vexed when the Circuit Rider said such a long blessing, for they'd had their appetites ready since morning.

". . . And don't fergit to say a hunderd words or so about the bugs that's liable to get it swallowed down afore us!" whispered Mrs. McCutcheon with a snort.

They had bear, deer, turkey, pigeon, squirrels, even quail. They had greens, lettuce, boiled cabbage, radishes, and pickled cucumbers left from winter. They had pumpkin butter, wild honey, and wild strawberries. Seemed like there was all manner of good things, but the cedar keg of rum was the most popular of all, and even the women slipped their noggins down to Simonton, who was doing the filling.

As a special treat they had white man's bread, for a mill had opened down the river, and now there was no reason why they couldn't have white flour instead of corn meal. But the young ones spit it out.

"I never tasted nothin so flat and flavorless!" Lannard's girl said.

After they ate there was dancing. Nathan got down the fiddle, and he and Jonathan took turns coaxing tunes from it. "Who Will Show Your Foot?" . . . "Possum up a Gumstump" . . . "What Are You Riding Here For?" . . . and "My Man John" were all favorites. When Nathan ran out of tunes, he made up some. His music was a bit sour at times, but who could hear it, with all that stomping and shouting? Even Mrs. McCutcheon got into a reel and swung her heels so hard, she kicked her shoepacs off. The young ones danced with each other, if you could call it dancing. The old dogs, Sin and By Hokey, too smart to stay close to all those swinging feet, went down the trail and watched from there. Firelight kept close to Nathan, for she had never seen folks cut up like this, and she was half afraid of them.

The grass was beaten into the ground and dirt flew up. When dark fell, they brought torches, but the breeze from the dancers' skirts put them out as fast as they could light them. Cowhide shoes were tossed aside, along with boots and shawls and moccasins. They laughed and sweat and beat their feet like they'd never live to see another frolic.

It was Sally Carson who put an end to all the fun. She climbed up on a bench and shouted that it was time to put the newlyweds to bed.

All gathered around the doorlog of the medicine cabin and a steaming kettle of water was poured over the doorlog. It dried quickly in the sultry air, and the young girls cast their eyes at Nathan, for it meant that one of them would soon be wed, and to a man who'd stepped over that log many times.

"Ain't no use lettin a preacher go to waste," one of them called boldly, and Nathan flushed at their giggles.

The women followed Tibby into the cabin. More quickly than they'd dressed her, they undressed her, pulling a new bed gown over her head. When they finally had her under the covers, they lingered on with bits of advice that made her blush and cast her eyes down. But when they started talking about their own wedding nights, Strange Rain shooed them out.

The door had hardly closed when it flew open again and the men came, fetching Earthwild. Tibby pulled the covers over her face and lay still. She wouldn't let them see her in her bed gown, nor would she look on her man's nakedness. It was taking him a long time to get rid of the men, she thought, but then she heard the door pulled shut and the bar drop in place, and saw the quilt go dark as Earthwild blew out the bear-oil lamp.

Nobody went home that night. Toward daybreak, the men who were still on their feet sprawled out on the grass and slept. The women crowded into the living cabin.

The next day was infare day. Again they rode for the jug, but this time Abe was the lucky one to yank it from Tibby's hand. They ate the layovers of the day before, cleaned up the clutter, and sat down for Present Time.

Tinch had whittled them a plow, working on it night and day, ever since he'd first heard about the wedding. "Ain't even got my winter hides traded!" he said proudly, so every one would know how important the present was to him. They all nodded approval and ran their hands down the white-oak moldboard that was scraped so smooth. The plow-share and bar were of one piece, and the stock was cut from cherry. They each had to tip it and feel its weight, while Tinch stood back and tried not to look puffed up.

"Now," he told Earthwild, "all you got to do is hang it in the chimney and let it season. It'll last you good, and will cut the earth without bruisin. Them iron plows is cruel to the earth."

"Whar'd you learn so much about plows?" Lannard raised his eyebrows.

"Well," Tinch hedged, "I . . . I ain't allus been a hunter." He added, looking shamed, "I was . . . a settler, once."

Abe had turned his hand to making them a pitchfork, but it wasn't like the common ones made of saplings. No, it had a four-pronged fork made from elk antlers. He told how he'd traded for it up north, and it had cost him three deerskins and a fisher fox. They were downright impressed at that, for it was a mighty stiff price. The antlers were set in a circular head of cherry, with fanciful designs carved all around it, and several of the men asked how many beaver skins he'd take to make them one.

Most of them gave seed. The men gave crop seed, and the women garden and flower seed. They'd stinted their own planting to save it, and it was sewn in muslin bags that could later be used to start a quilt.

Rocreuse gave them a soapstone skillet. It was three-legged and rubbed smooth with sand. All the women were envious, for meat wouldn't stick to soapstone.

Tanned hides, bearskin rugs, calabashes, and trenchers carved from maple were stacked up under the Present Tree, where all could come and look at them and handle them.

Lannard gave a copper kettle.

"That's to warsh your young ones in," Dove Callis called, in her jealous voice. "For cookin, they ain't worth a hang!"

The others glanced at each other, for they knew Dove had hankered for a copper kettle for years, and just couldn't stand seeing anybody else have one. They didn't see a present there from Jonathan and Strange Rain.

"It's been hidden down at Lannard's," Jonathan grinned.

Nathan fetched it back, and they marveled when they saw it—a dainty little filly, pale buff color, with a saddle trimmed with bells that tinkled when she stamped. She was a far cry from the mud-and-plunge horses you saw back here, and it was plain to all that she would never drag a plow.

"No," said Lannard. "She's jest to fetch them whar they want to go."

Near sundown, they reckoned it was time they went home. Now they talked about a cabin for Earthwild, and asked when did he plan a raising? But he smiled shyly, and told them it was already done.

"Me and Nathan built it ourselves, sneakin away and workin late. It's even got two glass windows. I saved the skins for months."

"Well, let's have a look at it!" cried Simonton, and they all got their young ones and started out down the trail, laughing and chattering, with Tibby riding the mare and Earthwild walking beside her.

"Land!" said Sally Carson, after they had walked for some time. "Did you go and build it clear to the Susquehanny?"

The sun was halfway down when they came on to the clearing and saw the new cabin, set back in a clump of dogwood and redbud trees. The green logs had put out shoots and trimmed it with leaves. Nathan had started morning-glory vines, and the wild trumpet vines had taken hold along the walls. There was a rail fence that had wild roses in the corners.

"Now that's a real purty place!" Ellen Simonton said softly, and the others nodded.

Strange Rain had brought some of the precious coals from her own fire, and now she built a new fire on Tibby's hearth. Never would it go out, if Tibby was a proper wife and tended to her chores, for it should last till her young ones were grown up and wedded.

They finally left the wedding couple standing on their doorlog. The new moon cast a faint light here in the clearing, but in the woods it was black. They pulled shellbark for torches and lit them from Tibby's fire, and broke into singing as they went off on their separate trails.

Tibby stood looking after them, watching the bobbing lights, hearing their voices call to each other and their singing fade off into the distance. She called a last good-bye to her folks, but it was Nathan she would miss the most, and he stopped and turned as if he knew what she was thinking. Even in the dusk, she could feel his half-moon eyes looking back at her.

"Come real soon, Nathan," she said softly.

"I will," he called, and she knew he understood her feelings, for no two people were closer than twins.

It was dark now, too dark to see when he turned away and padded off, but she thought he stood there for a long time, holding Firelight by the hand. And when the night dogs howled in the woods, she wondered was he safe?

18

IT WAS Falling Leaf Moon when word came that the war
was ended.

"Heard it up at Fort Wayne," Lannard said. "Got home as
fast as I could." He sank down on a stool and fumbled for his
pipe. "Yep, it's done . . . and I hope that's the last of them
danged British and their danged Injuns!"

Nathan and Jonathan pushed aside the herbs they had
been sorting, and pulled up stools.

"Maybe now things will settle down," Nathan commented.

But Lannard shook his head.

"No, not ever. There'll be folks jest pourin in here, now
that the danger's past. There'll be sun a-plenty in these old
woods, the game'll thin out, and cows'll graze the trails. The
earth'll be cut to pieces by iron plows, wagons'll be bouncin
over the trails, and folks prayin and preachin to the Injuns.
We'll be right in the middle of what we've all run from . . .
white man civilization!"

Jonathan nodded gravely.

"There's no doubt that it's coming," he agreed. "There are
thousands of people down at Cincinnati now. . . ."

"I still call it old Fort Washington," Lannard muttered.

". . . smiths, coopers, glassmakers, stonecutters, cabinet-makers, weavers, carpenters, the Lord knows who all and what all!" Jonathan continued. "There are seven stores now, in Columbus Town, over east, and more than a hundred people in Dayton Town. Eighteen stores, a newspaper, even an academy at Vincennes."

"Folks still called it *Chippecoke* when I come out here," Lannard said sadly. "Seems like all the old Injun towns are gettin white man's names, any more. We'll be a state next. Once we was hemmed in by Ohio and Kentucky. Then they took off some for Michigan Territory, and four years ago, some for Illinois Territory. All that's left now is to name us and state us. And we're done for!"

"*Ae,*" Nathan murmured.

They were silent. A bird perched on the doorlog and sang. After a while, Lannard got up.

"I run from it before, and I can run from it again. Now that my young ones is growed and my woman gone, there ain't no need for me to wait around."

He shuffled his feet toward the door.

"Seems like I hear that horn a-blowin, myself. . . ."

He started down the trail, shaking his head, and once Nathan saw him stop and wipe his sleeve across his eyes, as if they were teary.

Like the *wendigo,* the horn was only a woods story, but just the same, folks talked about it as if it were real . . . the Hunter's Horn that sounded through the forest, turning men's hearts restless and calling their feet back to the trails.

"Guess he heard the horn," they'd grin, when a man suddenly picked up his family and his plunder, and moved on.

It could call to anybody, any time, woodsies, settlers, even men with book learning, like Shawn or Jonathan. Nathan wished privately that it would call the Indians out of their ravaged villages and put their feet on far-off, unspoiled trails.

During the Long Night Moon, he went down to Asanzang Town again, but afterward he wished he hadn't seen it.

The People were a miserable lot. Their buckskins were

219

old and stained, their cloth skirts hung in rags. Some even wore the cast-off clothes of white men. One had on a soldier's hat, another shivered in a white woman's shawl. Even their hair looked tattered, for they had no will to roach and braid it now. The ribbons, beads, and gay trinkets were all gone. The bright colors were faded. The porcupine quillwork was forgotten. There was an emptiness in their voices and a loneliness in their eyes that wrenched his heart.

"*Ae*," he thought painfully, "it is gone, all gone. It will never come again."

Gone were the dancers with their plumes and their many-colored rattles. Even if the drums were warmed by the fire, they could never sing the joyous songs of other years. The hands that had made the drumbeats to call men from far-off places were now crossed bones in the buryholes of distant trails. The Hunter of Men sat by the village fires and waited. No longer was there talk of great battles and mighty hunters. No longer did runners come, with feathers round their arms, bearing wampum messages. Their swift feet were fastened to the earth like the roots of the monster trees.

He remembered something Far Thunder had told him.

"The People have many worlds," he had said. "In some, a man crawls on all fours, like a beast, in others he walks like a hunter, and in others he glides on his belly like a snake. We live in the last."

He found Cripple Foot and asked him for news of Far Thunder.

"Dead," the man told him. "Killed beside Tecumseh."

Nathan caught his breath.

"And White Moth?"

"None has seen her since the Battle of Tippecanoe."

Nathan started to turn away, but Cripple Foot reached out to him.

"Do not mourn them, brother, for they are fortunate. They have gone on the blessed journey of the dead. But we go on the journey of the living, a long walk that leads to nowhere."

The heavy token-feeling that Nathan had been noticing

grew stronger now, and he could not make it out. It was as if all things were coming to an end.

The war cries of the white men and The People had stopped now, and in their place had come a deathly quiet. It was like a dark, sultry, woods-still day when there was a storm off somewhere, the kind of day that made you pull off your hunting shirt and gasp for your breath and lie on the cool moss.

As he went down through the forest, he tried to imagine it as Lannard said it would be. He couldn't bear to see it overrun with stranger-folks who didn't understand it, who didn't both hate and love it, who hadn't fought for it, and who hadn't fought against it. It was hard to protect something so big you were like an ant beside it, and he felt helpless to save it. He wanted to put his arms around his woods and hold on to it . . . but it couldn't be.

When he saw Firelight sleeping beside the doll Tibby had made for her, he reckoned there were some things that always stayed the same and never changed. The young ones that grew up went on, and didn't die inside till they saw their own loved things coming to an end.

The winter was a quiet one. The hunting and trapping were good, and many a man fattened his purse with the hides he fetched in. A person could trade for salt now at any one of the settlements, and a lot of folks were eating white man's bread every day. Some things were easier, that was certain, but there was no pleasure to be seen in people's faces. No, only a kind of sadness, as though they were already on stranger-ground. All felt the change that was coming. Some, it made restless, and they packed and repacked their fixings, and talked vaguely about moving on. Others were so troubled, they sat staring out from their dooryards, and didn't even have the heart to do their chores.

It had been over a year now since Nathan was captured and taken north, and the *tchibai* of Broken Knee didn't haunt him any more . . . over a year since he brought home the little stranger-girl. She had taken Tibby's place in the cabin, had even learned to sing the same songs at her chores. Tibby had been wed for more than ten months, and it surprised him that she was not making a babe.

"Never you mind!" she laughed, when he dropped in to see her. "I'll find my own twins behind the chopping block some of these days!"

She had peeled a new broom with her cabin knife, and swept a little dirt in over the doorlog for luck. After that, she wiped the dust off the logs with her buckskin rag, and scrubbed the puncheon floor with a brush made from swamp rushes. There was no doubt that Tibby was a born home body.

Nathan sat watching her. She sure was a pretty thing. Her dark red hair was as shiny as a winter hide, and her skin as creamy as a May-apple bloom. She chattered as she worked, and when the noon hush set down, she dished up trenchers of fresh greens cooked with bear bacon.

"Earthwild won't likely be home before dark," she said. "When he goes to the settlement, he makes a day of it."

They talked some more after they'd finished eating, while Tibby busied herself with some pickup mending, and Nathan cleaned the rifle he'd fired earlier. He ran oily hunks of rag through the barrel on a hickory rod. He polished the metal until it was shiny clean. He rubbed the cherry stock with his open hand, for his pa had taught him that nothing was better for a gunstock than human-hand oil. He counted out the rifle balls he had left.

Tibby kept on about Earthwild.

"You'd think a body raised in the woods would crave the woods till he died," she said. "Specially a body that knew game and streams the way *he* knows them!"

But, no, he was always talking settlement talk, and how nice it was when he lived with Shawn at Harrodsburg and worked for the smithy. A settlement wouldn't be so lonesome for her, he argued, and their young ones could go to a school and get learned something.

"Like we had us a houseful!" Tibby laughed, but her eyes

were worried. It troubled Nathan to see her like this, for she was usually as gay as a red-winged blackbird swinging on a stalk.

"I reckon he's just lonesome for man-talk," he told her. "He's been on the trails by himself most of all winter. But now that summer's coming. . . ."

Yes, Tibby agreed, spring was about played out. Faded dogwood petals were underneath your moccasins everywhere you walked. Nights were warmer, so that you kicked at the quilt, and moved your pallet away from the hearth. Earth-wild had come on a copperhead down by the creek, a sure sign that summer was on its way, for that lazy thing was the last to drag out of its winter hole. Yes, Nathan was right. The winter had been long, and spring late and cold. Likely they'd all feel more like themselves when the days turned warm.

On the trail he met Jonathan going home, slumped tiredly over his mare, and all of a sudden it struck him like a branch across the face that his pa was an old man. Tight-chested, he asked himself when had it happened? On what day did Jonathan's broad shoulders stoop, on what morn did he wake with hollows around his eyes and a slowness to his always-brisk step? *Ae,* he said to himself, it had been coming for a long time, for years, but only now did he see it with his own eyes.

And Strange Rain? When they went inside the cabin, Nathan gazed at his mother with fear at his throat. But Strange Rain still had a gal-look about her, maybe because she was small and straight, and then too, she was a lot younger. But now he could see that when she turned to Jonathan, here eyes held worry and grief, as though she were thinking, "*Atawa,* my husband!" with the ashes of mourning already on her heart.

Afraid, he put aside hunting and trapping and stayed off the trails to be with his pa. And it was a good thing he did, for before the summer months ended, a new ailment had come to the woods, a *wendigo* of horror called milk sickness.

Nothing was ever so strange. Just as the honeybee came ahead of settlers, the milk sickness followed them. Where land was cleared and dumb beasts fetched to work it and graze on it, the sickness came. It had crept in on the west of them, from the Spanish settlements. Now it had spread all over Kentucky and Ohio. It had them trapped just like a forest fire, but there was no digging a burn-break for this!

Jonathan didn't know what caused it or how to cure it. All he could say was that somehow it got into a person's blood. Maybe it came on the air, maybe it was in the ground. Maybe it was in the very food and water they put into their mouths. There was nothing to do but ponder it, and pray.

The woodsies and settlers gave up hope. If Jonathan couldn't lay a cure to it, they reckoned they were done for.

Nathan and his pa made the usual cabin rounds, birthing babies, dosing the sick, folding the hands of the dead. When they found milk sickness, they carried the stricken one out to a half-face camp and told the others to stay away, except to give him food and drink, for nobody knew whether it was catching. Sometimes, even after that, whole families came down with it. But at other times, a wife or mother who stayed right beside the sickness never had a trace of it. Nobody understood it.

One thing they did understand, people came down with the sickness after drinking milk. Jonathan had an idea that maybe the settlers' cows got it first, from eating some poison plant * in the woods, and passed the poison on. Still, how could this be? The forest was full of poison things growing, but animals wouldn't touch them.

"Wild animals knows better!" Lannard argued. "It's them tame, brought-on animals that's too stupid to know what to eat!" They laughed at this, the truth none of them had stumbled on.

Later, though, there were cases where folks died of milk sickness without drinking a drop of milk, only water from a branch or pool. But couldn't a death-plant grow

* Believed to have been the white snakeroot.

224

there, and poison the water, too? Maybe sometime other doctors would think the same, Jonathan said. But who could know a hundred years would pass before that day?

Until this summer, Nathan had been only a lad wanting to help his pa. Now he was a tall young doctor desperate to help woodsies and settlers and womenfolks and young ones, all who turned to him on their pallets, waiting for him to do them a miracle. At night their eyes haunted him, eyes full of trust, believing in him, praying to him the way people prayed to God.

"Please, please help my babe. . . ."

"My woman, she's all we got. . . ."

It stirred him and hurt him, and made him weak and afraid and strong and confident all at once.

He learned a lot that summer about gentleness and humbleness, but he learned sureness, too. His hands no longer fumbled, awkward and uncertain, but dosed babes and set the bones of old men and held the clutching hands of women in torment. Soon they asked for him up and down the trails. "Send either Jonathan or his boy, don't matter much which."

Sometimes he thought of The People and wondered if he could ease their suffering, heal some of their wounds, kindle a spark of hope in the ashes of their spirits. He longed to sit by a village fire and talk to some of the old medicine men of the tribes, and tell them how much he had learned of what they had always known, that doctoring could be done with herbs and splints, but healing belonged to the gods. Many times he had prayed silently above a sickbed, saying in a mixed tongue the prayers of his pa and of The People.

It came to him that his life might be well spent if he took his skills to the tribes who had none to help them. But always then, he thought of Shawn, and the office never visited by either white men or Indians.

When he passed the Simonton cabin, he found them loaded up and leaving, fearing the sickness that had killed their nearest neighbors, a family of nine.

"At a time like this, we ain't go no druthers," Simonton said, hard-faced. "We're goin to build us a raft and float downriver. Ain't no sense in stayin here to die in our beds."

"Ef you get a chance," Ellen Simonton clutched at Nathan, "would you please warter my glories? I fetched them back from your brother's buryhole, and it seems jest a shame for pretty things like them to die for lack of human care."

Nathan watched them down the trail. Ever so often, Ellen would turn and look back at the cabin her man had built for her, and the only cabin they'd ever had. But Simonton never did look back. He was already thinking of the game on the far-off prairies, hurrying after the sound of the horn.

They weren't the only ones taking to the trails and rivers. The very mention of milk sickness brought a new kind of fear. But though they flocked like birds running ahead of winter, there was no escaping. Fresh buryholes dotted the lonesome trails. Some were axed out so quickly that not even a crude cross stood there to mark them. Sometimes Nathan found folks on the trail who had been by themselves and died where they fell. One of them was Tinch, but he didn't scoop out a hole for Tinch, there in the lonesome woods. He carried him home on his back, and they buried him in the graveyard on the hill.

Tibby was on his mind, though Earthwild said she was still pert and sassy, when Nathan met him on the trail to the settlement. Neither Strange Rain nor Firelight showed any signs of the sickness, but both doctors, young and old, kept to the medicine cabin and slept there, afraid of carrying the dread thing in to them. None of them used milk, and they drank only from their own well. Nathan and Jonathan carried water on the trails.

As the days passed, however, the sickness seemed to pass too, and by the time the katydids began to shrill in the woods, they had nothing worse to worry about than bringing Arlie Ransom's sixth babe, and dosing Mrs. McCutcheon's stiff joints. Jonathan perked up and looked rested. Strange Rain turned cheerful, and Firelight went back to singing the songs Tibby had taught her. Anxious to bring in hides and game again, Nathan took to the trails.

He came back in early fall, much sooner than he had thought, drawn by the bothersome token-feeling that had never left him. By the time he struck the fork that led to Tibby's cabin, the feeling was so strong inside him that he started to run.

"Likely she'll be waiting for me," he thought, to ease his fears. Close as they had always been, it didn't surprise him that Tibby could sense his coming. She said she could tell the minute he started for her cabin, and time after time, she'd met him on the doorlog with a soft pleasure in her eyes, and he would spy behind her a trencher set out for him.

This time, though, the cabin seemed empty. The puncheon door stood wide. He called her name, but her bright face didn't come to the window, her gay voice didn't answer back. His eyes turned dark. A feeling was gone from the place. The feeling of Tibby.

He called to the dogs, but no floppy ears came out from behind the spicewood. He stood still on the doorlog, and suddenly there was a noise of live things that was deafening to his ears. A flock of pigeons whirred overhead, dimming the light. A squirrel chattered. A jay called. But there was no human sound.

He looked at the wall pegs and saw that Tibby's shawl was missing, and Earthwild's rifle was gone from the rack. He ran out to the shed and saw that the mare was gone, too.

Then he leaned against the shed, feeling relieved. It was plain that Earthwild had gone long-hunting, and she was visiting a neighbor, or maybe had ridden over to his pa's cabin. The dogs went where she went, always had.

He went back to the cabin and was about to push the door shut when he saw that the fire was out. *Fire is life,* he remembered. Tibby should have thought of that.

He dragged in a backlog and started a new fire with wood chips. He struck it with his flint and steel and watched it

227

flare up. When Tibby came home this night, her cabin would be as cozy and warm as a wild thing's nest, and Earthwild couldn't rail at her, if he ever did, for letting the fire go out.

But as he left and read the sign of the dooryard, he saw that the mare had gone over the ground many days back. His heart sank. There was no use to deny it and talk around it; something had happened, something was wrong. All the way home, wild thoughts and imaginings chased each other through his mind. Tibby was dead. The milk sickness had taken her, and Earthwild couldn't bear to stay in the cabin any more. No, he had left her for some settlement gal, and she had gone back to her pa's cabin, to cry on her ma's breast. Then he shook his head. Only a man with the crazies would think such a thing, for Earthwild loved Tibby more than his own life.

He was on the swamp trail when Firelight saw him and came flying to meet him, calling his name joyfully in her softly accented speech.

"Nath'n! Nath'n!"

She hugged him with her slender brown arms, but he scarcely looked at her, and when he started to speak, he found himself as quivery as an aspen.

"Where's Tibby?" he fetched out. "Is she here?"

"Oh," she drew back, hesitating. Then, with a break in her voice, she said, "Tibby and Earthwild went West, to live in some settlement on the prairies that Earthwild heard about."

She was alive, she was all right. It should have been a wild relief, but he felt cold and empty. Tibby was gone.

He turned and strode to the cabin and his ma met him and held him close, and for the first time in his life, he saw her cry. And when he looked in his pa's eyes, he knew what parting from little Tibby had meant to them.

Earthwild wanted to get started, they told him, before the cold set down, but Tibby hoped and *hoped* her twin would come back before they left. Many's the time she had looked for him, out her doorway. But she was a gay little thing, and even when they had to leave, she didn't talk as if she and Nathan were parting.

"He'll ketch up with me after awhile," she said confidently. "Tell him I'll be lookin for him."

Nathan couldn't picture her following the streams and traces, for even though she had wigiwam blood, she had a cabin heart. When he thought of her, he saw her busy with her weaving, sweeping off her doorlog, kneeling to stir her pots and kettles in front of the fire. She was small and soft and tender, and her feet were not used to trails chilled by winter cold, beaten by winter storms.

Every time he ran onto a trader or peddler or hunter come from the prairies, Nathan wanted to seize him and demand, "Tell me about my sister. You must have seen her, you must have! And if you saw her once, you'd not forget her. Young and pretty, with dark red hair and crinkly eyes and a way of laughing. . . ."

Instead, he'd inquire politely, "I don't reckon you happened to meet my brother-in-law out there. Shawnessey's his name . . . and his wife Tibby. . . ." But they shook their heads and looked vague, all except one who said sourly, "Ef I talked to everybody I'm ast about, I'd never git no tradin done!"

Winter came with a blizzard that bellowed like a wild bull herd. The trails stood deep in snow. Many's the night Nathan lay awake, unable to sleep for thinking of Tibby, wondering if it was the same with his ma and pa.

No Indian and no hunter knew the woods better than Earthwild, he kept telling himself. Likely they'd reached the prairie settlement long since, maybe even had a cabin by now. Cabins were raised quickly in the settlements, where there were plenty of hands to help.

The thought was a comfort, and yet he was afraid, for many's the bride he had seen dragged to her death on the trails. Less than a year after her wedding day, she might be lying in her buryhole along some lonesome Indian trace, dead of ague or chest sickness or, more common, of trying to birth a babe.

And many's the time her kinfolks never even knew what became of her for, like Tibby, she couldn't write, and if she sent home a message by a hunter or trader, like as not he forgot it, or maybe never came.

Sleet splintered against the windows. The wind swerved from the trail to rattle the door latch and moan in the chimney. Nathan rolled over on his pallet with his head in his arms and thought, in anguish, "Oh, God, I'll never see Tibby again."

19

The next summer Jonathan died. He came home lying across his horse, and they never knew when it was that the Hunter of Men struck him down.

Nathan carried him into the cabin and stood there, staring down at him. The thin night fog drifted in and hung around the bed. In the dim light, his pa's cheek bones stood out as sharp as skinning knives. Nathan reached out to touch the grey, tangled locks and then drew his hand back slowly.

"*Atawa*," he murmured, "even his hair is dead."

"My son. . . ."

He lifted his head at Strange Rain's voice, but he wouldn't take his eyes away from Jonathan. He said to himself that this was not his pa, but only a worn-out body that had been cast off like a snake skin. His pa had lived in it for a while, and that was what made it dear to them.

"Nathan . . . ," she said gently, and when he turned to answer her, he saw that she had the heavy ax in her hands. Then he understood that she wished him to cut the ritual doorway for her husband's body to pass through. She wanted his pa to have an Indian burial, like the burial of Night Dog.

"He waits for me on the Pathway . . . ," he muttered.

"He does not wait on the Pathway," she said quietly. "Not yet. He waits here in this cabin for you, his son, to bury him."

Nathan stared at her with dazed eyes.

"You are living," she said. "He is dead. The two are never together."

She took both his hands and put them around the ax and left him standing there, facing the wall.

It would be well, he thought, to bury him in the Indian way, with none to stare or whisper. The picture of Dove Callis wailing out a false grief set him to shuddering. Lannard and Rocreuse were long-hunting and couldn't be told, anyway. As for the others . . . there had been a lot of sickness in the cabins, and if all of the people came together for a funeral, who knew what plague would spread among them? It would be well, just as well, he thought, and lifted up the ax.

Curious night beasts crept close to the cabin. Great white moths came into its light. Even a hill-hooter flew down from the woods and sat on the elm branch over the door.

But Nathan didn't hear them. He was listening to another sound, thinking he heard a mourning-drum in one of the villages. He thought he could hear the voice of a singer lifted in the prayer for the dead. Slowly, he began to chop a hole in the wall under one of the windows, and when he came to himself again, the doorway was done, and the fine glass of one of the windows had been broken. It was morning. He was sweating all over, and the drum and the singer had stopped.

He turned and looked at the cabin. His pa was still on the bed, only now his clothes were different. He had on a ceremonial shirt of black, with beaded designs, his new buckskin breeches, and soft new moccasins.

Then Nathan saw his ma. She was huddled beside the bed with her hair loose on her shoulders, and she had on a black short gown and plain black leggings. She was barefoot, and she had smeared ashes over her hands and face. Wordless, stricken, she crouched there, clutching one of Jonathan's hands, looking at nothing, seeing nothing. Pity filled Nathan's heart to bursting. Who knew what memories of their love were with her now?

Like an intruder, he slipped outside, still carrying the ax. In the entry he found the adz and auger, and then went off to the woods. Firelight trailed after him, weeping silently, frightened by the way he looked.

He had in mind a fallen poplar where he and his pa had spent many hours in talk. It was a monster tree, well seasoned by wind and rain. He thought it would be fitting to make Jonathan's coffin from it.

He stripped its branches and made his ax-cuts in the trunk, top and bottom. Then he set his wedges and split the tree apart. It was hard, slow work and his back and shoulders began to ache. Every time he brought the ax head down on the wedges, he could feel pain all through his body. But he didn't mind, for at least he had stopped feeling numb.

He dressed down the puncheons with the adz and whittled the wooden pegs last. When he got the box put together, he was proud of it, but it had to be finer than all others, and so he crouched down and carved some wood-designs on the top.

All day he stayed in the woods. Dusk was coming on when he went back to the clearing to fetch the mare. Firelight went with him, holding on to him.

"You'd best stay at the cabin," he said to her. "I can't watch after you, and you might get hurt when the box is dragged back."

The mare pulled the box back for him, but it took a while, for he had to go ahead of her and cut little whips of trees out of the way, and snake dead logs aside. When they reached the edge of the clearing, she broke loose and ran, with the box bumping along beside her. He caught her and tied her to an elm, for she was skittery now, and spun around kicking up rocks and dirt. It was as if she knew what she had hauled back from the woods, and why. Nathan stood soothing her.

"I guess even horses mourn," he thought.

When he went into the cabin, he found Strange Rain dividing Jonathan's things into equal piles, one to be buried with him and the other for Nathan to keep. But Nathan shook his head at her and put her gently aside.

For himself he took a few books, all the boughten medicine, and the instruments. The other things he left. Strange Rain had already made heaps of Jonathan's clothes, even down to his sashes, but Nathan went through them again. He took his pa's boots, his saddle blanket, his rifle and horn of shot and powder, his pipe. All the rest he put back.

Then he remembered something else. He took off his own belt and his gold ring and the new blanket from his pile. These he set aside for Jonathan. Then he went to the bed where his pa lay and slipped his hands down inside the shirt. There was a gold chain with a lucky piece on it which Jonathan had always worn. He was extra fond of it. Nathan slipped it off and put it around his own neck.

Going to the Bible, he ripped out the pages that had the *Psalms* on them. He took his good moccasins, his good breeches, the first four arrows he had ever made, and his flint knife, and laid them in Jonathan's pile. Finally, he decided it was right.

He spread a new quilt in the bottom of the coffin. Then he went back into the cabin, slipped the gold ring on Jonathan's little finger, and laid the new blanket over Jonathan's body. Then he and Strange Rain carried Jonathan out of the cabin through the new doorway he'd cut, after the way of The People.

They lit torches to see by, and laid Jonathan gently in the box. By his right hand, Nathan put the medicine he had gathered and brewed. By his left hand, he put the arrows and the knife. At his feet he put the books. All the rest was folded up and tucked in around the body.

When Nathan pegged down the lid, it seemed that he

could feel every peg go right through his heart, for he was shutting his pa in and himself out, for all the rest of his life.

He looped one end of a vine rope around the box, and the other around the mare's saddle. She was scared and trembly when he tried to back her, and reared up frantically. Finally, he wrapped his sash around her head, and calmed her down with quiet talk. Slowly, they started up the hill. Ever so often, a root or a hump in the ground would catch the box, and then Nathan would have to tie the mare and smooth the ground with the ax. He hadn't minded it bumping the ground when it was empty, but now his pa was in there.

Up on the hill, he began to hollow out a hole with the wooden shovel. He picked the open place next to Micajah. He found the roots of his Birth Tree down there, and though Strange Rain tried to stop him, he lopped them off with the ax.

They lowered the box with vines for ropes. It slipped, and landed with a bump. They stood there and looked at it for a long time before he began sifting the dirt back over it.

"He's never coming back," said Firelight, in her low voice, and sank down beside the buryhole.

When the box was covered, Nathan went back to the cabin and yanked off his shirt and rubbed ashes over his skin. He took off his earrings and bracelet and moccasins, and laid them down beside the lock of his pa's hair which he had cut off.

When he got back up the hill, Strange Rain had already lit the sacred fire. There was no need to stay by the grave, but none of them wanted to leave. The cabin was cold, for all its warmth was down here in the ground. There was no place else they wanted to be.

"*Oh, my father, farewell!*" he began the old prayer. "*You have taken yourself beyond the great river. Your spirit is on the other side of the forest. I will not see you for a hundred winters.*

"When the warriors of our totem meet they will say, 'Where is Jonathan? Where is the bravest of men?' And one will answer, 'He fell on the warpath.'

"Oh, my father, I will come to you. I will be with you across the broad river."

Nathan looked up at the night sky. The Pathway of Souls was brighter than he had ever seen it.

"Because *he* is there," he whispered.

He could see Jonathan crossing the black rocks that struck fire when a mortal foot stepped on them. He could see him drinking from the honey stream. And then he'd be standing at the Gateway, and many he had loved would be there to meet him . . . Micajah, Kerman, Tinch, Night Dog, Far Thunder, Shawn. Maybe . . . his eyes were blurred with tears . . . maybe Tibby, too.

Suddenly he was very tired. He leaned back and when he looked up again, it was daybreak.

He got up quietly because his ma and Firelight were asleep. He was as stiff as buckskin in wintertime. He took the ax and went up into the woods again, and hunted for a wild cherry tree. When he found one that was just a whip, he cut it down and made a cross from it. Then he searched for a slender parasite vine, peeled off the bark, and soaked it in a stream until it was soft. With this, he lashed together the two pieces of the cross. The rest of the day he spent in carving symbols of The People on it. Toward sundown, he carried it back to his father's grave and pounded it into the ground.

Night came, and Firelight slept against him. Strange Rain sat across from him, with slow tears trickling steadily from her eyes.

"Do you remember . . . any white men's prayers?" she asked, brokenly.

He thought of the stories Jonathan had told him, the white men's stories of Kije Manitou. And the prayers of parting . . . many's the time his pa had said these to him as he set his feet on the trails. Nathan's voice broke as he said them back to him now.

"The Lord bless and keep thee . . . the Lord make his face to shine upon thee, and be gracious unto thee. The Lord lift up his countenance upon thee, and give thee peace.

"And now may the Lord watch between me and thee . . . while we are absent, one from the other."

When the morning light came, he was pained by the stiffness of his body. He made Firelight and Strange Rain get up and walk with him a while. But when they were out of sight of the grave, Strange Rain was worried and kept looking back.

"Some beast might disturb him," she whispered. "I cannot be gone from him."

Nathan left her and stumbled into the cabin to fetch some creature-comforts. He sent Firelight back with quilts, and he brewed a pot of dittany and rum.

Strange Rain slept well that night, but it began to rain and he had to go back to the cabin and get his wild bull robe and cover her and Firelight with it.

He had a hard time keeping the fire going in the rain, and once when he went down to the chopping log, some beast was crouched behind it, and he heard it snuffling at his tracks all the way back. He threw a hunk of wood at it, and didn't worry about it. Death was in the cabin, and that was worse than any beast.

The next day he made a totem marker for Jonathan, fixing on it bits of cloth, beads, and feathers he'd been saving. When his ma saw the marker, he could tell she was pleased.

That last night, the trees stirred with a lonesome sound, and thunder muttered far off. Just before daybreak, it began to storm. The little *animikes* called out in their flight, their voices the thunder, their sharp beaks the lightning. The god of the forest drove them away with his tree spears.

"They are fighting over our very heads!" Strange Rain shouted, above the noise.

They stumbled back to the cabin. It seemed dark and strange, a place that had never known their thoughts or words. They were restless on their pallets, jerked awake at every sound, groping about them for some weapon, feeling oddly fearful. It was only after they lit the bear oil lamps that they could sleep.

Nathan did not wake until the noon hush. He lay there on his pallet for a long time, thinking. He had dreamed he heard a voice that kept saying, *"Things are coming to an end. . . ."*

"Ae, it is true," he murmured. Tibby lost, his pa dead. Now he knew what the fearful token-feeling had meant. He thought of his pa lying in his buryhole, and knew he had not died of any certain illness. No, like many a man before him, and many a man yet to come, he was just worn out.

When he stepped outside into the sun, the first thing he saw was his Birth Tree. A piece of its top was twisted and hanging down, and when he went up to it, he could see the lightning mark running down the bark and into the ground. Tenderly, he touched it.

"Both you and I have seen the end of spring," he said to it. This, too, was a token. It meant the end of all that was past, and the beginning of all that was to come.

He stared at the totem marker, where the feathers blew in the fresh summer wind.

"Ae," he murmured to his pa down there in the earth, out of sight. "I am there. The boy is buried with you, and now I have become a man . . . someone I do not yet know."

Firelight's doll was sitting on the grave and he picked it up and started back to the cabin. But she met him on the hill.

"I meant to leave it there," she said, in her soft tongue. "I thought maybe . . . he might be lonesome. . . ."

Nathan's eyes softened. He went back up the hill and she trudged beside him. He dug out a little hollow for the doll and set it down.

"I didn't have anything else," she said suddenly, with tears starting up.

He reached out and pulled her against him.

"That's a God's plenty," he told her.

20

THE trumpet vine pulled itself over the patch that Nathan
had put in the cabin wall; the summer rains came and
went. The maples yellowed, and the staghorn sumac turned
bright. The time of mourning passed, and they washed their
hair, ate meat and salt again, hunted game and gathered
wild grapes.

Woodsies came to stand by Jonathan's grave most every
day, and many's the tear that had fallen on the leaf-strewn
mound. Sometimes the womenfolks brought a flower and
planted it there, wanting to do some loving thing. And once
a timid gal-child had fetched a bunch of wood asters limp
from the warmth of her hand.

Nathan could not help seeing, with a catch in his chest,
how few remained of the folks he had known in his boyhood. Some, the woods had killed with its fevers. Several
men had died in the war, and their women had turned back
East. Others, like the Simontons, had fled from the milk
sickness or, like the Stiles, from the idea of being friends
with an Indian.

The woods seemed full of stranger-faces now, and stranger-
cabins had been raised along the trails. Every now and then,

Nathan passed where a babe cried, or a young woman sat alone on the doorlog, looking homesick and lost. Dear God, whatever had fetched them out here, where there was nothing but hard times and heartbreak?

Maybe the women didn't know, but their men did. Maybe the men couldn't put it into words, and that's why they mumbled about the game back home giving out, or the land back home being sour. But the thing that had fetched them was the steady call of a far-off horn.

It had wakened them as they lay in their safe and warm settlement beds, of nights. It had called to them as they walked down the streets on the way to their everyday work. They heard it as they ate boughten food from china dishes. But not all men heard it . . . only those who knew tormented moods that told them there were greater things than the sameness of settlement life. That was why they had hefted up their guns and started west, with their womenfolks and their young ones trailing after.

The folks they had left behind called them drifters, but if they drifted it was because they were lost. Among them were creative men whose tongues had never learned to spell out a sound or write a word, rough hands that could have painted a picture, tormented minds that groped toward master thoughts. No, they couldn't do these things, but they followed the same horn that blew for the men who did.

Lannard came the nearest to putting it into words when he said, "Jest to leave somethin behind to show that once you lived and was here, even ef it's only a blaze-mark! And tarnal! A blaze-mark's a whole big book to a man that can read it!"

It was a long-hunt the horn had led them on, one that would last their whole life, for when settlements moved into the places they'd made safe, the horn would blow again farther off, and the woodsies would set out to follow it.

Fall came. Abe and Lucy got wed and Mrs. McCutcheon died. Auntie Gentry came to swap doctoring talk with

Nathan. Rocreuse's oldest boy ran off to work in a store at Vincennes. The Carsons moved into Tibby's cabin.

It seemed that fewer Indians were seen on the trails. Many of the villages were abandoned now, and those of The People who stayed had forgotten Tecumseh's teachings, had gone back to the cheap trade cloth and tomahawks, the worthless trinkets and the rum. They hunted little, drank a lot, and listened no more to their medicine men.

A Frenchy trader came by one day, looking for Nathan. He'd stopped at a prairie settlement to have his horse shod, and when he and the smithy got to talking . . . yes, the smithy had asked him to set and eat, and the smithy's gal-wife had made him swear he'd take word to her folks. . . .

Nathan was half-stunned with joy. *Tibby* . . . somehow her Indian blood and her love for Earthwild had taken hold, had made her strong enough for the hard trails, the stranger-rivers, the lonesome campfires. They had them a cabin, the trader said, and no longing for anything else, 'ceptin a longing to see their folks. . . .

A new restlessness came over Nathan after that. Sometimes when he went to the far spring with the wooden yoke over his shoulders, he'd stand and stare out into the trees as he had done in his boyhood, and forget that his ma and Fire-light were waiting for the water he'd gone to fetch. On rainy days, he'd lean back in the half-light and listen to the soft sound of the rain on the bark roof and leave his medi-cines untouched. Sometimes the cabin seemed to take his breath, and he'd leave and beat the feeling out of himself on stranger-trails. And when he came back, tired and short-spoken, Firelight would ask him what was wrong. But he couldn't answer, because he didn't know.

His ma never asked. No, she would only nod to herself as if she had been expecting him to change this way. And when she cleaned out the holes at the foot of each grave (left for the shadow-soul to come and go by), he thought he saw her lips moving as if she were talking to someone. And of nights, when she sat at her sewing, she would hum the old song of

The People that told of the many lives a man was born to live. It began: *"He is born with his face turned to all things. . . ."*

He began to spend more and more time down at the Delaware villages on the Whitewater, for though he had been raised in the Potawatome way, he craved to learn more of his totem-people. But their misery saddened him, and he was only more restless when he came back again.

He spent a lot of time talking to the traders that drifted east and west, and could scarcely keep his moccasins from walking in their tracks. When he dressed in white men's clothes and went to Cincinnati for boughten medicines and doctoring-books, he watched the big Kentucky flatboats heading downriver to New Orleans and had a sudden hankering to see that settlement. Even the soldiers he saw coming and going at the new territorial capital of Corydon filled him with the urge to be on the move. Late in September, he went to the north prairies to hunt, along with Lannard and Rocreuse.

"Why the prairies?" he had asked them.

"We jest want to see what it's like out thar," Lannard had answered slowly.

But they hadn't done much real hunting, for Lannard and Rocreuse had seemed far more interested in just prowling the trails, squinting at the grasses, the prairie sign, and the different look of the sky. It was when they turned back toward home that their real reason for wanting to hunt the prairies came out.

"We been thinkin," Lannard said. "Rocreuse and me . . . we been thinkin more'n more . . . of headin West."

"West!" said Nathan. "For good?"

"Yep."

"It's . . . mighty different there."

"Yep."

"Don't you think you might be just a little too set in your ways to be starting a new life . . . in a new place?"

"Nope."

"The game's thicker'n flies, they say," Rocreuse put in. "And you can see the wild bull herds, like used to be in here. Them herds stretch from horizon to horizon, they say, farther'n a man can look, goin on forever."

"Yep. And they got deer, antelope, game a-plenty. And folks a-plenty who need a good doctor." Lannard slanted his eyes at Nathan, but Nathan acted as if he hadn't heard the last.

"They say the grass is so sweet tastin, you can boil it and never want for corn. And they got Injuns out thar that talk with their hands. I want to see *that!*"

"You can allus see the sky, and there ain't ever blasted kind of a beast hidin in the shadder of some monster tree. And as fer the Injuns . . . wal, they ain't too friendly, but leastways, you can see 'em comin!"

Nathan caught at his breath, for he could see it all as they told it, and he ached to be going with them. And he could see Tibby. . . .

"Come on. Trail along with us," Lannard said softly.

"I would sure like to!" Nathan answered.

"Wal, then?"

"Come on, Nathan," Rocreuse wheedled.

Nathan shook his head slowly.

"You know I can't. I can't go off and leave my ma and my girl to look out for themselves. Who would keep them in game? Who would do their trading for them? And I couldn't take them along. We wouldn't know where we'd be heading, and you can't just drag womenfolks . . . ," he broke off.

Rocreuse and Lannard looked at each other and nodded.

"Nathan, thar ain't nothin else you *can* do!" Lannard said gently. "There ain't nothing here for any of us now. The time has come to git, and you know it, too!"

Nathan squinted at the sign along the trail, as though he didn't know what Lannard was saying under those words. But he knew well enough.

All that was left to him and his family was the old cabin where they lived, once the finest in the Territory, but not even as good as common now, for the new folks coming in from the East craved better.

The hunting was bound to give out in a few more years, and then what would they live on? The price of hides and pelts had fallen already, because so many settlers had taken to trapping that winter. And he didn't think they could live on what he'd bring in by doctoring!

The thought made him bitter, but he'd seen the stranger white men looking away from him because they'd heard he was a breed. When they could, they went to a doctor at Fort Wayne. Once at the settlement, he'd heard a woman say, "We've got to bring a doctor here that's a white man!" He tightened his mouth.

"How you goin to find a man for your girl when she's growed?" Lannard went on. "It won't be long, you know."

Nathan looked down. Yes, he'd noticed that her body was filling out, and she was getting curves where women had them. Even her voice sounded more grown up, and her touch embarrassed him, so that he'd scolded her for crawling onto his pallet of morns, and told her that was no way for a near-grown girl to act. He'd even gone to Fort Wayne and got calico so she could have some new skirts, for her knees were peeking out from under her short gowns, and her knees didn't look like a little girl's.

"Now, I don't aim to hurt you, Nathan," Lannard said kindly, "but *who* is goin to want to marry a past slave girl of the Winnebago, who don't even know was her ma and pa white, or Injun, or some of both?"

Nathan flushed.

"We'll get along some way!" he said proudly.

"You ain't going to get along a-tall, lessen you leave here and find somewhar else to go!" Lannard flared. "A place whar you can doctor folks, and there's huntin and trappin a-plenty, and it don't matter what mixture of blood you got!"

Lannard stopped then, and pulled a twig, and began twisting it nervously between his fingers.

"Another thing," he said, in a low voice. "The time's comin when the Injuns is goin to be asked . . . mebbe not even asked, but *made* to move out'n here. Likely they'll be lumped together on a piece of land set aside for 'em, whar the game ain't good, nor the water, nor the weather, nor nothin! You want yer ma and yer girl made to live like that? You want to live like that yerself?"

"But we're only *part* . . . ," Nathan began. Then he saw their faces. "Why, they wouldn't do that! They *couldn't!*"

Lannard and Rocreuse looked steadily back at him.

"You've heard talk!" Nathan said, and they nodded. His face went dark. He remembered they'd been down at Corydon a little time back.

Lannard threw down the twig.

"It's comin . . . and soon."

They went on slowly. They were back among the trees now. It was hot, and they stopped and pulled their shirts off and drank from a spring. A flock of passenger pigeons went over, the whir of their wings like a hard wind. The air they raised rocked the treetops. The woods grew black, then the green light came back as the wings passed.

"I reckon . . . maybe Abe would keep them in meat," Nathan said slowly.

"And I'll see that Sammy does their tradin," Lannard offered.

"Have some sang," Rocreuse suggested, cutting off a hunk of ginseng from the root he carried.

They walked on, chewing thoughtfully.

"My ma and my girl . . . maybe they won't understand," Nathan said once.

Lannard shrugged.

"It'll come to 'em," he said. "They ain't stupid."

They went faster over the trail then. The words they spoke about their going popped out of their mouths as fast as seed from weed pods.

"Good-bye, you plagued Injuns!" Lannard called, as they passed Kuwosi village. "We're headin West!"

245

"Hesh!" Rocreuse ordered. "They're liable to shoot at us, jest out'n plain jealousy!"

When they hit their homeward trail in the night, they lit torches and kept on.

"I couldn't sleep, noways," Lannard laughed. "I'm jest too purely glad to be up and goin . . . goin *some* place . . . goin *any* place!"

21

THEY stayed together, each man going to his cabin to pack his plunder, and the others trailing along with him. They felt that if they separated, something might happen to keep them from going after all. They talked with Sammy about doing Strange Rain's trading, and Abe said quick enough that he'd keep her in game.

"Nathan," Abe said, "how about if me and Lucy take our plunder and jest move on down thar? Thar'd be a man on the place then, and you got two cabins."

Nathan looked up in pleased surprise.

"It sure would mean an awful lot to me," he said.

"It's settled then."

"I'll send you back all the hides and pelts I can, so it won't be a hardship on you," Nathan promised.

But Abe shook his head.

"I don't want your hides and pelts," he said. "What I want from you is jest to find a good place to go. Cause when you come back to get your ma and girl, Lucy and me are goin with you."

The closer they got to Nathan's cabin, the slower they went, thinking of the woman and girl.

"Don't know how I'm going to make them understand," Nathan said.

"We'll talk up fer you," Lannard offered.

Strange Rain listened to their words as though she'd already heard them. She put her hand on her son's arm.

"*Ae,* I know why you must go," she said. "I only wonder that you waited so long." She added, "Find Tibby, and a place for us. We'll be ready when you come again."

But Firelight wouldn't look at Nathan when he told her. He watched her out of the corner of his eye as they sat at the table and ate. She stayed by the hearth, saying she was watching the stew and too busy to eat. But he knew she just didn't want to sit near the man who was going from her, and when he spoke to her, her eyes turned on him, hurt and fierce. "I fought for you that day at Fort Wayne!" they seemed to say. "Even though I believed I'd be killed, I stayed by *you!*"

While they lingered at the table, Nathan took a piece of firewood and pared it down to make a calendar stick. He made eighteen notches down its face, and he explained to his ma and his girl that they were to cut a mark across each notch for every moon.

"Before they're all cut, I'll be back," he said.

But Firelight turned away, and he could see she didn't believe that he was ever coming back.

As the day turned late, they rolled in the keg of rum from the entry. They meant to make this last night a frolic night. They sang and stomped their feet, and when Abe and Lucy came with their first load of plunder, Nathan got down the fiddle and they bobbed their heads to its tunes.

"Bet you never heerd nothin finer than that!" Lannard teetered on the doorlog and yelled out into the night to the swamp and the woods.

The false dawn wasn't far off when the men went to sleep in the medicine cabin. But they dreamed of the prairies, and squirmed and mumbled so, they woke each other up.

"There's a trader at Vincennes," Lannard said, "has got a map, sort of. It tells whar is the water holes, and the best game, and such-like. We'll have to see him."

They'd doze then, but one would wake and shake the others.

"Ain't it somethin, jest to be goin!"

Abe would raise himself up, and listen to their rummy talk, and laugh. But then he'd turn serious.

"Now, Nathan, I ain't foolin," he said. "You look for some good land out thar, close to whar you plan to be. Lucy and me, we'll go back with you next time." Later he rolled over and jabbed Nathan awake and said, "We jest got to go with you, cause who else could doctor us? We wouldn't trust no other hands to poke at us, or mix our medicines. You *know* us."

Sometimes one of them would just rise up and whoop for all he was worth, and pound his heels on the floor and shout, "G'bye, plague take it! G'bye! G'bye!"

At last the false dawn came, and all slept soundly but Nathan. He was still worrying about Firelight and how hurt she had looked. Finally he got up and pulled on his breeches and moccasins. He went quietly into the living cabin and woke her with a touch, for she was sleeping on the outside edge of the bed. She got up without a word, and he could hear her pulling on her dress and running the haw comb through her hair.

"Come outside," he whispered.

She went out into the dooryard ahead of him and didn't quit walking, but just stopped once in a while to see where he was taking her.

"Down by the cottonwood," he said.

He could see in the early light how straight-backed she walked, as if she didn't care that he was leaving, but he could see too that she had been crying.

They sat down under the cottonwood. She didn't look at

249

him, but kept her eyes on her skirt and traced its calico pattern with her finger.

"I . . . I know you think I ought to take both of you with me . . . ," he began.

She turned quickly.

"We're strong! We could go! Your ma told me she was raised on the trails. She said it wasn't bad. . . ."

"You're not going to be raised that way!" he told her shortly. "It's no way. You're going to live in one place, in one cabin, the way my sister did. A place where folks respect you and you can have plenty, and you don't always have to be worrying about how you'll live, or where you'll camp, or will the next village be friendly!"

She opened her mouth again, but he got his word in first.

"No!" he said firmly.

She began to sniffle, but he paid no attention to it.

"You must understand," he said, "I have to go without you this time. But not the next. Not once I've got a roof to put you under, good land in a place where there's game. We can have a little corn patch, and there'll be folks who *want* my doctoring. . . ."

She jumped up.

"I don't care about all that!"

He pulled her back down beside him.

"There's more," he went on quietly. "I aim to find a man for you."

She stared at him.

"You must be thirteen . . . fourteen . . . maybe even fifteen by the time I get back." He looked at her sideways, at her body filling out, her blue eyes, her soft hair curling from the dampness of the morn. "You're going to be mighty pretty. I guess there'll be a lot of men coming around the cabin while I'm gone, just to see you."

He added sharply, "But I don't aim for you to marry any of them! I've got in mind some man who can read and write, and who owns a nice cabin. Maybe a lawyer, or a preacher. Somebody who *is* somebody, and who can buy you dresses like I've seen the women wear down at Cincinnati. Someone who's not always going to be traipsing across the country, and who won't care that . . . well, never mind. I can't find him here! But I don't want to come back and find you've run off with some stranger-man, a sweet-talking hunter, or some young Shawnee. I want to come back and find you *here!* Do you hear me?"

She nodded slowly.

"I won't run off with anybody," she said, in her low voice. "I don't want to. And I don't want you to find me any man. I want to stay with you."

"Well, now, that just can't be," he said quickly. "I mean you should find a man you love, and get married and have babes. I . . . I reckon I'll get married myself, someday. But I sure can't do that if I have a daughter, full grown, to look out for!"

She jumped to her feet and stood looking at him.

"Nath'n . . . ," she began to cry, and ran off through the willows. He ran after her and caught her and held on to her, even though she fought him.

"I didn't aim to hurt your feelings," he burst out. "You'll always be my little girl." He took a deep breath. "Firelight! That day on the lake when I made you my daughter . . . it didn't mean anything. It wasn't binding!"

She turned quickly so that she could look up at him where he stood, tall above her, with the light coming behind him.

"I only did it to make you come with me. I hoped maybe you'd seen someone adopted . . . maybe you'd remember. You wouldn't come with me, you fought me like a panther, so . . . don't be angry. I've kept you and looked after you, just the same as if it was binding."

"It was, it *was!*" she cried.

He shook his head.

"Not without a chief."

She gasped.

"You didn't want it to be! You always meant to go off and leave me and never come back. . . ." She burst into tears.

"No! I . . . ," he felt the flush rising on his skin. "Firelight, I really do love you," he blurted out. "I was going to find you a fine man, but I wonder . . . do you reckon I'd do for your man?"

She sobbed all the harder, and wouldn't look at him.

"I guess I didn't mean that," he whispered, worried. "I'll get you a man, the kind I said. Don't worry. Don't cry. . . ."

But as he tried to comfort her, somehow his lips brushed hers, and he could only hold her and kiss her clumsily.

"Don't you run off," he whispered fiercely, his fingers tangled in her hair. "Don't you run off unless . . . you don't want to be my woman. If you don't, I won't come looking for you."

He let her go suddenly.

"Get on back to the cabin," he said gruffly. *"Get!"*

She stepped back from him hesitantly, not wanting to go, but he turned from her and stared out over the swamp. Finally he heard her moccasins scuffing on the trail and he knew that he was alone.

"What'd I have to go and do that for?" he muttered.

But later when he walked back to the cabin, he said quietly, "I do love her." And then he said it again so that his Birth Tree, the shadow-souls of the dead, his gods, the woods and swamp and all the little living things could hear it and witness it. "It's true."

The sun was over the clearing when the men got up. Lannard and Rocreuse had aching heads, and they put their feet down gingerly as they walked into the living cabin.

"Watch how you're shovin me! Tarnal!" Lannard flared at Rocreuse. "My head feels like it's the size of a punkin, and I think some of the seeds is loose in it!"

They sat down to the meal the women had fixed for them, but they ate slowly, for now that the time to go had come, they tortured themselves a little by dawdling, savoring the fact that they were going and the woods didn't know, and they were coming and the prairies didn't know. It gave them a feeling of power to know that they could control their going, as if they had stepped off the world and were watching it go by, but they could climb back on any time.

Each of them sat thinking of the unknown country ahead and would they be welcome there, would they be liked, how would it be? The thoughts made their hands tremble a little.

"It was a good life we had here," Lannard said quietly.

It was hard to be going away from all they knew, and suddenly they longed to stay where they were, and they sat back and smoked their pipes and listened to the comings and goings of the wild things outside, and each hoped the other would say, "Let's just stay here!" They looked shamefacedly at each other.

Nathan went about packing his *parfleche*, putting in his grandpap's medicine bag, some things of his pa's, and all else he would need to carry with him. Firelight helped him, and every time their eyes met he flushed, thinking of what he had said to her that dawn. She was still a little girl, he told himself roughly.

"Reckon I'll go out to the graveyard," he said then, and the others followed after him.

All stood over the graves of their folks, Lannard over the grave of his woman, so long dead, Rocreuse over the graves of his little girl, and his first woman, and his second.

"Wonder if they'll mind that we ain't goin to be here," Rocreuse said softly. "Wonder if they'll know we had to go . . . same as them."

And when they went back to the cabin, all the old life had gone out of it.

"Let's git!" Lannard said suddenly. "This place gives me the chills. Too many hants in it."

They stopped on the doorlog with their packs on their backs and their rifles in their hands. It seemed they heard other steps and voices, skirts rustling, and Jonathan's boots.

"Them was the times!" Lannard licked his lips as if the words tasted sweet. "But they've gone."

The four men went slowly down the hill. The women trailed after them. Firelight walked behind all the rest, so she could look at Nathan with none to see.

Now they lingered over the sign, the sounds, the smells, but they wouldn't remember the woods as they saw it this day. They would remember it the way it had been, the long-past way. The cabin smoke of new settlers had no place in their memories, nor the new-fallen trees, nor the changed blazes that said the trail ahead was no longer Indian.

They held up at The Bucks, the monster-trees that had seen so many farewells.

"Listen!" Lannard said. "Do you hear it . . . the horn? We ought to . . . it's blowin fer us."

They fell still and turned their heads a little, as though to listen for this woods-talk sound.

"I been hearin it for a long time now," Abe said quietly.

But when they turned back to the women, they could see *they* didn't hear it, and never would.

"Nath'n," Firelight pulled him aside shyly. "I . . . I'll be lookin for you."

"I won't hold you to that," he said softly. "You're just a little girl. But when I come, if you haven't found anybody else, then. . . ."

"I'll watch the trail," she said, casting her eyes down.

He stood beside her a moment longer, wishing the time was past and he was coming home instead of going away, wishing the new cabin was built, wishing that she was grown enough to wed. He saw the woman that she would be, and it made his mouth go dry.

"You sure are pretty," he whispered, touching her cheek with his thumb. "The same," he said, "same blood as mine."

He turned from her to Strange Rain.

"You take care," he said to her. "Those legs of yours are going to have to take you on one last trip. You . . . just take care . . . *ninga*."

"Such a tall, strong son I have!" she burst out, and he saw that she was crying. "Now I cannot call you little son. *Atawa*, surely it was only a few nights ago that I was walking down the trail to Asanzang Town, and your father came to me. . . ." She broke off and bit her lip. "Come back soon."

They left quickly, and their feet went easily over the ground.

"I've walked a good piece, over this continent," Lannard said, "but I don't plan on hikin clear acrost it! Soon's we hit Vincennes, let's us trade fer some horses. Out whar it's flat, a man can ride lots easier than back here."

Nathan nodded and grinned, but Rocreuse balked.

"I've never rid a horse," he said. "I . . . I'm skeert of 'em."

They stopped and looked at him and their grins grew wider.

"It ain't no joke!" he sulked.

"Wal, either you're goin to have to learn," Lannard guffawed, "or you're goin to have to run awful fast to keep up with us."

Where they struck the west-running trail, they stopped again for a last look. The long tunnel through the woods was dark and cool, with little patches of green light dancing through it. The leaves rustled. The birds gave their cries. The beasts scuttled in the brush. The wind touched their faces and blew the loose hair across their necks. They sniffed the fern-sweet air.

"It's enough to make a man cry," Lannard said.

They looked away from each other, blinking.

"We're like a bunch of old women," he went on softly. "I reckon I know now how a woman feels, when she's bein carted off from some place she loves. Maybe it ain't a woman-feelin only, though. Maybe it's a feelin every mortal has."

They were silent for a minute, then Nathan spoke.

"Come on," he said with a sudden grin. "There are trails and trails just waiting. . . ."

A faint squaw-rain began to fall, and they could hear it way above their heads, on the topmost shingles of the roof of leaves.

"It's cozy down here at that, ain't it?" Lannard nodded. "Them trees, they pertect us. But them prairies. . . ."

"We may have to take to carryin them things . . . umbrells . . . out thar," Rocreuse said seriously, and the others laughed.

"Wal, I'm an old man!" he added, in defense. "I don't want to ketch cold!"

They started on down the trail, keeping quiet and wary as always. Then Lannard cried out, "What are we tippy-toein along for? Land's sake, we ain't huntin, we ain't dodgin In-juns, we ain't askin nothin from these old woods any longer, and I plan to go out of 'em makin noise a-plenty! *Here we come*," he began to sing loudly, tunelessly. "Here we come, we're a-comin, look out fer us, cause we're a-comin. . . ."

The sound of their soft-walking moccasins soon was gone. The tree branches closed in behind their swinging shoulders. The wind caught a vine and threw it across their trail. Their voices faded to a last faint shout. The forest was still. The fern, broken when they stumbled against it, began to stop its bleeding and heal. The moss smoothed itself, losing the im-print of their heels. The rain fell softly, its freshness taking away their mixed scent of hides, kinnikinnick, buckskins, jerky, and ginseng.

Nathan's gods pattered after him with their quivers slung from their shoulders. The deer grazed slowly, moving west, and a family of night dogs followed them with stranger-seeds stuck in their matted coats. The ancient villages, the half-face camps, the broken cabins, the woods, the trails, the streams were empty, for the heart-soul of the forest had gone, and now only the shadow-soul stayed behind.

A lark called, and a honeybee came up the south trail, darting in and out. The trees shivered, hearing the lark and the bee, and the sound of axes behind them. They drew into themselves and braced themselves, for the settler men were coming, walking strong in cowhide shoes and carrying iron plows on their backs.